I0746814

TOGETHER
WITH
You

Books By Leah Dobrinska

Love at On Deck Café
Good To Be Home
Together With You

TOGETHER WITH *You*

LEAH DOBRINSKA

Copyright © 2022 by Leah Dobrinska

All rights reserved.

No portion of this book may be reproduced in any form without written permission from the publisher or author, except in the case of brief quotations embodied in critical articles or reviews.

In accordance with the U.S. Copyright Act of 1976, the scanning, uploading, and electronic sharing of any part of this book without the permission of the author is unlawful piracy and theft of the author's intellectual property. Thank you for your support of the author's rights.

This book is entirely a work of fiction. Names, characters and incidents portrayed in it are either the work of the author's imagination or are used fictitiously. Any resemblance to actual persons, living or dead, businesses, companies, events or localities is entirely coincidental.

Editing: Jenn Lockwood

Cover Design: Ana Grigoriu-Voicu with Books-design

Author Photo: Beth Dunphy

Library of Congress Control Number: 2022913766

ISBN: 978-1-7374483-4-1 (paperback) | 978-1-7374483-5-8 (ebook)

For my family. I love celebrating Christmas together with you.

Chapter 1

LANEY

NO ONE WARNED LANEY McGregor how humiliating failure would be.

The large wooden door to her office closed behind her with a hollow thud, and Laney allowed herself a couple seconds to rest her head against it. Hard as she worked to shove down her feelings, traitorous tears burned the backs of her eyes. She blinked them away and readjusted the box of her belongings under her right arm. She hadn't become one of the youngest state congressional assemblywomen in history by blubbering. Even though she'd lost her seat in the assembly to some high-rolling lawyer who spent a ton of money on campaign advertising, she was going to leave the Wisconsin State Capitol with her head held high.

Laney wedged her purse more firmly into the crook of her opposite elbow and took a deep, steadying breath. The familiar scent of ink and copy paper laced with a fusion of indiscernible cologne tickled her nose. She shot a quick glance around before setting off down the second-floor corridor.

It was the Wednesday before Thanksgiving. Most of her colleagues—soon to be former colleagues—had left earlier in the day. Maybe she was a coward, but Laney intentionally waited to make her departure until she was pretty sure everyone else was long gone. She didn't want to face them, knowing they'd be looking on as she cleared out her office. Their stares would have been filled with pity, and hearing their whispered gossip about the girl who couldn't hack it for more than one term would have felt like taking an icicle to the eardrum.

Laney swallowed hard as she made her exit. Her black high-heeled shoes clicked against the tile floor. She usually loved the sound, imagining the clicks ringing out like cymbals heralding her power and purpose. Now, each step she took taunted her. Click. *Failure.* Click. *Disappointment.* Click. *Flop.*

The rotunda floor was vacant. Soon, the walls would be lined with bedecked Christmas trees, and the balcony banisters would be covered in white twinkly lights. Seasonal tourists would be clambering up the Capitol steps to take in the holiday extras. But right now, everything looked bare and empty.

Kind of like my job prospects.

Laney sighed, pushing open the Capitol's exterior door. She stopped on the landing that overlooked East Washington Avenue and filled her lungs with frigid air. She'd spent most of her life succeeding in everything she did. Her perfectionism was born out of necessity. She was the daughter of humble farmers. That meant scholarship money had been her ticket to college. She'd worked hard to be the best in school, and the mindset had carried over into her professional life. Needless to say, losing in November's election had rocked her—and not in a good way. For the past month, unease hovered over her head like Olaf's stationary flurry—except a lot less cute.

After depositing her box of belongings on her passenger seat, Laney made the quick drive a few blocks west and tucked her car into a spot in the small lot behind Madison Children's Theater. The place was deserted as Laney entered and cut down the hallway that ran between the stage and the dressing rooms. She paused outside an open office door and gave a courtesy knock before peeking her head in. "Hey, girl, hey."

Sally Hennessey's eyes popped up from the computer in front of her, and a grin spread across her freckled face. "Laney!" Sally stood and walked toward her, her artsy denim jumper, burnt-orange tights, and low-heeled booties a stark contrast to

Laney's creased black dress slacks and high heels. "I'm glad you stopped by."

Laney hugged her best friend. "I wanted to say goodbye in person."

"Well, thanks. Can you sit for a second before you go?"

Laney checked her watch. She was headed home to Mapleton to lick her wounds and try to regroup. She had a two-and-a-half-hour drive ahead of her, but she wasn't too keen to be alone with her thoughts just yet, so she gladly sank into the worn fabric-covered chair opposite Sally's messy desk with a huff.

"Yikes." Sally smiled as she plopped down in her swivel chair, her clay, turkey-shaped earrings swinging back and forth at the motion. "What's up?"

"Just feeling the weight of the complete and total collapse of my career extra heavily today. You know, the usual."

Sally rolled her eyes. "I deal with enough drama queens in my day job, thank you very much. I never pegged you as one."

Sally and her husband, Ron, owned and ran Madison Children's Theater. They coordinated theatrical productions, private lessons, workshops, summer camps—you name it. If it had to do with the arts and having fun, Madison Children's Theater put it on.

Laney rubbed her fingers against her temples. "I'm serious! My time in the Capitol is over—just like that. All my purpose? Gone. I need to find another job, but I have no idea what that might be."

"Hey, it's going to be okay." Sally held out her hand, waiting for Laney to take it. When she did, Sally squeezed. "You're good at a lot of things, Lane. You'll figure something out. You always do. Everything's going to work out just fine."

"Easy for you to say, Ms. *My Life is Picture Perfect*. You've got your dream job and your dream guy. Oh? What's that?" Laney cupped her free hand to her ear. "I think I hear the Hallmark Channel calling. They want to make a movie about you."

Sally rolled her twinkling eyes, a giggle escaping from between her plump lips. "I wish. Can you imagine the publicity?"

Laney shook her head. "You don't even need it. Your business is thriving. Everyone loves you. But me? My constituents didn't reelect me, so now, for the second year in a row, I'm facing down a bleak holiday season, heading home with my tail tucked between my legs. It's so embarrassing." Laney's shoulders slumped of their own accord, but she sat up straighter in her chair when Sally's eyes took on a conniving gleam. "What? What's with that look?"

"I just realized something. It's you. *Your* life has the makings of a Hallmark movie."

It was Laney's turn to laugh. "Hardly. My life is in shambles."

Sally snapped her fingers. "Exactly."

"Wow. Thanks."

"You said it, sister, not me. But hear me out. Big-city girl is down on her luck around Christmas time. She goes back to her small town where her family just so happens to own the local Christmas tree farm." Sally punctuated the last words, circling her finger in Laney's direction. "And general merriment ensues." She sat back and clasped her hands in delight, as if she'd just solved all of Laney's problems.

Laney pinched her brows. "I'm afraid I'm not following."

"You are going to have a holiday season to remember, Laney McGregor. I can feel it. You just have to agree to follow these steps." Sally retrieved a sheet of loose-leaf paper from somewhere within the bowels of her desk.

"What steps?" Laney scooted forward in her chair. "What are you talking about?"

"You're a Christmas cliché in the making, and I think you need to lean into this role and see where it takes you."

Laney looked on as Sally scratched out "Operation Christmas Cliché" on the top of the page. Underneath, she started listing different events and activities.

Laney tilted her head so she could better read the upside-down list. "Go ice skating. Drink hot cocoa with friends. Cut down a tree. Wait, what are you writing there?" Laney craned her neck. "Go on a holiday-themed date? Sally! That's going to be a giant nope. I don't want or need a holiday season to remember. I just need to get through the next month so I can move on."

"Trust me!" Sally added some doodles to the list and then brandished the paper, holding it out for Laney to review. "If you actually try to enjoy the holidays by doing these Christmas clichés, I bet you'll be better for it."

Laney dangled the list between two fingers, eyeing it with a grimace. Sometimes, her best friend's optimism was exhausting. But she knew Sally's heart was in the right place, and Laney loved her for caring so much, even if the absolute last thing she planned on doing was embracing the seasonal spirit—at least this year.

After her whole personal life imploded last Christmas, she was feeling a little touchy toward the holiday. Laney had rearranged her schedule for the next month so she could hole up at home alone. The assembly's floor periods were over, and all of her remaining committee meetings she'd attend virtually. Her goal was to survive the Christmas season and draw as little attention as possible to the massive failure that was both her personal *and* professional life.

"I really don't think so, Sal."

Sally narrowed her eyes and steepled her fingers under her chin. "I'm going to have to make this worth your time, aren't I?"

"What do you mean?"

"I mean if you complete this list…" She pointed at the paper in Laney's hand. "Really complete it. Like, put your whole heart into it. Then, I will talk to Ron's uncle about a potential job opportunity."

Laney sucked in a breath and tightened her grip on the paper. Ron's uncle was US Senator Larry McClaren, who split his time between Washington D.C. and Madison. Laney had never met him, never asked for a referral.

Like everything else, she was content to work her way up the political ladder on her own. She'd never wanted it to seem like she was using Sally and Ron for their connections. That wasn't the kind of person she was. Even the thought of Sally offering this referral made Laney squirm. She was a do-it-yourself kind of girl—sometimes to a fault.

Still, what Sally was offering? It could be a game-changer for her.

But no.

"I can't take your charity. Don't get me wrong, I'm super grateful. But it's not how I'm wired."

For better or worse.

Sally looked triumphant, as if she had been expecting Laney to say that. "It's not charity. It's an equal exchange. You complete the Christmas Cliché list for me, and we'll give you the referral."

Sally snatched the paper back from Laney and made an X at the bottom of the sheet. "Sign here, please."

Laney hesitated. Her plan had been to stick close to the farm—not cowering, per se, but definitely not going out of her way to insert herself in the community she'd failed in her election-day loss.

Then again, her hometown did nothing halfway, and Christmas was no exception. Mapleton could give the North Pole a run for its money in the holiday-spirit department, so she wouldn't have any issues finding opportunities to complete the list.

Sally's offer to connect her to Senator McClaren *was* tempting. Since the referral wouldn't be a full handout if Laney followed the list, she did feel better about the arrangement.

And deep down she knew she wouldn't be able to avoid the people of Mapleton entirely. They would sniff her out. She could think of a couple of village residents in particular who had detecting senses that would rival bloodhounds—at least where gossip or town news was concerned.

"Really, what do you have to lose?" Sally asked, as if sensing Laney's crumbling resolve.

"My dignity."

At that Sally just snorted and crossed her arms over her chest.

Laney squinted one eye shut and peered across the desk. Sally beamed back in a smug way that told Laney she knew she'd already won.

"Alright, fine." She scrawled out her signature and held up the paper in proof. "Are you happy?"

"Delighted." Sally reached for the sheet and signed her name below Laney's. "There. This is now contractually binding." She winked. "I'm going to be checking in to see how you're doing. If I feel like you're not holding up your end of this, then no referral for you."

"You're incorrigible." Laney chuckled, but then her smile slipped. "Haven't I been through enough?"

Sally's face softened. "That's exactly why, as your best friend, I couldn't allow you to leave my presence until I figured out a way to make sure you weren't going to go back to Mapleton and wallow the rest of your year away. Mission accomplished, I'd say." Sally dusted off her hands dramatically. "Have fun with it. Keep an open mind. You know clichés became clichés for a reason—they've worked before. Besides, if this all works out like a Hallmark movie, maybe you won't even need me to talk to Senator McClaren."

Laney issued an unconvinced grunt and perused the list with a skeptical eye. She didn't know how Sally thought that singing Christmas carols and building a snowman was somehow going to solve all her life's problems, but when she glanced up, her friend looked at her with such an earnest expression that Laney figured *what the heck.* She could suck it up and be merry for a month if it meant she'd have a decent job opportunity on the horizon.

She pocketed the list of holiday to-dos, mustered up a smile, and hugged Sally goodbye.

"Christmas in Mapleton, here I come!"

Operation Christmas Cliché

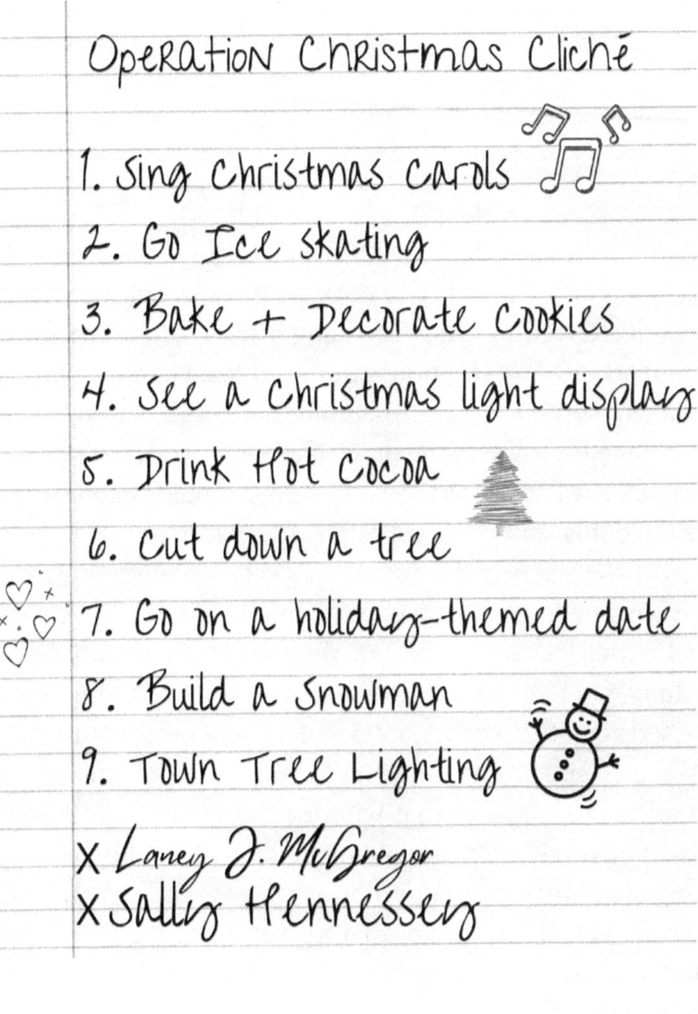

1. Sing Christmas Carols
2. Go Ice Skating
3. Bake + Decorate Cookies
4. See a Christmas light display
5. Drink Hot Cocoa
6. Cut down a tree
7. Go on a holiday-themed date
8. Build a Snowman
9. Town Tree Lighting

X Laney J. McGregor
X Sally Hennessey

Chapter 2

FORD

IT WAS A MAPLETON tradition to gather at Hal's Diner—the village's only bar-like establishment—on the Wednesday of Thanksgiving week to catch up with those returning to town for the holiday.

Hal's was already packed to the gills at seven o'clock when Ford Marshall showed up. He was riding a wave of adrenaline after passing off the keys to a house he'd sold to a young couple who'd decided to settle in Mapleton. From there, he'd driven to the old barbershop on Mapleton Avenue. If all went well next month and he passed the Real Estate Broker Exam, it would become the new location of his very own real estate agency.

Ford wove his way through the crowded restaurant, savoring the feeling of accomplishment. It had taken him a while to think that he, the less successful of the two Marshall siblings, had anything much to offer. With a famous sister like Isabel, who had amassed something of an interior-design empire, complete with a TV show—and given his history as something of a miscreant—it was difficult to believe that what he did would ever match up. Slowly but surely, he was building up his self-confidence.

Days like today helped. When Ford matched a family with a home, it made him feel like what he was doing mattered. He was proud to be able to provide a service to the community, and that was something.

"Ford! Good to see you! What can I get ya tonight?" Hal, the owner of the diner, smiled a weathered smile as he waited on Ford. He wore a faded flannel shirt, and his graying hair was in a low ponytail.

"A Spotted Cow would be good. Thanks, Hal." Ford tossed a tip into the jar as Hal handed him the amber bottle of Wisconsin-brewed beer. He took a sip but pulled the bottle quickly away from his lips as a hand thumped him on the back.

Ford turned to find Eric McGregor grinning back at him. The two shook hands. Eric was a couple years older than Ford, but they had played on the same basketball team in high school after Ford got moved up to varsity his sophomore year. They found a pair of barstools on the far side of the counter. Ford hooked his thumb over his shoulder, gesturing to the collegiate crowd. "Is it just me or do they get younger and younger every year?"

"Either they're getting younger or we're getting older." Eric laughed.

The two made small talk, catching up on each other's lives. Ford hadn't told many people about the prospect of opening his own agency, not wanting to count his chickens before they hatched, as the saying goes. But since Eric was an accountant and Ford hoped to get a meeting on the calendar and tap into his expertise, he explained his plans to his friend.

Eric thumped Ford on the back again. "Good for you. You must be stoked."

Ford just nodded. He refused to get his hopes up too high in case things didn't pan out. He may be finding his footing, but self-preservation and a low bar was still his default.

"We've got a little lull before tax season, so I'm pretty open," Eric continued. "Text me on Monday, and we'll get something on the calendar."

Ford agreed and took a sip of his beer.

"Anything special going on at the Marshalls' house for Thanksgiving?" Eric asked.

"Not really. It'll just be the four of us, plus Daniel and his grandfather." Daniel was Isabel's fiancé. "My mom is making her famous pumpkin pie, though."

"I would jump in the Squirrel River for a piece of Val Marshall's pumpkin-cheesecake pie. Want to save me one?"

"Only if you promise me an extra mug of Joan McGregor's tree farm hot cocoa."

"Deal. Just come to the farm anytime between Friday and Christmas Eve, and my mom will be serving it fresh."

Ford salivated at the thought. McGregor Tree Farm hot chocolate was legendary.

"As a matter of fact"—Eric set down his beer on the bar—"Laney's probably twisting Mom's arm and getting an early batch of cocoa out of her as we speak."

Ford's pulse spiked at the mention of Eric's sister, but he directed all his energy toward picking at the label on his bottle. "Is Laney back in town?"

"She texted that she got home before dinner, which would give her just enough time to eat and weasel some hot cocoa out of Mom." Eric made an exasperated face. "What a little sneak."

Cocoa was suddenly the last thing on Ford's mind. "How's she doing?"

Ford and Laney had been classmates in high school. Where he'd barely skated by, graduating with a C- average, Laney was the class valedictorian. They ran in similar circles since several of their extracurriculars overlapped, but the only time Laney paid him any attention was when he was antagonizing her—which he did fairly often. It wasn't that he'd singled her out. It was just that she was a rule follower, and since he was typically pushing boundaries and breaking rules, they often wound up butting heads. In his defense, it was never mean-spirited, and he'd liked to believe Laney had known that, too.

She had always been equal parts intimidation and intrigue to Ford, if he was being honest—like a one-woman wrecking ball, plowing through any obstacle standing in her way en route to achieving her goals. Where it had taken Ford a while to figure out his path, Laney had known what she wanted from the beginning, and she'd gone after it. From what Ford could tell, observing her at a distance over the years, Laney had single-handedly gotten what she worked for.

At least until this past election day when she'd lost her seat in the state assembly.

"She's alright, I think. I'm not too sure. She was so busy in the lead-up to the election, and since then, she's been pretty closed off, so I haven't gotten a good read on her."

"Laney always hated losing." Ford thought back to some of the pickup basketball games they used to play behind the old barn at McGregor Farm. Laney had the skills—basketball and otherwise—to back up the big game she always talked.

"Don't I know it. Speaking of her...Laney!" Eric was looking over Ford's shoulder, waving his arm in the air. "Over here."

Ford turned to see Laney standing just inside the door to the bar. Their eyes connected for a brief second, and Ford forced himself not to look away. Not for the first time, the sight of Laney did something funny to his insides. In the past, Ford chalked it up to being insecure around someone who clearly had her life much more together than he did. But he was a grown man now, and he knew better. Seeing her framed by the bar door, hair tousled and cheeks rosy from the wind, it was time to admit that he'd been half in love with Laney McGregor since he knew that being in love was a thing to be.

Ford swallowed down the breath that was lodged in his throat as Eric stood up next to him. "There she is. My favorite sister." Eric opened his arms, and Laney stepped into the hug.

"I'm your only sister." Laney's low, melodic voice held a hint of amusement.

Eric pulled out his barstool for her to sit on. "A technicality. We were just talking about you."

"Oh?" Laney's shoulder brushed up against Ford's as she sat down. He caught a whiff of her vanilla perfume, his entire body thrumming with awareness. Ford hadn't been around Laney for any length of time in years.

After high school, she'd gone off to college—to conquer the world, he imagined. He kept up with her on social media, so he knew she'd gotten a clerking job in Madison immediately after graduation, and she'd worked her way into an elected position two years ago. She'd rarely been back in town the past two years unless she was campaigning or on official business. He saw her at a village bonfire the summer after she'd been elected, but that was about it. At the time, she'd had a serious boyfriend—or so he'd gathered.

Ford chanced a glance at her left ring finger. Relief swirled around his gut when he found it empty. He wondered if she was still with the guy, whoever he was. Ford took a slug of beer to try to erase the sour taste that image conjured.

Laney swiveled in her seat toward Ford, knocking into his shoulder again and sending his nerve endings rocketing. "Is my brother behaving, or is he spreading rumors about me?"

Ford screwed up his mouth, faced her fully, and tried not to let the tap dance his heart was doing affect his voice. "That depends on whether you'll confirm or deny your hot chocolate consumption tonight."

Laney's eyes widened in a quick show of surprise, gold flecks glinting in the low light of the bar. She pulled her top lip into her mouth before she said, "No comment."

"Unbelievable. Didn't I tell you, Ford?" Eric pointed at Laney. "Mom totally likes you more. She hasn't made me any all month."

Laney just laughed. Her dark hair was longer than Ford remembered, falling past her shoulders. Shaggy bangs covered her forehead and fell into her eyes, and his fingers itched with desire to brush them away so he could get a clearer look at her. But he was not going to do *that*.

Instead, Ford tipped his chin toward her. "It's good to see you."

Laney cocked her head. "Not sure if I'm brave enough to say the same, but it's been a while."

Ford sat back. "Touché."

He couldn't blame her for that slight dig since the last significant memory she had of him was likely their high school graduation.

As valedictorian, Laney had been tasked with giving the commencement address. And since Ford was an idiot as a teenager, he'd decided to sneak his duck call into the gymnasium and be obnoxious with it during her speech. He'd started with the basic quack sound, and Laney had stopped mid-sentence while a buzz had zipped through the packed gym. Everyone was mumbling about what was going on and who'd made that insufferable noise.

From the podium, Laney's gaze had locked onto his. While he'd intended to be discreet, she'd been onto him. She always was two steps ahead of everyone else. Without breaking eye contact, she had said straight into the microphone, "What the actual duck?"

After a beat, the entire gym broke out into laughter and applause. Ford put the duck call away, and when the crowd settled down, Laney flipped her long hair over her shoulder and picked up right where she left off.

She was lightning on her feet, that one, and Ford was completely enamored with her wit and her tenacity.

He had been then, and he'd bet if he spent more than a couple minutes with her, he still would be now.

Chapter 3

LANEY

A McGregor family Thanksgiving was a sight to behold. It was the only time of the year that the entire extended family gathered. All of Laney's mom's siblings—there were five of them, four brothers and one sister—and their spouses and children, and now, some of their children's children, descended on Laney's parents' farm at noon on Thanksgiving Day. Everyone brought a dish to pass. They ate spread out on makeshift tables in every nook and cranny of the house, wherever Laney's parents could fit them. Laney's uncle grilled nearly thirty pounds of turkey, and her aunt roasted another fifty pounds of potatoes to feed the crowd. It was loud, it was chaotic, and it was one of Laney's favorite days of the year.

Usually.

But this year, she was the center of attention—and not in the way she preferred.

"I can't believe you didn't get reelected. What is *wrong* with people?" Laney's Aunt Renee said from where she stood stirring the gravy at the stove.

"You're preaching to the choir, Renee." Laney's mother, Joan, slung her arm over Laney's shoulder. "But we know Laney will land on her feet. I can't wait to see what she'll do next."

"You and me both, Mom. You and me both."

"No plans yet?" Aunt Renee asked, wiping a bead of sweat from her forehead with the back of her hand. Gravy making was not for the faint of heart. "What about on the boyfriend front? Any movement there?"

Laney took a fortifying breath. She loved her family. She did. They were only peppering her with questions because they loved her back. It wasn't their fault she was still so sensitive a year after everything went south with Dustin. And why *was* she so sensitive, anyway? Dustin had done her a favor. She knew that. But it all still made her feel weak and like she lacked control. Like she'd failed. All things she hated.

It also had stunted her ability to consider dating. That, or she just hadn't come across anyone who piqued her interest.

"Not really," she answered her Aunt Renee.

"You've got time." Her mom gave her shoulder a squeeze.

Laney smiled to hide her grimace.

· ♥ · ♥ · ♥ · ♥ · ♥ ·

When the last of the family left at just after six o'clock, Laney flopped down onto the couch.

"I'm stuffed." Eric sat down in the chair across from her. "Unless there's more pie. I always have room for more pie. Which reminds me..." Eric ferreted out his phone and started typing.

"What are you doing?"

"Texting Ford."

"Why?"

"He told me he'd save me a piece of his mom's famous pie. I've got to remind him. Hopefully I'm not too late."

Laney let her head fall back against the couch cushion and closed her eyes, dialing up an image of Ford's deep-set eyes and angular jaw.

Ford Marshall had given her a run for her money back in the day. He seemed to get his kicks from making mischief. He was always nettling her, too—playing devil's advocate, pushing her to clarify her points on the debate stage, or challenging her in some way or another in class. She hadn't minded. Actually, it had been kind of thrilling. Most people didn't try her, but Ford did. And she'd enjoyed systematically swatting away each and every one of his attempts to throw her off her game.

But he *had* thrown her off her game when he got the last word at graduation. Not during her speech. No. Then, she'd had a smart comeback for his ridiculous duck call. But afterward, when she'd confronted him about it? That had been another story.

She'd snuck away from the dozens of cameras snapping photos of her and her friends, because she wanted to drop a thank-you note off under the door of one of her favorite teachers. The rest of the school had one more day of classes left, and she knew Ms. Sholtz would find her note the next morning. When she'd rounded the corner of the history hallway, she'd nearly run into Ford.

"You!" Laney's hands had flown straight to her hips.

Ford smirked at her, rocking back on his heels. "What?"

"You know what. Are you pleased with yourself?"

"I don't know what you're talking about."

Laney jutted a firm finger into the center of his Milwaukee Bucks t-shirt, visible under his unzipped gown. Because *of course* Ford wouldn't have been bothered to wear anything dressy for the occasion. "Don't you? I'd watch it, Ford, or I'll have everyone calling you Mallard Marshall."

They had been standing nearly nose to nose, close enough that Laney had seen the shadow of stubble lining Ford's jaw and felt the warm breath escaping from and being drawn back through his lips. When she'd met his eyes after no less than a millisecond of cataloging the rest of him, Ford was staring at her with a look she couldn't place. His gaze held fire, and for the briefest moment, she wondered if he was going to kiss her.

For all of Laney's academic and extracurricular accomplishments, she hadn't dated much in high school. Check that. She hadn't dated *at all*. Standing there in that deserted hallway with Ford, the lights buzzing overhead, her stomach had made a pleasant swoop, and she'd licked her lips.

But then, Ford blinked and cracked a grin, taking a step back. "Mallard Marshall, huh? Has a nice ring to it. Later, Laney." He'd skirted past her before she could utter another word.

Laney waited for the memory to clear before she trusted herself to speak, and even then, her voice came out sounding a little pitchy. "How is Ford these days?"

"He's the most successful realtor in this part of the state."

"Really?" Laney wasn't sure why she was surprised. While Ford had never applied himself in school, he'd always been whip smart. "Good for him."

Eric's phone pinged. "A-ha!" He turned the screen for Laney to see. "He's a man of his word."

Laney glanced up at a picture of Ford holding a piece of pie inside a Tupperware container.

"See that?" Eric tapped his knuckle against the screen. "That pie's got my name on it. Literally."

Someone had scrawled *Eric McGregor* on a piece of masking tape and affixed it to the front of the container. Laney chuckled at the sight, even as her eyes bounced from the pie to the man holding it. His face held just the trace of a smirk, like maybe he had a secret. Laney wondered what it was, wondered if he'd tell her if she asked. What made a guy like Ford tick? Who was he really? Why did—

Eric clicked his screen to black, jarring Laney from her runaway-train thoughts. "He promised to bring it by tomorrow. His family is coming to get a tree."

Laney had to stop herself from groaning at the mention of the tree farm. She was usually ready and willing to help out with her parents' business, but making small talk with everyone from around town and feeling like a letdown was going to be brutal. If she could just get through this opening weekend, she'd make herself scarce from here until Christmas.

Except for Sally's blasted list.

Laney bit back a curse. "This holiday season might be the death of me."

"Don't look so glum. I'll ask him to save you a piece of pie, too."

"I'm not glum. And I certainly don't want Ford's pie." Laney snarled out the words, trying to ignore the fingers of heat slipping up her neck.

"Easy! It's not Ford's pie. It's his mom's."

"Whatever. Christmas and men...I could do without either."

Laney's parents joined her and Eric in the living room, and they all took a collective breath.

"What a nice day that was." Joan eased into a seat on the couch next to Laney. "I'm always so glad to get everyone together."

"It's too bad Eliot and Carly couldn't come this year," Eric said of their brother and his wife. They hadn't made the four-hour drive from Chicago because Carly was thirty-three weeks pregnant with twins. "I miss seeing Johnny."

"Me too." Laney perked up. The last time she saw her four-year-old nephew was almost a year ago. Her schedule hadn't aligned with Eliot and Carly's since then. "Didn't you say they were going to try to check in at some point today? Have you heard from them?"

Her dad, Jeff, wedged his phone out of his pocket. "I don't have any missed calls."

"Me neither. I got so tied up with the day. I didn't have a chance to reach out. I'll call them now." Joan scrolled through her contacts, and her phone rang as the video-call worked to connect.

A couple seconds later, Eliot popped up on the screen. Laney scooched closer to her mom so her face would be in the frame.

"Hi!" Laney and her mom chorused. But when Laney took in the harried look on her brother's face, her smile fell. "What's wrong?"

"Nothing." Eliot dragged a hand across his face.

"It doesn't look like nothing." Joan leaned forward, peering at the phone as if she could get a better diagnosis from her son that way.

"Everything's fine for right now. I was just about to call you," Eliot said. "Carly started having regular contractions about an hour and a half ago. She's on the phone with her OB right now."

Laney sucked in a breath. She wasn't well versed in the ins and outs of prenatal care, but she knew Carly's doctors had been hoping to get her to at least thirty-five weeks before delivering the twins.

"What do you need, El? What can we do?" Their dad had come to stand behind the couch. Eric joined him, a serious look on his usually relaxed face.

"I don't know, you guys." Eliot glanced over his shoulder and dropped his voice. "I have a feeling these babies are coming sooner rather than later. The timing is...not ideal." Eliot frowned. "I know we planned for you to be here to take care of Johnny when we went to the hospital, but it's the biggest day of the year on the tree farm tomorrow. Can you still come?"

"Of course we'll come." Laney's mom didn't even hesitate.

"Are you sure? It's late. I mean, I can try to find someone local to watch him. It's just with the holiday weekend and short notice, most of our friends are tied up."

"I'm going to pack right now. We'll stay as long as you need. Right, Jeff?"

"Absolutely."

"That's the other thing..." Eliot shook his head. "If the babies are born soon, chances are we'll have a long NICU stay ahead of us. We might need your help around here for the foreseeable future. I can't ask you to leave the farm. Not now. It's Christmas tree season."

Joan wagged her finger at the phone. "Our kids and grandkids come before the farm. Always have, and always will. We'll figure it out on this end. Don't you worry."

In the background of the call, something crashed. Laney flinched, and Eliot's head jerked to the side.

"Crap. Johnny's into the pots and pans. I've gotta go. But you guys are coming? Like now? You're okay to drive through the night?"

"Give me half an hour, and we'll be on the road. We'll be to you before eleven o'clock tonight. If you need to go to the hospital before we get there, just let us know where we should pick up Johnny."

Laney's mom tossed her the phone as she rushed up the stairs, barking orders at Laney's dad, who was grabbing the keys and walking out the back door to start the car and get it warmed up before they set off.

Laney studied her brother's image through the screen. She wasn't used to seeing Eliot so strung out. He was an attorney and, like her, prided himself on being put together and in control. Calm, cool, and collected. Now, though, his face was lined with worry and his jaw clenched.

"It's all going to be okay, El. Carly's got this. She's in good hands. Mom and Dad will be there soon to take care of Johnny. You're doing everything right."

Eliot blinked and then blew out a breath. "You're right. I can only control what I can control. I'm just worried about the babies—and Carly."

"It'll be good when Mom and Dad get there." Eric's tone was subdued. "They always make everything better."

Eliot let out a forced laugh. "That's true."

"All this stress and worry is going to be worth it when you see your babies. I can't wait to hear that my new niece and nephew are here." Laney vowed to herself, then and there, that whatever her next job was, she would make more time to see her family.

The smile on Eliot's face said it all. "I can't wait for them to get here. Thanks, guys. I'm going to go now. Tell Mom and Dad to text me when they're on their way."

Eliot disconnected, and Laney sat still, listening as dresser drawers opened and shut upstairs. Her dad came back inside, snow dusting the collar of his jacket. He rushed past Laney and Eric, flying up the steps to pack his own bag and calling to them over his shoulder. "We're going to want to leave ASAP. Snow's starting."

"Well, shoot." Laney leapt off the couch. "Help me pack them some food for the road," Laney directed Eric.

She got out the leftover turkey and placed slices onto buttered buns. Eric schlepped yellow Jell-O into a plastic container.

"Really, Eric? You think that's going to travel well?"

"Jell-O is a comfort food." Eric narrowed his eyes at her as if she was the crazy one before he scooped another helping of the lemon, banana-chunked concoction into the bowl and sealed it.

Laney opened her mouth to argue but decided against it. "Fair point," she conceded. "Grab some carrot sticks and some bottled water. I'm going to brew some coffee. I worry about them driving so late at night with a long day already under their belt. The snow is going to mess with visibility."

"They'll be fine. They're farmers. They're used to dealing with the elements on very little sleep."

Laney slid the food into a travel-sized cooler just as her mom came down the stairs, two suitcases in tow. "All set?"

"I think so." Joan opened the junk drawer, pulled out her phone charger, and shoved it in the side pocket of her purse.

"Here." Eric took the cooler from Laney and handed it to their dad. "Food for the road."

"Good thinking. Thanks, guys."

"No problem. Anything else we can do?" Laney rested her hip against the counter.

"You can run the tree farm for us for the next month."

"Sure thing," Laney answered out of habit before she processed what her mom said. "Wait. What?"

"The farm. Someone's got to be here to run it. Like Eliot said, it's our busiest season—our only season," her dad added pointedly.

Laney plastered a smile on her face. "Of course. I can handle it."

"Eric, you'll help, too, right?" Her dad studied her brother.

"Happy to be here as often as I can," Eric said easily.

"Thank you. Love you." Her mom and dad hugged them both and hurried out the door.

As Eric rifled through the rest of the leftovers, making himself a second (or third) dinner, Laney stared at the taillights of her parents' truck until they disappeared over the hill that led out of town.

Somehow, instead of helping out on the tree farm here and there, she'd be running it. So much for steering clear of the locals. Sally would be thrilled.

This had "Hallmark movie" written all over it.

Chapter 4

Ford

FORD ANGLED HIS CAR down the long driveway next to the McGregor farmhouse. The heavy, overnight snow had turned to light flurries. He followed the tire tracks to an open space on the right of the red barn where an area had been plowed to serve as a makeshift parking lot for tree-farm goers. Ford managed to squeeze into a spot between two other vehicles. The fresh snow made it nearly impossible for anyone to park in any sort of order.

He rubbed the three-day-old scruff he had growing on his jaw and peered out his windshield. Set against the backdrop of Christmas trees that seemed to endlessly unfurl toward the horizon, the teal-sided farmhouse and worn red barn looked straight out of a movie.

Ford's parents and Isabel were waving at him from where they stood at the entrance to the tree farm. Ford opened his door and then remembered his promise to Eric. He reached behind his seat and retrieved the container of pie. A surge of nervous anticipation hit him when he recalled Eric's last message from the night before.

I think Laney wants some, too. Bring it by tomorrow.

Ford knew he was reading into Eric's text too much. But he couldn't help but think about how it would feel if Laney wanted something from him...beyond a piece of his mom's pie.

How it would feel if she wanted *him*.

He'd never let himself believe it was a possibility, and he really shouldn't get his hopes up now. Who knew what her plans for the future were, but he highly doubted they included a small-town, former-goof-off-turned-mid-level-successful guy like himself.

"About time!" Isabel's voice echoed through her cupped, gloved hands and silenced his thoughts.

"I'm not late." Ford strode in her direction.

"Yes, you are."

Ford heaved his shoulders up and let them fall down. "You're the one who wanted to have family bonding after we just spent all day together yesterday. Then, you went and scheduled it for first thing in the morning. I'm here, aren't I? Where's Daniel? How did he manage to get out of this?"

"Daniel's playing cribbage with his grandpa and Cheryl, thank you very much. If he were here, he certainly wouldn't be complaining. He'd be keeping me warm." Isabel rubbed her hands together.

"Gross. Could we not?"

Isabel smirked and opened her mouth, undoubtedly to say something else that would raise Ford's hackles, but then Ford's mom, Val, held up her hand, making the *stop* sign. "For heaven's sake, would you two quit your bickering? You're fighting like cats, and I'm allergic to cats. Come on, this is going to be fun."

She marched off in the direction of the trees, and the rest of her family fell in line behind her.

Isabel matched Ford's steps. "You know I'm just giving you a hard time, right? Someone has to keep you on your toes, and it's not like you have a girlfriend to look after you."

Ford scoffed, even as his thoughts boomeranged to Laney. "Now we're talking about my relationship status? Really, Iz?"

"I'm just saying." Isabel shrugged, a grin hanging from her lips.

Ford decided not to engage further. Instead, he held up the pie. "I'm going to set this in the barn for Eric, and I'll meet you back out here."

He cut to his right and walked through the open barn door. The homemade sign that championed Joan McGregor's famous hot cocoa rattled on its nail in the wind. Eric was behind the register.

Ford walked over and deposited the pie. "Don't say I never gave you anything. My family's waiting. We've got to find our tree, but I'll swing back in."

Eric shot him a toothy grin before his attention was taken up by the line of folks waiting to check out and get their complimentary cocoa. Ford looked around for Joan, but he didn't see her...or Laney. He shook his head.

Quit pining, you ridiculous welp.

·❤·❤·❤·❤·❤·

Outside, the scent of pine was invigorating. It brought Ford back to a childhood spent tromping through the farm with Eric and Eliot and some of the other kids from the village. They used to play hide and seek, freeze tag, and their own version of the last event in *Harry Potter's* Triwizard tournament—minus the horror.

Today, a couple of kids ducked in and out of the trees, screaming out made-up rules and taunts. One younger boy hung his head and pulled up short as the others ran ahead. Ford recognized him from church. It was Bobby, the youngest of Emily and Pat Kimber's kids.

Ford spotted the boy's parents standing a ways off, chatting with a group of adults. He glanced up and waved to them before turning to Bobby.

"Hey, buddy." Ford bent down. "You okay?"

Bobby's lower lip, just visible above the scarf that was wound tightly around his neck, quivered. "I'm not fast enough."

Ford motioned to the group of kids who darted between trees ahead of them. "What are they playing?"

"They said we were playing snow tag, and I'm it. I'm supposed to try to get 'em."

Ford's heart went out to Bobby. The tree farm should have been a magical place, not one that made anyone feel sad. Ford dropped his voice. "You want some help? I think the two of us can take them."

Bobby nodded his head up and down so fast his stocking hat slipped over his wide eyes, and he had to reach up and shove it into place. "What do I do?"

"Here, climb on my back. But first, grab a snowball so you'll be ready when we get closer."

"Really?"

The eagerness in Bobby's voice made Ford smile. "Really. We used to have snowball fights in these woods all the time when I was a kid. Hop on." Ford crouched lower and waited for Bobby to hoist himself up.

"You good?" Ford asked once it felt like Bobby was in position.

"Uh-huh." The little boy clung to Ford's jacket.

"Alright. I'm going to run at them, and when we get close, fire away."

Bobby giggled, and Ford couldn't help but grin. "Here we go."

Ford took off in a jog, and Bobby's laugh grew louder. With Ford's longer strides, Bobby was in prime position to strike in no time.

"Go for it!" Ford shouted.

Bobby shifted his weight and launched a snowball. It smacked into the back of his older brother, William.

"Gotcha!" Bobby cheered.

Ford lowered him to the ground. "Come on, we're not done yet!" He scooped up some snow and handed the ball to Bobby. "Press your advantage, kid!"

Bobby looked at him like he was crazy but seemed to get the idea. He threw another snowball, and the older kids stopped and started firing snow back and forth.

Bobby's older sister came and took him by the hand. "Come on, little Bob. You can be on my team."

Bobby's smile spread from one rosy cheek to another as he trotted off, grateful to be included. Before he got too far, he turned back to Ford. "Thanks, mister!"

Ford gave him a salute before setting off to try to find his family.

When he spotted his mom and sister, he snuck over to the next row of trees. Inspired by his recent snowball-fight success, Ford bent down and wadded up a pile of snow, packing it into a tight ball. He waited until his mom and Isabel stopped to inspect a particularly large Douglas Fir that would never fit into his parents' living room, and then he launched the snowball right at Isabel's back.

Isabel squealed, spinning around.

Ford chucked another snowball at her. This one hit her in the shoulder.

"Oh, you're on." Isabel ducked behind their mom.

Val stood between her children with her hands on her hips.

Ford stood up from his crouched position and came out from behind a tree. "Isabel, that's cheating. You know darn well I can't throw snow at Mom."

"It's not cheating. It's strategy." Isabel lobbed a snowball in his direction, but he easily sidestepped it.

"Is that all you've got?"

"No. It's not all I've got, you big weenie."

Their mom looked to the sky, as if asking the Lord where she went wrong in raising them.

Isabel bent over to collect more snow.

"You can't hide behind Mom forever. You're never going to get me from back there."

"You sure about that?" Isabel stood upright again and peeked out from around Val. "I've got a secret weapon up my sleeve."

Ford feigned a yawn. "Unless you're hiding one of Dad's old mechanical pitching machines in your coat, I'm not too worried."

"Okay, then. You've been warned. NOW!"

Chapter 5

LANEY

ON ISABEL'S CALL, LANEY lined up her pitch and fired. Her snowball pelted Ford square in the back. Laney clamped her lips together but not before a gleeful giggle escaped. When Ford whipped his head around, Isabel nailed him from the other direction. The look on Ford's face was priceless, and Laney let her full laugh loose.

"Ouch. Sorry about that." She came out from behind a tree, not feeling sorry at all.

Isabel joined them, dusting snow from her gloves. "Told you I had a secret weapon."

"Yeah, yeah. Where did you come from, anyway?" Ford pointed at Laney, who found herself transfixed by the snowflake droplets that clung to his eyelashes and the start of an impressive-looking beard. She must've been more overtired than she thought because the idea of running her hands along Ford's snow-damp jawline and through his hair crowded its way into her head.

The idea was so out of left field it startled her, but she chalked it up to stress and her exhausted brain. She'd stayed up late the night before, waiting on pins and needles until her parents texted her that they made it to Chicago. She proceeded to get up before dawn to run the snowplow and make sure everything was ready for opening day at the farm while also trying her best to replicate her mom's famous hot chocolate for their guests.

She was dragging, but all her tiredness and lingering resentment at being saddled with running the tree farm melted faster than Frosty in the greenhouse when she saw Ford piggy-backing a little boy who was sad and left out.

Dustin would have never done something like that. Heck, most of the guys she brushed shoulders with in her political spheres wouldn't have.

Ford's interaction with Bobby was so pure it had sort of made Laney want to cry. She found herself weak in the knees with the aching sweetness of it all. She could liken it to the kind of total-body sensation that one gets when reading the last page of a book and finding the story tied up so perfectly that you well up with tears of contentment.

She'd cut behind a row of trees to collect herself and so Ford wouldn't see her staring. She'd watched him pick a snowball fight with Isabel, and when his back was turned, she stepped out. Isabel caught Laney's eye, and Laney knew exactly what she wanted her to do. She'd silently scooped her own ammunition, happily replacing her peculiar emotional reaction to Ford with the excitement of a bit of payback. High school may have been a long time ago, but it felt a little like Laney and Isabel had bested Ford at his own game.

"I got lucky"—Laney high-fived Isabel in response to Ford—"and was in the right place at the right time, I guess."

"Unfair home-field advantage is more like it," Ford complained.

"Don't be a sore loser," Isabel said. "You started it."

"Yeah, Ford. You started it," Laney echoed, not even trying to hide her smile.

"You both better watch your back. That's all I'm saying." Ford glanced from Isabel to Laney. When his gaze landed on her, Laney felt something arc between them. Her smile faltered as a fizzy sensation uncurled from her sternum and rolled into her stomach. Laney sucked in a breath of cold November air.

She really needed a nap.

She cleared her throat. "I'll be on guard against mallard mating calls for the rest of the time I'm in town, then."

Ford narrowed his gaze. "Get serious. All the smart ducks have migrated or are hunkered down at this time of year."

Laney rolled her eyes. "You're calling yourself a smart duck?"

"Obviously. Now reindeer, on the other hand, have a very particular call, and this is their season to shine. So, I'd stay alert if I were you." Ford tapped the side of his nose, and Laney snorted out a laugh.

Val came over to the group, and Ford stepped back so his mother could have Laney's ear, severing whatever weird connection she thought she felt with him.

"Laney, dear. I'm glad you're here. I have a question for you. I can't seem to find either of your parents anywhere."

"They're in Chicago." Laney explained the situation with Eliot and Carly. "No babies yet, but my phone is turned up as loud as it can go."

"Oh, my stars." Val clutched her chest. "How exciting...and a little nerve-wracking. Glad your folks can be there. How good of you to run the farm for them. That's a big job for you, now, isn't it?"

"I've got it all under control."

Val's husband, Dave, joined them, and Laney greeted him before turning back to Val. "You said you had a question, Mrs. Marshall?"

"Yes, and please call me Val, dear." Laney nodded, and Val continued. "I like a strong pine scent to last into the New Year, and I can never remember what type of tree I should get."

"A Balsam Fir will be your best bet if you want fragrance."

Fortunately, all the fun facts about Christmas trees Laney's dad drilled into her as a kid stuck through the years, and Laney could answer with confidence.

Isabel scrunched up her nose and surveyed the forest around them. "How do you tell the difference between all of the species? These look exactly the same to me."

"You're right, and that's because they're from the same family of trees. Fraser Firs, the ones over there"—Laney pointed to the quadrant of trees her dad had grown across the path—"are derived from Balsam Firs, so they're very similar." Laney ran her hand over the needles on the Balsam Fir closest to her. "You'll spot a slight difference if you look closely at the needles. See how these are primarily green? If you go and peek at the Frasers' needles, you'll see they're two toned. They're a little more silvery in comparison to the Balsams."

The Marshall family crowded around to get a closer look.

"You're going to be on our trivia team, right, Laney?" Isabel asked.

Laney turned and bumped into Ford. He held out his arms and steadied her. She took a giant step back.

"I promise I won't bite."

"I know that." She put her hands on her hips. "But I don't trust you not to douse me with snow at your next opportunity." She faced Isabel. "What trivia team?"

"For the second annual village-wide Christmas trivia tournament. We launched it last year as part of the Merry Mapleton Christmas Celebration. I'm claiming you as part of our team this year. We could use your holiday expertise."

Trivia was sort of right up Laney's alley, and somehow, she figured this would go a long way in pleasing Sally—maybe even get Laney out of some of the other Christmas clichés—so she nodded. "Sure, I guess. Let me know when it is."

"Don't worry. Julia is going to call a planning meeting."

"Julia Derks?" She was another one of Laney's former classmates who owned the local coffee shop, On Deck Café.

"Yep. Julia Baker now. She married Samson, our village administrator, this past spring."

Laney made a hum of acknowledgement. She remembered meeting Samson at a village bonfire, and she'd communicated with him after he took over as administrator. "Cool. But do we really need a planning meeting for town trivia?"

"You have no idea," Ford said dryly.

"Ford's right. Town trivia is cutthroat."

"You guys are just sore losers." Val stabbed a finger at her own chest. "Us old folks beat them last year."

"We've only had to hear about it for the last eleven months." Isabel rolled her eyes. "Like I said, Laney, we need you."

Laney laughed. "No pressure or anything."

Talk returned to Christmas trees, and Laney kept as much distance between herself and Ford as she could without drawing extra attention—only so he wouldn't catch her off guard with another snowball fight, of course.

After the family picked a stout five-footer for their living room, Laney snapped a picture of the four Marshalls in front of it and followed them to the barn.

"There you are!" Eric rushed from around the counter. "I was trying to call you. The babies are here."

"What?" Laney grabbed for her phone and frowned at the screen. "It's dead. It must've been working hard to pull a signal out here and drained my battery faster than usual. What happened? Is everyone okay? Who called?"

Eric put up a hand, halting her questions. "Dad called. Everyone's doing pretty well. The babies are in the NICU. They are each a little over four pounds. Asher and Gwen."

Tears welled in Laney's eyes. "So small. How's Carly?"

"She had to have a c-section. They tried to stop labor all night, like Mom said they were going to do. But one of the babies' heartrates kept dipping, so they decided to get them out."

Laney pressed her lips together, overcome with a myriad of emotions, when a strong hand settled on her shoulder.

Chapter 6

FORD

FORD DIDN'T THINK BEFORE he tried to comfort Laney. Sure, it was just a stoic shoulder pat, but he was compelled to do *something*.

Laney stiffened under his touch, shooting him a questioning look through watery eyes.

He immediately dropped his arm back to his side.

Val marched past Ford and wrapped Laney in a hug. Laney was stiff as a board when Val embraced her, too, and that made Ford feel marginally better. Laney wasn't just prickly when he tried to be there for her, but when *anyone* tried to be there for her.

"Everything will be okay." Val stepped away from Laney. "And how wonderful that you two stepped up to take care of the farm. I'm sure your parents appreciate not having to worry about a thing here while they're gone."

Eric didn't look convinced. "It's a big undertaking. I'm not sure how Laney's going to be able to handle it while I'm at work."

Laney waved him off. "I'll be fine. If Mom and Dad can do it, I can do it."

"The key word there is *and*. Mom *and* Dad have each other." Eric pointed at Laney. "Unless you have a secret boyfriend who'll step up to the plate and help you while I'm at work, I don't know how this is feasible for one person."

Laney turned bright red. "I don't *need* a boyfriend. I said I'll be fine, Eric."

She shot a look at the Marshall family, and Ford could tell she would rather not be having this conversation in front of them.

"Not to butt in here, but Ford can help."

Ford spun around to face Isabel, who was expertly avoiding his gaze.

"Pardon me?" Laney said.

"Ford," Isabel said his name as if that explained everything. When everyone else just stared back at her, Isabel went on. "He'll help you. Right, Ford?"

"That won't be necessary." Laney spoke before Ford could get a word in. "I mean, he has to work, too. Don't you, Ford?"

Again, Ford opened his mouth, but Isabel cut him off. "He was just telling me earlier in the week how the month of December is his slowest month. I'm sure he has the time to spare, right?"

Isabel finally turned to him. The look on her face said *Don't screw this up.*

"Sure," he said easily.

Laney's eyes went wide before she narrowed them. "No, no. I couldn't put you out like that. I'll be fine on my own."

Her brisk tone made it clear Laney wasn't going to budge on this issue, and it would be useless to argue with her.

Isabel clapped her hands, evidently coming to the same conclusion. "At least you know Ford is around in case you get desperate."

"She's already desperate. She just doesn't know it yet," Eric said.

He dodged a punch from Laney. "Watch it, Eric, or I'll tell Santa to put you on the naughty list."

"I've been on the naughty list for as long as I can remember," Eric said, unfazed. "Now, it's your turn to man the register. I need some fresh air."

Laney slipped behind the old wooden counter as Eric sauntered outside. She closed her eyes and breathed in through her nose as if re-centering herself before addressing them again. "I'm sorry about all that."

"Oh, honey. We've been parenting these two for going on thirty years." His mom motioned between him and Isabel while his dad stepped forward and paid for the tree. "That was nothing we haven't seen before."

Laney smiled, but it looked like it took serious effort. She handed back the credit card and glanced beyond them at the sound of the barn door squeaking open. "Help yourself to some hot cocoa. If you'll excuse me..." She waved the new patrons forward so she could assist them with their payments.

Ford let his parents and Isabel go ahead of him before he ladled himself a drink. Steaming cup in hand, he chanced one last glance at Laney before he left. Dark circles were just barely visible beneath her eyes, and the urge to take care of her hit him hard—to make her smile and to ease some of her load.

If only she'd let him.

Laney must've felt him staring, because she looked in his direction, her gaze sharp. Ford lifted his cup awkwardly before ducking his head and leaving the barn, but not before some of his cocoa splashed out and stained his jacket. Ford silently cursed his complete lack of finesse where Laney was concerned.

When he emerged from the barn, Ford found Eric helping his dad hoist the Christmas tree into the bed of his truck. His mom was shouting out instructions.

Isabel had hung back, and now she wheeled around and pointed at him. "Ford, you're coming here on Monday."

Ford frowned. "Laney doesn't want my help."

"Didn't you see her? She's clearly overwhelmed, and while she may not like to admit it, she's going to need a hand around here when Eric goes back to work."

Ford rubbed his newly formed beard. He would love to help Laney, but he didn't like the thought of showing up unannounced. Ignoring her wishes didn't seem like the best way to prove to her that he wasn't the same guy who had set a dozen chickens loose in the school commons as a senior prank.

Isabel narrowed her gaze. "Don't tell me you're scared to face Laney McGregor's wrath."

Ford bit his tongue because...yeah, he was.

Isabel pursed her lips and stared him down.

"Fine." He held up his hands in surrender. "I don't mind swinging by on Monday. I like it out here."

Ford glanced around the tree farm, filling his lungs with the scent of pine and fresh snow.

Isabel wiggled her eyebrows. "You like *who's* out here, is more like it."

"I don't know what you're talking about."

"You can keep up the act, but I see right through it. So, I guess you should be thanking me for getting you more face time with her."

Ford frowned. "Isn't she dating someone?" Based on the way Eric had joked, Ford didn't think so, but he'd like to know for sure—merely out of curiosity.

"According to social media, she's single. Don't worry. I checked for you." Isabel patted him on the shoulder, a self-satisfied shine in her pupils. She crossed to where their parents were still chatting with Eric before Ford could formulate a retort.

He groaned. The last thing he needed was his sister trying to make something happen between him and Laney. That was so like Isabel. Hadn't she heard Laney?

I don't need a boyfriend.

Clearly, Laney didn't want anything to do with a relationship—with him or anyone else.

Chapter 7

LANEY

LANEY STOOD LIKE A sentinel at the opening of the tree farm. Over the outdoor speakers, "It's the Most Wonderful Time of the Year" played, adding an extra bit of holiday cheer to the crisp, picturesque morning. The dusting of snow overnight was just enough to make the grounds look like a holiday greeting card but not enough to require more snow plowing. Thank goodness.

She and Eric had survived a busy opening weekend, but now she was on her own, which, quite frankly, was well within her comfort zone.

Laney had made a list and checked it twice. She had enough spare change in the register in the barn. She'd prepared back-up batches of hot cocoa so she was sure not to run out. She'd stacked sleds near the entrance to the farm so families would be able to tow their trees back to their cars on their own since, much to her chagrin, she wouldn't be able to be in two places at once, both taking money and out among the trees helping.

She'd gone through all possible scenarios, and she was ready to take on the day.

It was a good thing, too, because a line of cars rolled down the driveway toward the parking lot near the barn.

She checked her smartwatch. Twelve noon, on the dot. It was go time.

As the cars kept coming, a slight twinge of panic crept down Laney's spine, but she shook it off. She'd taken on stuffy politicians without batting an eye. She could handle running a tree farm.

·♥·♥·♥·♥·♥·

Four hours later, Laney was drowning in pine needles. As it turned out, the tree farm was running *her*. She hadn't stopped moving since the families arrived at noon, and it had still been impossible to keep up with all the requests.

So. Many. Requests.

Everyone needed her ear and wanted her expertise on the trees, and she was happy to oblige. But that meant the check-out line was longer than usual because she had to go back and forth between the barn and the lot.

She felt like a licorice rope, all twisted up and then yanked in opposite directions. A small part of her wanted to throw up her hands and yell, "I give!" before burying her face in some of that leftover yellow Jell-O.

She spit out a strand of tangled hair that had worked its way into her mouth. She had foolishly spent forty-five minutes with the curling iron this morning, wanting to look good for the villagers she encountered. Now, her hair hung in limp strands, and she was sure she looked like an overworked elf.

She waved goodbye to her most recent customer and took a second to check her watch, groaning when she saw it wasn't even five o'clock. She had at least another hour or two before she could close, depending on the foot traffic.

Laney started for the barn so she could assist the next paying customer.

"Laney! Can we get your help over here?" Mable Glasheen stood near the entrance to the tree line, flagging her down.

"Sure thing." She redirected her route and proceeded to spend a precious ten minutes she didn't really have to spare helping the Glasheen family decide between a Douglas and a Fraser fir.

Finally, their decision made, Laney took off in a jog toward the barn, certain that she'd have a pile-up of customers waiting to pay for their trees. She cringed at the lack of customer service she was providing, but when she burst inside, she stopped short at the sight before her.

Ford stood, towering over the register, making small talk with her patrons, directing them to the hot cocoa bar, and taking their payments—as if he was right at home.

As if he'd done this all his life.

As if he was just what the Christmas doctor ordered.

Laney's skin bristled, but she couldn't tell if it was because she was annoyed that he'd blatantly disregarded her when she'd specifically said she didn't need his help or because she was secretly relieved that he was here.

He caught her eye, and a hint of red colored his features. Laney could tell by his sheepish expression that he felt guilty.

As *he should.*

Before she could deepen her scowl, he turned back to the job at hand, focusing all his attention on the people he was helping.

Laney squeezed her fingers into fists at her sides before releasing them, telling herself not to be a jerk in front of paying customers. She really shouldn't be a jerk at all. Ford *was* helping her out of a major bind. She'd deal with him later.

For now, she trailed her most recent customer out to the parking lot and helped him secure his tree to the roof of the car before she flitted back through the trees. She took a deep breath of piney air and tried to collect her scattered nerves.

That was her first real breath of the day, and she'd only been able to take it because the barn and the register were in Ford's capable hands.

It was jarring. Around Ford, she usually found herself *holding* her breath, waiting to see what trick he would yank out of his bag and how she could deflect it.

But he didn't seem to be trying to one-up her today. He was just *here*. Present. Helpful.

Laney wasn't sure how to deal with that.

Relying on others—thinking that they'd be there for her in the long run—didn't work for her. Case in point: her cheating ex-boyfriend, Dustin. It was better to do things by herself.

Then again, maybe just for today, she'd take Ford's help.

Because even though it dinged her pride to admit it, she needed him.

Chapter 8

FORD

FORD SHIFTED HIS WEIGHT where he stood behind the register. He'd been at the farm for almost two hours and had helped more families than he could count. He hadn't seen much of Laney since she'd come into the barn and given him a death stare before retreating outside. He'd have to face her at some point, but he was trying not to think about it.

Then again, if she really laid into him, he was perfectly prepared to blame his sister.

He took the break in paying customers as a chance to peek his head outside the barn door. He spotted Laney immediately, almost as if his gaze was attracted to her like a magnet to steel.

Steel was a good descriptor for the unflappable woman in front of him.

She was aiding an older couple whom he recognized as Gladys and Wilbur Reynolds. Laney was hauling their tree toward him. A quick scan of the area revealed only one remaining car in the lot—besides his—which meant the Reynolds were the last customers of the day.

He crossed the opening between the barn and the tree line and reached out to take the trunk from Laney. "I'll trade you."

Her eyebrows shot up so high they almost reached the winter hat she was wearing. "I've got it."

"I know. But you must be freezing." He directed his next words to the Reynolds. "Why don't you all go ahead, and Laney will get you checked out in the barn. There's plenty of cocoa. I can take this to your car."

The older woman smiled a broad smile at him, tucking her hands into her pockets. "How lovely. Isn't Ford charming, Laney? What a nice beau he would make."

"What? Oh no. We're not…I'm not in the market—"

"I would make a nice beau, Mrs. Reynolds. Thank you for noticing." Ford shot Laney a smug smile. He'd promised himself he wouldn't provoke her unnecessarily, but he couldn't help teasing her a bit. The flames that lit her cheeks made him grin. He may never be able to be her real-life beau, but he could enjoy pretending he was good enough…at least in the presence of Gladys and Wilbur.

"You go ahead." He placed his hand on the small of Laney's back and pressed her forward.

Wilbur readily agreed and hit the unlock button on his key. He took his wife by the elbow and walked with her in the direction of the barn.

Laney aimed her gaze at Ford, and if the ground wasn't already frosted, she might have frozen it with her icy glare.

"Easy does it, Elsa." He beamed back at her, and before she had a chance to take him to task, he angled away, whistling a Christmas tune as he headed for Gladys and Wilbur's car.

When the older couple appeared five minutes later with Laney following them, Ford had everything ready to go. They climbed into their car, but not before he heard Gladys comment on what a handsome couple he and Laney would make.

He tried to ignore the way Laney scoffed next to him.

The two of them waved as the older couple drove off.

When their car disappeared onto the main road, Laney spun and faced him, her hands fisting at her hips. "What are you doing?"

"Helping you run the farm. I thought that was pretty obvious."

"I said I didn't need your help."

Ford struck a surrendered pose. "I know, but I had a feeling maybe you'd be in over your head, so I swung over after I was done with work for the day. When I saw the check-out line in the barn winding all the way outside, I stepped in."

Laney closed her eyes and held her mittened hand to her forehead, as if she suddenly felt faint. "I didn't realize it had gotten that long. Were people upset?" She opened her eyes and fixed him with another piercing stare.

He had to tell himself not to look away from her. She was so beautiful...his breath failed him. "Not at all. Everyone understood."

Laney nodded, and some of the fight seemed to seep out of her. "That's good. Folks are usually pretty cheerful when they come to cut down their Christmas tree. Still"—she pivoted toward the barn—"I promised Mom and Dad I would take care of things. I can't have the place falling apart on my watch."

Ford had to hurry to keep up with her. "I'll come back to help tomorrow."

Laney whirled around so quickly he almost ran into her. She opened her mouth to say something—maybe shoot him down, he wasn't sure—but Ford pressed his gloved finger against her lips. Her eyes widened.

"Face it, Laney. You can either take my help or run yourself into the ground alone here. I know I haven't always made life easy for you, but I want to be here now—if you'll let me. No strings attached."

She blinked several times in a row as Ford dropped his finger from her lips. He could practically see the argument she was having with herself in her head. He prayed that she'd relinquish the grip she held on her independence just enough to let him in.

"Fine," Laney huffed. "No reindeer mating calls, though. It'll scare off the guests."

Ford bit down on his cheek to keep from grinning. He loved the way her mind worked. He'd just thrown her completely off, and yet she'd still managed a witty barb. "Understood. Do you need help closing anything up tonight?"

"Not much to do. I'll just bring the hot cocoa inside, lock up, and kill the music and lights."

Ford thought about offering to stay to assist, but something told him Laney needed some space, and he didn't want to push so hard that she pushed him away. "I'll be back at noon tomorrow, then. Or maybe a little earlier so you can give me a crash course in Christmas trees?"

Laney nodded.

"Alright. Goodnight, Laney." Ford turned to walk to where he parked his car at the backside of the barn.

"Hey, Ford."

He glanced over his shoulder to find Laney glaring at him with an unreadable expression. "Yeah?"

"Thanks."

They stared at each other, and after several seconds, Laney gave him a reluctant smile.

She was a sight to behold, backlit by the string lights of the barn, her dark hair blowing in the winter wind, tangled beneath an oatmeal-colored stocking cap. A large part of him wanted to stride back over and take her in his arms, let her lean on him after a long day. Maybe a more self-assured man would have—or a more reckless one.

Ford's reckless days were behind him, so he just nodded in acknowledgement, dipping his chin into his coat and doing the level-headed thing—walking the rest of the way to his car. After all, he'd just secured himself more time with Laney tomorrow. He'd take that win for tonight and live to fight another day.

Chapter 9

LANEY

THE FARMHOUSE DOOR SLAMMED shut behind her as Laney stepped out onto the tree farm grounds. The sun was high in the clear sky, and the air was freezing as it spanked against her cheeks. It was her second day of running the place on her own.

Well, not *completely* on her own.

At the thought of facing an entire day with Ford, Laney shivered. She told herself it was from the outside temperature, but she knew better. What she couldn't figure out was why? Why, all of a sudden, was Ford having this sort of effect on her? She'd always been able to go toe to toe with him and come away unscathed. She'd never felt as unbalanced as she was feeling right now. He was the same guy, so why did everything feel different when he was around?

Laney's phone pinged in her pocket. She fetched it and read the message from Sally.

Sally: Hey, girl! What's on tap for the day? Hopefully crossing off some items on your list! <santa emoji>

Laney: <eye roll emoji> You'll be glad to know I'm holding up my end of the bargain, aka I'm now in charge of running my parents' entire tree farm for the holidays. <wide eye emoji> <pine tree emoji>

Sally: WHAT? What happened?

Laney tapped back a message, filling Sally in on the news of Asher and Gwen.

Sally: Sweet babies! That's amazing news! And this is even better for YOU and Operation Christmas Cliché! <winking emoji>

Laney: Hardly. I can't talk now. I'm waiting for Ford to get here, but I can call you later.

She cursed under her breath the second her message sent. Why had she mentioned Ford by name? Sally would be all over her in—

Sally: Ummmm...who's Ford??

—no time. Laney's face heated in spite of the cold.

Laney: He's no one.

She could practically hear Sally's snort of disbelief from one hundred and fifty miles away.

Sally: Laney McGregor, you better not be holding out on me...I demand details.

Laney: Fine. We went to high school together. He's helping me out on the farm while I cover for my parents.

Sally: He must be a nice man if he's rearranging his life for you like that. Do you two have a history? An old flame to rekindle, perhaps?! <heart eye emoji>

Laney shook her head, even though Sally couldn't see her.

Laney: No! I wish you could have seen how hard I just rolled my eyes. There's never been anything between Ford and me. There isn't going to be anything between us now.

Sally: Sounds to me like you're just trying to convince yourself of that.

Sally: Send me a picture of him!

Laney groaned.

Laney: I don't have a picture of him. Why would I have a picture of him?

Sally: Take one today. You know what they say: Picture or it didn't happen.

Laney: No! Nothing happened. Nothing's happening.

Sally: "The lady doth protest too much, methinks."

Laney: Really? Shakespeare? You're impossible.

Sally: And you love me!

Laney glanced up at the sound of a vehicle and recognized Ford's car pulling into the driveway.

Laney: I've got to go now. We'll talk more later.

Sally: OMG he's there, isn't he? Tell him I say hi! Send me that picture. Details, McGregor. I want DETAILS.

Laney clicked her phone off just as Ford unfolded his tall frame from the front seat of his car, and *details* were suddenly all she could think about. Like the deep set of Ford's dark eyes framed by the lashes that went on for days. And the sloping angle of his jaw beneath her favorite kind of facial hair—not too long and not too short. He had on worn jeans with a brown Carhartt jacket. A hint of a flannel shirt peeked out from the collar and at the hem.

Laney wondered what he smelled like and then told herself to knock it off.

Ford joined her at the opening of the tree line, and whether she wanted it to be or not, her question was answered. He smelled clean and spicy...like oranges and cloves. A little voice in her head made an exaggerated slurping sound, like she was a cat and she wanted to lap him up, and *honestly*, what was going on with her?

"Morning, Laney."

She pulled her wool mittens more firmly into place to buy herself some time to unstick her tongue from the roof of her mouth. "Hey. You ready to work?"

"Absolutely. Just show me what you need me to do."

Laney turned and walked into the trees, thankful for an excuse to put some distance between them. She began pointing out the different species to her right.

"We need to stick mostly in these quadrants. These trees over here"—she gestured to her left—"are a bit smaller because Dad plants on a cycle, so they aren't technically ready for sale yet."

"Got it. So, steer people in this direction."

"Yep. Twine and hot cocoa are complimentary in the barn. Kind of like yesterday, one of us will have to man the register while the other one floats out here and helps people take photos and load trees up. We can switch off."

"Sorry, I stopped listening at the mention of more of your hot cocoa."

"You thought the cocoa was okay?" Laney's ridiculous inner cat perked up its ears, evidently happy to live on Ford's scent and his compliments. She hated that it mattered so much to her what he thought of her silly batch of hot chocolate, but it did. She was barely clinging to her frayed belief in her ability to do anything well anymore.

"It was delicious."

Laney nodded once, ignoring the meowing sound that rang out from somewhere in the back of her brain. "Glad to hear it. Unlimited hot cocoa for you today. I really appreciate this, Ford."

"You know I'm just doing it to strategize my next snowball attack, right?"

"I—wait, what?"

"That was a joke, Laney. You should see your face."

She evened her features and hit him with a no-nonsense look. "I can never be sure with you. No messing around on the job."

"Says the woman who nailed me with a snowball while on the job not three days ago."

"I make the rules around here." Laney stuck her nose in the air and strode toward the barn.

Behind her, Ford chuckled. It was a deep, comforting sound that reminded Laney of a rumble of thunder during a summer night storm when she was safely tucked into bed.

In a word...electric.

She closed her eyes. It was official: Operation Christmas Cliché was totally going to her head.

Chapter 10

FORD

LANEY RAN A TIGHT ship, but to her credit—aside from the brief interlude when he'd found her rolling balls and constructing an admittedly pitiful-looking snowman in the front yard—she'd been right there in the trenches, doing the work alongside Ford all day. When he asked about the snowman, her mumbled response was indecipherable, and her cheeks turned the color of the red stripe on a candy cane. He'd dropped the subject but not before telling her that it added an excellent ambiance to the farm.

That earned him a wry grin.

They'd been at it for over six hours at this point. The sun had set, and the already freezing temperature had dropped with it. Ford's body ached the good ache that comes with worthwhile labor.

He hoisted the umpteenth tree onto the top of the final car of the day and secured it in three places like Laney taught him. He waved as the family drove off and turned to see Laney propped against the barn door. In each hand, she held a cup with steam rising into the night air.

She pushed off the red wood of the barn and walked in his direction. Her cheeks were tinged pink from the cold, and her eyes were lit only by the dim glow of the light from the barn and the string lights along the fence at the opening of the tree farm. She was windblown and smelled like pine and peppermint. Her presence seemed to push the oxygen back into his lungs, bringing him to a more fully alive state.

Laney met his gaze and offered him one of the cups. "You've held up well today."

Ford grabbed for the drink and took a quick sip, grateful for something to do with his hands. "I could say the same for you. It's like you do this for a living."

Ford had been amazed at how much Laney knew and at how effortlessly she seemed to handle everything the farm threw at her—from lines of customers, to the frigid temperature, and even a fight over a particularly impressive spruce.

Laney tucked her chin into the high collar of her coat. "It's sort of like riding a bike, I guess."

"You mean you have muscle memory for running a tree farm?"

She chuckled. "Something like that."

They sipped their cocoa in silence until Laney spoke again. "Though it pains me to admit it, it is way easier with a second set of hands around." She looked up at him through her lashes. "I hate to ask, but is there any chance you're around to help some tomorrow?"

Ford twisted his back, trying to work out the kink between his shoulder blades. "I can be, though I'm going to feel all this manual labor in muscles I didn't even know I had. Aren't you exhausted?"

Laney shrugged, even as her gaze dropped lower on his body before she shook her head and met his eye. At her transparent appraisal, a pleasant rush of warmth spread through him. "In my line of work, I don't get to be tired. Everything that's not a perfectly presented front is a sign of weakness and will be leveraged against me."

Ford thought about that for a minute. He could only imagine the stress of always having to be perfect—or at least appearing so. "That sounds awful."

She shrugged again. "I'm good at it."

"I don't doubt that." Ford said it quietly, but judging by the way she stilled, Laney heard him.

She took a long drink from her cup, giving Ford a chance to study her. Her eyes held the same flicker of unbridled determination as he remembered. If it was possible, she seemed to carry herself with even more self-confidence than she had in high school. The only time he'd seen her waver was when she thought she was failing the tree farm patrons on Monday. His blood hummed with desire to truly get to know her, and he could only hope she'd give him a chance. "What else are you up to this month? When you're not running the farm, I mean."

Because he was watching her so closely, he saw her wince before masking it and arranging her mouth into a level line. "I've got to start the job hunt one of these days."

"Any prospects?"

Laney tipped her head back and forth. "Sort of."

He waited for her to share more, but she took another sip of her drink and changed the subject. "I thought I'd try to hit up the tree-lighting ceremony in town. It's tomorrow, right?"

"Yep."

Laney's jaw clenched, and she nodded. "Okay, then. I'll be there."

Ford couldn't help but chuckle. "Don't sound so excited about it."

Laney squished up her cheeks and rolled her mouth to the side. "Sorry. It's just that...well, I'm not. Excited, I mean. But I'm trying to be a good sport about all this holiday stuff. It's not really my scene."

Ford made a show of stroking his chin, a picture of Laney's life forming in his mind. "You know what I think?"

"No, but I'm sure you're going to tell me."

Ford smirked. "I think"—he leveled her with a stern look—"that you need to have some more fun."

"Who says I don't have fun?"

Ford actually snorted at that. "I'm not even going to justify that deflection with a response. But if you need someone to show you a good time this month, I know a guy."

Laney let out a slight gasp before narrowing her eyes. "What sort of fun are we talking about here?"

Ford held up his hands. "Good, clean fun. Just keep me in mind, okay? I know your parents are gone, and Eric's presence is spotty at best."

That earned him another twitch of Laney's lips. "Thank you. But I'll be good, really."

"If you say so. Consider the offer always on the table if you ever need company."

Ford waited for Laney to acknowledge what he'd said. When she dipped her chin ever so slightly, he glanced out over the tree farm. "Same time tomorrow?"

"Yeah." He felt Laney turn next to him, and when he looked down, she, too, was staring out over the field of pines. "It's so peaceful here."

Ford remained quiet, wondering if she'd go on, wondering when the last time was that Laney took a breath and let her guard down.

In the distance, the bare branches of quaking aspen and maple trees creaked in the evening breeze. The pine boughs rustled as if whispering a story only they knew.

Next to him, Laney shifted. "I should get things taken care of here. You don't have to stay."

"I don't mind."

"I'd rather be alone."

Ford took his time, peering into Laney's eyes. What he saw was a mixture of staunch stubbornness and vulnerable uncertainty. Real emotion. It made her even more stunning, and now that he had a glimpse of it, he wanted more. But he'd pushed her so often in the past he was determined to show her a different side of him, so he settled for a compromise. "Why don't I give you my number in case you need anything."

Laney hesitated but then reached into her coat pocket and pulled out her phone.

Ford rattled off his number.

"Got it. Thanks." She typed something else and then put it away just as he felt his pocket vibrate. "I texted you so you have mine, too."

Be still, my high-school heart.

He nodded, not trusting his voice to betray his thoughts and come out all high and squeaky.

"Goodnight, Ford."

"Bye, Laney."

They parted—Laney toward the barn and Ford toward his car.

Behind him, as the wind gusted, the trees picked up their tale once more, and Ford couldn't help but hope they were telling the beginning of a love story.

Chapter 11

LANEY PRESSED HER PHONE firmly to her ear so she could hear her dad through her stocking cap.

"Everything sounds like it's going well," he said.

"So far, so good." Laney cut through the tree line and popped out into the clearing. The lights hanging from the fencing and the spotlight overhead shone a warm glow on the grounds and made everything seem twinkly and magical. A family was exiting the barn where Ford was inside, manning the register.

"Is Eric there?" Laney's dad asked.

"No," she grumbled. "He has been conveniently tied up at the office this week." Laney explained how Ford was acting as her number two.

Laney had been shocked at how well they worked together. He'd turned out to be a great partner. He anticipated what she needed from him and was quick to jump in and help out. She appreciated that. She appreciated *him*.

She was also actively choosing to ignore the way her heartbeat went from soft snowfall to raging blizzard when he was around.

"That's just like Ford," Jeff said.

"What do you mean?"

"He's always been willing to step in and help me out around the farm."

"Really?" Laney turned as Ford pushed open the sliding door and exited the barn. He immediately went to provide the family he just checked out with some assistance loading their tree.

"After that huge storm, summer before last, he came by and helped me get the farm all cleaned up. He also helped Eric install the new basketball hoop for the court behind the barn earlier this year."

"I had no idea." Laney said it more to herself than to her dad.

"Yep. Ford's a good guy. Please tell him thank you for us."

"I will, Dad. I should go and get things closed up here. The village tree-lighting ceremony is tonight."

"That's right. One of our finest will be on display."

Laney smiled at the pride in her dad's voice. "I'll take a picture for you. Give Mom a hug, squeeze Johnny for me, and tell Eliot and Carly we're thinking of them and the babies."

"Will do. Love you, Laney."

"Love you, too."

Laney ended the call and glanced up to find Ford lingering to her left. As soon as she pocketed the phone, he walked over to her.

"Everything okay?" He was wearing the same jacket he wore all week, but thanks to the warmer temps, no hat today. His dark hair was shaved close around his ears and longer on top. When he arrived at noon, it had been gelled into place, but after a day in the elements, a few relaxed strands fell across his forehead. Laney liked this undone look.

Scratch that.

She did *not* have any preference for Ford or his hairstyle. She was perfectly indifferent.

Laney cleared her throat. "My dad wanted an update on how things are going here, and I wanted to hear how the babies are doing."

"How are they?"

"As well as can be expected for preemies, but they have a long road ahead of them. They're getting supplemental oxygen until their lungs develop a little more, and they both have feeding tubes." Laney took a deep breath. Her mom had sent a picture from the hospital earlier in the day, and Laney loved seeing Asher and Gwen, but she hated how fragile they looked, drowning in the little blue and pink hats they wore constantly for warmth.

"They're being well cared for."

Laney bit her cheek. She refused to get emotional in front of Ford. "I know. I wish there was something I could do for them."

Ford was quiet, his gaze an odd mixture of gentleness and intensity. "You don't realize it, do you?"

"Realize what?"

"That you *are* doing something."

Laney lifted her brow in question.

"You're running the farm. That freed your parents up to help out Eliot and Carly with Johnny, which lets them focus solely on their babies."

"It doesn't feel like much to me, though."

"I bet it feels like a lot to your family."

Laney hitched up one shoulder. She wasn't sure what to do with this new self-aware and reasonable version of Ford. He seemed to have an uncanny knack for reading her and talking her down from the ledge—or at least saying exactly what she needed to hear before *she* even knew she needed to hear it. How did he do that?

Laney adjusted her stocking cap. "We should be just about ready to close up here, huh?"

"You tell me, boss."

"Don't call me boss." Laney nudged him and immediately regretted it when her body flooded with heat at the contact. It didn't matter how much she appreciated grown-up Ford. She didn't intend to flirt with him—or anyone else, for that matter.

Did she?

Ford held up his arms and took a step back, a slight smirk on his face.

Laney turned away from him to hide the blush she felt creeping into her cheeks. She needed to pull herself together when it came to Ford. She was teetering on the brink of dangerous territory, and her heart wouldn't appreciate another break.

"I'll lock up the barn. You can head home if you have stuff to do before the tree lighting."

"I can help you."

"It's really okay. I've got it." Laney stopped talking as Ford walked past her into the barn. He put the lid-locks on the hot cocoa crock and unplugged it before lifting it off the table and turning to her.

Laney scowled at him. This was the Ford she remembered—the one who had an unashamed disregard for her desire to be in control and who seemed to delight in provoking her.

Then again, was he really provoking if he was helping her out?

Laney decided to let him have this one. She hurried to retrieve the money from the register and slipped it all into a cash bag. She led Ford out of the barn, and they trudged in through the back door of the farmhouse. "You can bring that right over to the kitchen. I'll make another batch tomorrow morning."

Ford nodded and walked ahead of her.

Laney peeled off into her dad's office and deposited the money for the day into his wall safe. When she returned to the living room, she found Ford with his hands in his pockets, peering around. "You don't have a Christmas tree in here."

Item number six on Sally's list flitted across Laney's mind.

One cliché at a time!

"Not yet. Haven't had a chance."

Ford didn't say anything in response, and Laney fiddled with the sleeve of her jacket, pulling it down and gripping it with her fingers. "Okay. Well, I guess maybe I'll see you down there?"

"Probably so." Ford swept his hand out, motioning for her to lead the way back outside.

They split off, each to their own vehicle, but the second Laney caught sight of hers, her heart sank. "You've got to be kidding me." Her back left tire was completely flat. She shot a glance across the makeshift parking lot to where Ford was crunching his way to his car.

As if sensing her gaze on him, he turned. She grimaced, and he jogged over. He took one look at her car and said, "You can ride with me."

"No. That's okay. I can change it. It just might take me a while." Her voice wavered. It had been a long time since her dad taught her how to change a tire—like a decade and a half. But she refused to let Ford see her sweat.

"Don't be ridiculous. I'm here. Just hop in with me. We'll worry about changing it later. If you can't, I will."

She shook her head. "No. I can do this. You go ahead."

Ford shot her a skeptical, partially amused look. "You aren't going to take my help with this, are you?"

"I'll handle it. I don't want you to be late."

Ford held up his empty hands, walking backward in the direction of his car. "Fine. Have it your way."

Laney blew out a breath and turned her attention to the task at hand. She popped the trunk and got a brief morale boost when she spotted the spare. Laney slipped off her mittens and tried to pry away the lining that covered the tire. She yanked and tugged, breaking a nail in the process, but it wouldn't budge. She mumbled a few choice words. When she stood back with her hands on her hips, she spotted Ford leaning against his still-parked car with his arms crossed over his broad chest.

Conflicting feelings of annoyance and attraction fought for control in her mind. She didn't like the fact that he was watching her flail about in her attempt to change the tire. But she couldn't deny the pleasant wiggle her heart did at the knowledge that he stayed.

Ford pushed himself off his car and retraced his steps toward her. "This is dumb. Just come with me."

Laney cast a longing look at her car. She hated having to rely on him, and as much as she wanted to dig in, there was a lot riding on getting to this tree-lighting ceremony.

Because once it was over, it was over.

It wasn't like some of the other items on the Christmas Cliché list that were more...flexible.

Yeah, it was just a silly tree-lighting ceremony, and she could totally lie to Sally and say she'd gone even if she didn't make it. But she hated that idea, too, especially since they'd struck a deal, and she wouldn't feel right taking the job referral from Sally and Ron if she didn't hold up her end of the bargain. Laney scowled. That ridiculous list.

Here she was, trying to check off her first real item—she could hardly count that leaning tower of snowman she'd piecemealed together behind the barn—and already it was causing her nothing but problems.

Hallmark Channel, my butt.

"Fine," Laney grumbled.

Ford opened the passenger door to his BMW and waved her inside. She begrudgingly took her seat, and he drove them downtown.

"Downtown" was sort of an exaggeration. There was one main street that ran through the village—Mapleton Avenue. Area businesses lined the thoroughfare, along with a smattering of historic houses and picturesque green spaces.

"Everything looks great." Laney peered out the window of Ford's car. In spite of herself, she felt her spirits rising.

Evergreen wreaths with red bows adorned the streetlights. Small businesses were decked out with window displays full of multicolored packages and other holiday paraphernalia, and lights were strung on every fence post and roof line in sight.

This wasn't Laney's first Mapleton tree-lighting ceremony, but it had been several years. Since college, she had spent the lead up to the holiday working in Madison.

Last year, she'd been with Dustin...until she wasn't.

"If you like these light displays, you should hit up Candy Cane Lane at some point."

Grateful to have something to think about that wasn't Dustin or last Christmas, Laney questioned Ford. "Candy Cane Lane?"

"It's the nickname for the street Julia and Samson live on. A couple years ago, Julia got her neighbors together, and they all decided to deck out their houses with an absurd amount of Christmas lights and festive displays. You can walk down the street throughout the whole month of December. It's pretty remarkable."

"Sounds neat."

"Add it to your list."

Laney froze.

How does he know? Does he know?

"What did you say?" she asked.

Ford shot her an indirect look. "Not like an actual list. You said you were going to try to take in some of Mapleton's Christmas activities, right?"

"Oh. Right." Laney sat back in her seat. She shouldn't feel so mortified about the Christmas Cliché list. It really wasn't that big of a deal. But she'd hate to have to explain the whole thing, calling attention to the fact that, without the referral to Senator McClaren, her job prospects were as empty as toy shelves after the Black Friday rush.

No, thank you.

Ford pulled into an alley that ran along an empty building.

"Is this the old barbershop?" Laney leaned forward to get a better look.

Ford nodded. "It's empty, for now, so we can park back here." The alley led to a lot with four parking spots in it. Ford backed into one of them. "I'll grab your door."

"You don't have to—" Laney started to protest, but he was already out of his seat, shutting his door on her squabble, and walking around the front of his car.

When he opened her door, she glowered at him. "I can get out of a car on my own, you know."

"I know."

Laney turned her legs out and looked up at him. "That's it? That's all you're going to say?"

"Yep."

Laney rolled her eyes. "You're the worst."

Ford closed the door behind her and hit the lock button on his key fob. "And you're cute when you're disgruntled."

Laney scoffed at that, even as her heart did a backflip.

"Come on." Ford led the way back down the alley between the buildings. They turned right onto Mapleton Avenue and walked past the abandoned barbershop. Ford glanced back at it as they passed.

"Ford! Laney!"

They turned to see a couple flagging them down from across the street. Laney recognized Julia and Samson. She and Ford lingered on the sidewalk as the pair crossed the street and came toward them.

"It's good to see you, Laney!" Julia came in for a hug, and Laney warmed.

Okay, so maybe the Christmas Cliché list had its benefits. It was forcing her to get out and connect with the town. She did love the way everyone in Mapleton felt like extended family. So far, no one seemed to think less of her since she'd lost out on re-election, which was a relief.

"You've met Samson, right?" Julia stepped back and tucked her hand into the angle of Samson's arm.

"Yes, briefly. It's nice to see you, Samson."

"You, too. We heard you're going to be in town for a while. Not to start out the night talking work, but if you have some time, I'd love to meet with you to discuss a few business-related items."

"Of course. Mornings are good for me." Laney slipped immediately into assemblywoman mode, but then she paused as her stomach sank. "Though, I'm not sure what help I can be at this point. My term is basically over." If Samson wanted to discuss legislation connected to his role as village administrator, she wouldn't be able to offer him much in return.

"I'd still really appreciate the chance to pick your brain."

"I'll help in any way I can, just as long as you temper your expectations."

"Fair enough. I'm in the office every morning for the rest of this week and next. Stop by whenever."

Laney was struck with how different things were run in Mapleton than at the Capitol—slower, more relaxed...cozier. She didn't hate it.

She smiled at Samson. "Will do."

"No more business talk tonight." Julia tossed Samson a spirited scowl before looking at Laney. "We have more important things to get to. Isabel said she recruited you for our trivia team, and I couldn't be more thrilled."

"Julia has been strategizing this year's trivia efforts since we lost last year," Samson supplied.

"Is that right?" Laney said.

Julia bounced on her toes. "We're trying to give ourselves the best chance to win, and from the sounds of it, you're going to be our secret weapon."

"She's a ringer alright."

Laney snorted at Ford's deadpan declaration. "I am not."

"Are too. You know a ton of Christmas facts, and we all know how competitive you are."

He had her there. Laney grinned, a faint memory coming to mind. "Still bitter about that time I bested you in debate senior year?"

Ford pinched his brows. "You wish. I let you win."

Without any consent from her brain, Laney's lips curved into a smile. "Doubt it. That goes against your very nature, Ford Marshall, and you know it."

She'd become re-accustomed to their bantering the past couple of days, and she loved the push and pull of verbally sparring with Ford. It energized her in a way little else ever had, and try as she might, Laney hadn't been able to quit the game. What scared her was she wasn't certain she wanted to.

Because now, Ford was so much more than the teenage guy she once knew who had no direction and a penchant for haphazard pranks. Ever since he showed up at the tree farm in spite of her assurances that she didn't need him, Laney's eyes had been opened to the reality of grown-up Ford—a really decent guy with a big heart, who liked to have fun but was also reliable and kind. She found herself yearning to get to know him more even as her head repeatedly reminded her of why she was reluctant to strike up a new relationship—the loss of control, the proclivity to get her heart demolished in the process.

Etc. Etc. Etc.

Julia swished her hand, cutting into the charged air between Ford and Laney and interrupting their staring match. "You'll be on the same team now."

"Even better," Ford mumbled under his breath.

Chapter 12

Ford

"What's that?" Laney tipped her ear in his direction.

Ford kicked himself. He hadn't realized he'd spoken out loud. Thank goodness Laney hadn't heard him. He really needed to work on playing it cool. This was what he got for trying to match wits with a woman who was the definition of *too good for him.*

"Nothing," he said. "We should hurry." Ford pointed Laney in the direction of the town's tree, and Samson and Julia fell into step behind them.

The residents of Mapleton turned out in spades for the village's tree-lighting ceremony. The courtyard outside Hal's Diner, which sat almost at the exact midpoint of Mapleton Avenue, was packed with people dressed in colorful stocking caps, scarves, and mittens. Excitement crackled all around, seeming to warm the December air. The mild temperature had given way to the finest of snow flurries, making the event even more charming. Every fence post, bench, roofline, and tree branch in a two-block radius was wrapped with lights, all waiting to be illuminated along with the village's tree.

"Are you guys thirsty? Amanda is manning the café's drink cart." Julia gestured across the way to where another former classmate of theirs stood behind a contraption that reminded Ford of those moveable hotdog stands you saw in the movies.

"I shouldn't have caffeine at this hour, or I'll never sleep tonight," Laney said. "And I'm sort of hot cocoa-ed out."

Ford chuckled at that.

"We can make you a steamer," Julia offered.

"*Amanda* can make you the steamer," Samson corrected his wife. "You have the night off, remember?"

Julia rolled her eyes. "Yeah, yeah. But *you* don't have the night off, dear husband. You should probably find Neil."

"You're right. I'll meet you back here after the ceremony, okay?"

In response, Julia angled her face toward him, and Samson placed a lingering kiss on her lips.

Ford looked away, trying to bury the desire that kept welling up in his chest to kiss Laney. He needed to get serious.

Wake up and smell the cocoa.

Stop pining.

After all, he was the hired help, not someone Laney would ever think about kissing.

"Neil?" Laney asked after Samson left them to weave his way toward the makeshift stage. "As in Neil Schaumburg?"

Julia nodded as the three of them approached the drink cart. "Yeah. The village president. You know how he always gives the welcome speech? Well, he's got laryngitis and, apparently, no voice, so he tapped Samson to run the show this year as the village administrator."

"Gotcha." Laney stepped up, greeted Amanda, and ordered a vanilla steamer.

"You want anything?" Amanda asked Ford.

"Just a coffee for me. Black."

"Coming right up." The curly-haired barista went to work preparing their drinks.

Ford rotated around to find Laney staring at him, her eyes slightly crinkled. "What?" he asked.

"Nothing. I'm just learning a lot about you this week."

"Oh yeah?"

"Yeah, like you can drink coffee after seven o'clock at night, so that means either caffeine doesn't affect you, or you don't need sleep. Which is it?"

"You think I'd have a face like this without my beauty sleep?"

Instead of her usual quick comeback, Laney's eyes skimmed over him, back and forth between his temples, down to his jawline, as if she couldn't make up her mind where to settle them. She opened her mouth and closed it again before meeting his gaze. Were her cheeks rosier than they had been?

"I guess—"

"Hey, guys!" Isabel appeared with Daniel. Behind them were Ford's parents. Isabel reached out and hugged Laney.

Ford wanted to throw something. What had Laney been about to say before his sister's impeccable timing? Why had she been looking at him like that? Also, it was *not* fair that Isabel got to hug Laney whenever she pleased.

Isabel pulled back and extended her arms to Ford. "I'm glad you two can take in the festivities this year. What a great turnout!"

Ford arranged a smile on his face. He shook Daniel's hand and got separated from Laney, who Val and Isabel corralled into a conversation.

Amanda handed Ford his coffee before walking around and delivering Laney's steamer. Ford took a sip and kept one eye on Laney as he talked with his dad and Daniel about the Packers' schedule for the month of December.

Laney's brother, Eric, joined the circle, and he said something that made Laney punch him in the shoulder, but when he slung his arm around her back, she grinned into her drink. Ford caught her gaze from across the circle and lifted up his cup of coffee in a silent toast, earning him a slight smile.

She had a really nice smile. He sort of wanted to collect all the different varieties—like the Pokémon cards of his youth. Except, instead of trying to snap up a Charizard holographic and a first-edition Squirtle, he was setting his sights on drawing out Laney's wry smirk, her full-faced smile of delight, and every little quirk of the lips in between.

Gotta catch 'em all.

"Ladies and gentlemen!" Neil Schaumburg's raspy voice croaked over the speaker system set up in the courtyard. "Is this thing on?" He tapped the microphone, and the thuds echoed through the crowd.

A couple of people yelled, "Yes!" in response.

"He sounds terrible," Daniel said.

"Laryngitis," Ford supplied.

"Still, he just couldn't pass up one tiny chance in the spotlight," Julia muttered, and Ford chuckled.

"As you can hear, I'm a bit under the weather, so I'm going to turn the mic over to our administrator, Samson Baker."

Samson stepped forward from where he stood behind Neil. "Welcome, everyone, to Mapleton's annual tree-lighting ceremony." His clear and deep voice was a welcome relief. "It is my great pleasure to be here with you tonight on this unofficial kickoff to the holiday season."

A round of applause and some woops rang out. Julia let out a catcall, and Laney snickered at her.

Ford was watching her when Samson said, "As most of you know, we're blessed to have the best tree farm in northeast Wisconsin right here in Mapleton."

Laney's eyes flipped from Julia to the stage.

"Let's give it up for the McGregor family, who so graciously provided the village tree from their farm again this year."

More applause rang out. Some especially loud screeches came from Isabel and Julia. Ford shook his head at them, but Laney just smiled. This one looked a little forced to Ford's eye.

"It's tradition for Mr. and Mrs. McGregor to get up and say a few words, but I'm sure you've all heard Eliot and Carly just had their twins, so the McGregors are in Chicago, helping them out. But Laney is here."

Samson put his hand up and over his eyes, searching the crowd.

"Over here!" Eric hollered, and Laney shushed her brother, darting a glance around, almost as if she was afraid to be seen.

Samson spotted her and waved her forward. "Laney, can I convince you to come up here and say a few words?"

Laney rolled her lips into her mouth, and Ford sensed that she was summoning up her courage. She stood up straighter and handed Julia her coffee cup before grabbing Eric's arm.

He yelped. "What are you doing?"

"You're a McGregor, too," Laney sang sweetly, dragging him toward the stage. "You're coming with me—even if you cut out on helping at the farm."

"I told you I had to work, and you said you could handle it," Eric argued, but he shot Ford a wink as they passed him on their way to the tree.

Samson offered Laney the microphone and stepped back, giving her the floor.

"Hello, everyone! It's good to see so many of you tonight. As Samson said, our family has had the pleasure of serving Mapleton's Christmas tree needs for several decades. It has been a great joy to be a small part of your holiday traditions." Laney paused, and when the crowd applauded, she seemed to relax. Her posture softened, and she smiled more assuredly out at the throng of villagers. "I hope to see many of you at the farm this year. This beauty"—Laney pointed to the still-darkened tree off to her side—"is one our family planted fifteen years ago, which just goes to show you that good things take time, and they're better when they're enjoyed by all. I'm excited to see her lit up tonight. What about you?"

The crowd cheered. Laney was a public-speaking pro. What had made her nervous about getting up in front of the Mapleton faithful?

"Why don't you two do the honors tonight?" Samson called out and gestured to the giant button that sat on the stage. "What do you say, folks? Can we give the McGregors a countdown? In ten, nine, eight, seven..."

"Six, five, four..." everyone around Ford joined in.

"Three, two, one!"

Laney and Eric pressed the button together, and all at once, the tree was dazzling, illuminated from within with an array of iridescent, old-fashioned bulbs. The entire courtyard glowed with glittering strands of lights.

Oohs and *ahhs* and applause erupted, and "Merry Christmas" greetings rang out from party to party. A group of carolers struck up "O Christmas Tree."

Ford shifted his gaze from the tree to Laney. Her face shone in the reflection of the strands of lights. Next to her, Eric and Samson were in conversation, but Laney kept her eyes fixed on the top of the tree before closing them. It looked like she mouthed some words, but what she might have said, Ford couldn't tell. Samson spoke to her, and Laney turned in his direction, cutting off Ford's observations.

"Whatcha starin' at?" Isabel sidled up to Ford with Daniel at her side.

He turned to the pair. "The tree. Pretty gorgeous, isn't it?"

"Uh-huh. The tree"—Isabel made air quotes—"sure is."

"That's what I said." Ford kept his face impassive and glanced back to the stage, but Laney was gone.

Isabel smirked at him, and Daniel looked over Ford's shoulder. "There's the family of the hour."

Ford swung around as Laney and Eric rejoined the circle.

"Nice work up there," Ford said.

"Thanks, man. I'm really in my element in front of a crowd, aren't I?" Eric butted in.

Laney shot her brother an exasperated glance, but her eyes danced. "You really stole the show, Eric." To Ford, she added, "I was prepared for a rogue duck call, you know."

Ford's blood turned solid in his veins. Was that why she had been nervous? The thought made him hate himself a little bit.

"I'm not that guy anymore." He said the words quietly and spoke to the snow-dusted ground. He wasn't sure if Laney had heard him, didn't know if he wanted to face her.

She was quiet, so he chanced a look and found her staring back at him, like she'd been waiting for him to meet her gaze.

"I know," she said, offering him a hint of a smile. It was unlike any one he'd seen from her before. He felt the weight of it, like they were finally reading from the same page of the book.

Before Ford could say anything in response, Samson joined them, and the conversation turned to everyone's plans for the upcoming holiday festivities. Ford listened as Isabel and Julia invited Laney to their cookie-decorating girls' night. She hesitated, clenching her jaw before relaxing it and accepting the offer.

"Hey, mister!"

Ford felt a tug on the back of his jacket. He turned to find Bobby Kimber standing behind him, his parents and siblings walking his way.

"Hey, Bobster." Ford crouched down so he was at eye level with the young boy. "What do you think of the tree?"

"It's awesome!" Bobby jumped up and pumped a fist in the air. "Mom and Dad said I could say hi, but now I have to go home and go to bed." Bobby stuck out his tongue.

"You should listen to your mom and dad." Ford raised his gaze as Bobby's parents approached. He stood to greet Emily and Pat before bending down and whispering in Bobby's ear. "You know, if you get enough rest, you're only going to be a better snowball thrower."

"Really?" Bobby's eyes grew wide.

"Definitely." Ford made a cross over his heart. "Sleep helps your muscles grow."

Bobby studied him for a minute before nodding slowly. "Mommy, I'm ready for bed now."

"Is that so?" Emily chuckled and faced Ford as Bobby tugged on her hand. "We should have you come over at bedtime every night. It's usually a fight."

Ford smiled as Pat ushered his family away from the lit tree, but a pit of longing opened up in his stomach. He wanted what Pat and Emily had—a family to come home to and a wife and kids to love on.

"You guys talking strategy?" Laney's voice interrupted his thoughts, and Ford turned to see her staring at him with that same unfamiliar expression as before.

Something tingly lanced through the bottom of his stomach. "What do you mean?"

"I just figured you and Bobby were putting your heads together to plan your next snowball attack."

The tips of Ford's ears burned. "You saw me with him? At the farm?"

Laney blinked, looking to the side as if she was almost embarrassed to admit it. "Like I said, I've learned a lot about you lately."

In that moment, Ford dared to hope she liked what she was learning, that the look on her face that made the smooth skin around her buttery-brown eyes crinkle with awareness was the result of feelings of interest.

Laney turned to peer out over the crowd. "This has been a lot of fun. Thanks for making sure I made it."

Ford followed her gaze and stared up at the Christmas tree. "Do you get anxious? Speaking in front of people on the spot like that?"

"Not usually," she said in a low tone. "Tonight was a little different because of the way the election went down. Hard to know what people think of me."

She was self-conscious. Laney McGregor was worried about other peoples' opinions. Ford could hardly believe it. At the same time, he was thoroughly relieved that he and his past pranks hadn't been the cause of her discomfort. He shot Laney a glance out of the corner of his eye. She was transferring her weight from one foot to the other, and he sensed she didn't want to talk any more about the election, so he changed the subject. "What were you doing up there?"

"What do you mean? Samson asked me to say a few words."

"I mean after the tree was lit." Ford waited for Laney to meet his gaze. "You closed your eyes and said something."

Laney blinked and looked away. "Nothing. It's silly."

Ford stayed quiet, biding his time. As a realtor, he'd learned that silence was often the way to get people to keep talking. By giving them space to process, they eventually offered their own conclusions.

His patience was rewarded when Laney dragged her eyes back to meet his. "Promise you won't laugh?"

Ford nodded.

"I wish on Christmas tree stars."

Ford rolled his head to one side and digested her words. Laney always seemed so pragmatic and firmly in control of her own destiny. The thought of her making wishes on stars made her seem more human—in the best possible way.

"Really?"

"Yeah."

"What'd you wish for?"

Laney's eyes widened before narrowing at him. She crossed her arms over her chest. "If I tell you, then it won't come true. That's the most important rule of wish making."

"Fine." He turned toward the tree, closing his eyes.

"What are you doing?"

"Making a wish." He cracked one of his eyes open to find Laney watching him. "You want to know what I wished for now, don't you?"

Laney swallowed, her cheeks blossoming winter-berry red. "I do not."

"Good. Because I'm not telling you."
Ford wanted his wish to come true, too.

Chapter 13

LANEY

LIGHT STREAMED INTO THE window of Laney's childhood bedroom. She blinked one eye open and groaned, smashing a pillow over her face and rolling over as her brain picked up right where it left off before her fitful night of sleep.

She'd enjoyed herself at the tree-lighting ceremony, and much of that enjoyment was thanks to Ford. She liked being around him, liked his wit and the way he took in everything that was going on.

Her growing attraction to him scared her, so by the time they were in the car on the way back to the farm, she'd all but shut down in an effort to guard her heart.

Ford had tried to draw her into conversation, teasing her about how he was sure he would sell more trees than she would over the course of the holiday season, but she barely acknowledged him, instead giving him one-word responses, not playing along, and pulling out her cell phone.

Like a grade-A diva.

She'd panicked. The silent treatment had been the best defense she could come up with in the moment.

Laney buried her face deeper into the pillow for good measure, the embarrassment over her actions from the night before heating her skin even now.

Giving up on getting back to sleep, Laney scraped herself out of bed and trudged to the bathroom to get ready for the day.

Twenty minutes later, she clambered down the stairs and poured herself a cup of coffee. She stood, staring into her parents' living room and tapping her finger against her ceramic mug.

The farmhouse was still devoid of any decorations, and as Ford had noted yesterday, the room was missing the crown jewel of the season—a Christmas tree of its own. Usually, her family would cut one down on opening weekend, and they'd decorate it throughout the month of December, whenever time allowed. This year, that tradition had been shoved aside with the twins' early arrival.

Laney wasn't sure when her parents would get back to Mapleton—if it would be before Christmas or not—but either way, it felt wrong to run a tree farm and not have a Christmas tree in the farmhouse. She could remedy that. Picking out and cutting down a tree was on her list from Sally, and it was something she could do all on her own. Nothing confusing or uncertain about it. That was just what she needed right now. What better way to get her mind unstuck from Ford than with a little manual labor?

Determined to take back some control, she put on her winter coat, hat, mittens, and boots and trekked outside. Despite the tread of her seasonally appropriate footwear, the compact snow was slippery under her feet. Undeterred, she grabbed one of the hand saws and set off into the heart of the farm.

Laney took her time, ambling through the rows of trees, brushing her hand against the familiar needles. Her breath plumed out, and she relished the stillness and the silence of the early morning. The pine-scented air soothed her, and as she trudged farther into the depths of the trees, her shoulders relaxed. She walked all the way to the back line where the oldest trees stood. These were beauties, and the farmhouse had a pitched ceiling in the corner of the great room, which allowed her to pick out a nine-footer.

Deciding on a skinny, spindly one with enough room for ornaments to hang and be seen, Laney notched out the bottom of one side of the trunk, just like her dad taught her, before slicing through the other side. As the tree toppled and landed with a muffled thump of pine needles hitting snow, a thrill of merriment ran through Laney.

I just axed my own tree. Hear me roar!

Riding the wave of energy, Laney wasted no time hoisting up the trunk and tucking it under her arm.

·♥·♥·♥·♥·♥·

Halfway back to the barn, the merriment had been replaced by misery. Why hadn't she thought to grab one of the sleds her family kept on hand for this very purpose? She'd overestimated her strength and underestimated the effort it would take to lug a nine-foot tree nearly a half mile on her own.

By the time she made it to the house and leaned the tree up against the siding, she was wheezing and cursing her own ambition. Laney put her hands on her knees and filled her lungs with deep breaths. She needed to regroup before attempting to get the evergreen monstrosity she'd so happily—*naively*—selected inside.

She left the tree and went into the house in search of the tree stand. She brought it up from her parents' basement and busied herself with positioning it in the corner of the living room.

When she could put off the inevitable no longer, she squared her shoulders and readied herself to tackle the job of hoisting the tree that was three and a half feet taller than she was up the stairs and into the house. Piece of cake.

Back outside, Laney circled the tree...as if looking at it from all angles would somehow help her cause. She stopped and crossed her arms, staring down the fir. She didn't want to drag it up the concrete steps and risk damaging the branches or losing an unnecessary number of needles. But what, then?

With no apparent solution coming to her, Laney just started trying things.

First, she reached in through the branches and squeezed the trunk with both hands, but when she attempted to lift and walk forward with the tree, she tripped over it and nearly face-planted on top of it.

Laney brushed her hands. "Okay, that's not going to work." She needed to try to get the tree up onto her shoulder so she could walk with it, which was going to be easier said than done. Still, she'd gotten this far; she could do this.

She bent into a squat. "Here we go. Easy peasy. Like a clean and jerk."

Yanking the tree upright with all her might, Laney tried to position herself under it. She got it onto her shoulder, but the weight was distributed unevenly, and she tipped backward. She took a couple reverse stutter-steps to try to regain her balance, but the tree was so awkward and oversized above her, and the snow was so slick under her feet.

"Oh dear." Laney was about to fall flat on her butt, which, in the split second she had to think about it, just seemed like a cruel twist of fate after she started off on this tree-cutting endeavor feeling all but invincible. Then, all at once, her momentum was stopped, and Laney was held in place by two strong hands.

"What are you doing?" Behind her, Ford's deep voice held a hint of laughter.

Laney turned to look at him but ended up getting a face full of pine needles instead. Her own voice came out sounding strangled, and her lungs seemed to have forgotten their primary function with Ford standing so close to her. "What does it look like I'm doing? I'm moving this tree inside."

"Are you moving it, or is it moving you?"

"Very funny." Laney was acutely aware that Ford's hands were still on her hips. Even though they were meant to be steadying her, Laney felt the opposite of steady. If the tree and snow had caused her to lose her balance, then Ford's touch may as well have sent her into a complete tailspin.

"I've got this." Laney moved to take a step out of Ford's grasp, but his grip didn't falter.

"Pretty sure you don't."

Before Laney could bite out a retort, Isabel's cheerful voice sounded from somewhere behind her. "Hey, Laney."

Great. Now she had another spectator for what was quickly becoming one of her worst ideas ever.

"Hey, Isabel. Did you need something? I'm a little tied up at the moment."

Isabel laughed gaily. "You've definitely got your hands full. Ford will help. I'll grab the door."

Isabel moved forward and came into Laney's line of vision. Laney tried to regain her bearings as Ford released her.

"Move to the front of the tree, and I'll get the back," he said.

She couldn't think of anything smart to say, so Laney did as Ford told her. At this point, she was glad to put some space between them. Then again, the second he stopped touching her, she felt the loss. A stupid part of her wondered if her skin would be singed where his hands had rested, so hot was the current that flowed between them.

Laney cleared her throat. "Ready?"

"Whenever you are."

Together, they took the stairs up into the house, one awkward step at a time.

Laney led the way to the tree stand, and with a little maneuvering, Ford set his trunk-end down. Laney walked her hands one over the other and slowly pushed the tree upright. "Can you tighten the bolts for me?"

Ford was already bending and screwing the knobs into the trunk of the tree before she got the sentence all the way out.

Isabel wandered inside behind them. "This is such a great house."

"I think so, too." Laney's voice was muffled from where she still had her face half in the tree as she supported the trunk and waited for Ford to give her the all-clear to let go.

"I love what your parents did with the kitchen."

"Complete remodel about four years back," Laney grunted.

"You should be good." Ford sat back on his heels beneath the tree, and Laney gingerly stepped away, keeping her hands up.

"Are you expecting it to topple?"

Laney dropped her arms to her sides. "No." She scowled at Ford. "It just took a lot of work to get it in here, so I'm a little overprotective of it, alright?"

Ford smirked in response.

"It was well worth the effort," Isabel said, her voice tinged with delight. "What a beauty! I can't wait to see it all trimmed."

"Trimmed. Right." Laney cast a wary look at the tree. When she'd picked the mother of all trees, she'd failed to consider the extra work that would go into having such a beast in the home, and that included how she would decorate it. "That's going to be a big job."

"We'll help you! Won't we, Ford?"

Chapter 14

Ford

FORD WAS MINDING HIS own business under the tree, trying not to dwell on how darn good Laney looked with a gritty flicker in her eyes, but at his sister's excited declaration, he nearly toppled over himself.

"What? No, Izzy." Ford looked up at Laney. She stared at him with a slight frown on her face, but then she glanced away. "I mean," he hurried to add, "I'm sure Laney wants to do it herself, and we wouldn't want to impose."

He was trying to give Laney some space after the way last night ended, but his response felt about as productive as sticking his head into a giant snowbank.

"Of course, we'd never want to push ourselves on you or mess with your traditions." Isabel narrowed her eyes at Ford before turning to face Laney. "I just thought since your parents are out of town, maybe you'd like a couple of extra hands. We could get some other friends over here, too. Make a night of it. It could be fun. More fun than decorating it all by yourself, that's for sure."

"You really think people would want to come over and decorate my parents' tree with me?"

"I absolutely do." Isabel beamed, shooting Ford a rather exasperated look. "Don't mind my dimwitted brother. Leave it to me. Now, I need your help with something."

Isabel practically vibrated with energy as she described the pine boughs she wanted for a blog post she was writing on DIY holiday decor. The pair walked back outside and toward the barn together, chatting away.

Ford trailed them, and deciding to make himself useful, he grabbed a shovel and started clearing a path from the entrance of the barn to the parking area, hoping maybe the cold air would jolt some sense into him—that, or at least reinforce all the self-talk he'd done after the tree-lighting ceremony.

When Laney had basically ignored him on the drive home, he told himself to let go of the idea of her wanting anything more from him than his help on the farm. But he was fighting a losing battle.

If he hadn't figured out that he was completely caught up in all things Laney McGregor, the sensation of having her in his arms—even with a heavy Christmas tree hovering overhead—was enough to have his heart soaring higher than Santa's sleigh.

Isabel reappeared from the barn, her arms laden with trimmed evergreen branches. Ford set down the shovel and jogged over to her, taking some of the load.

"Thanks." Isabel was breathless. "Isn't this great? I can't wait to stage these on my mantel at home. I'm so excited! Thanks again, Laney," Isabel called over her shoulder.

Ford deposited the boughs in the trunk of Isabel's car and twisted his neck to see Laney had stepped out of the barn. She waved to Isabel, who got into her front seat, honked her horn, and drove off.

Ford walked back to Laney's side, completely at a loss for what to say to her.

"Are we okay?" he blurted out.

Not the most suave entry into a conversation, but it was effective.

Laney eyes flew wide. "What do you mean?"

Ford kicked his feet in the powdery snow. What *did* he mean? "I don't know. Last night, it seemed like you were mad or something. You got all quiet in the car."

"Last I checked, being quiet wasn't a crime."

Ford could tell she was trying to make a joke, but she didn't land it with as much force as her usual verbal punch. He chose his next words carefully. "That's fair. But I want to make sure I didn't do anything to offend you. You know, beyond the way I've inserted myself here on the farm."

Laney chuckled, and Ford's heart beat a little faster. "We're okay," she said. "I mean, I'm fine."

"Promise?"

Laney nodded. "I'd tell you if I wasn't."

Ford's gaze jumped back and forth between her eyes, not quite ready to let it go. Because while he felt like he'd been making progress with her—seeing glimpses of who the real Laney was—last night, it all seemed to come to a grinding halt. "Would you?"

Laney straightened. "That's what friends do, right?"

"Right." Ford kept his voice light, even though the sound of the word "friends" rolling off her lips made his stomach plummet. It shouldn't have because they'd always been friends—to a degree. But a pesky bird of hope had taken flight in his chest, making him want more. The friend label was a strong shot of reality.

"That's settled, then." Laney clapped her hands together. "So, Isabel's going to rally the troops to help decorate the tree tonight if you're available."

"I'll be here."

The smile she gave him may have been worth his inner turmoil. It would have to be.

Chapter 15

"I THINK THAT'S ALL of them." Laney shoved the last plastic bin onto the top step toward Isabel.

"I can see why you picked out a giant tree." Isabel hoisted the box up and brought it over to the rest of the containers she was piling in the main room.

Laney switched off the light to her parents' basement, her least-favorite part of the old farmhouse, and gladly followed Isabel into less-creepy quarters. "Yeah, getting it in here turned out to be more work than I anticipated. In hindsight, I don't know how I thought I could decorate it by myself."

Isabel offered her a knowing smile. "You're a lot like me that way."

"Oh?"

"I like to do things all on my own—or at least I used to. I spent four years blazing my own trail in California, and don't get me wrong, it was good for me. But it was also good for me to come home and realize that I thrive within a community."

Laney tugged at the hem of her sweater, making a noncommittal sound in response. She could see Isabel's point, but it flew in the face of the hard line she'd taken on maintaining her independence in the wake of the Dustin debacle and, when she thought about it, pretty much her whole life.

The doorbell rang.

"Good timing." Isabel plopped down on the couch and removed the lid to one of the bins as Laney went to welcome her guests.

When she opened the front door, Amanda, Seth, Julia, and Samson were standing together on the porch.

"I feel like we should sing a carol or something," Samson said as they filed in, bringing an immediate warmth and sense of rightness into the house along with them.

Laney was used to living alone in Madison, but she hadn't realized how lonely the farmhouse was until it was filled with people again.

"I wouldn't stop you," she quipped.

"Don't encourage him. The man's tone deaf." Julia nudged Samson, and he covered his heart with his hand, pretending to be hurt.

"In that case," Laney laughed, "why don't I take your coats. Help yourself to coffee or hot cocoa from the kitchen."

The two couples headed into the house, and Laney turned into her dad's office with their jackets slung over her arm. She placed them on the back of the chair behind the desk just as the front door opened, and Eric's voice sounded in the hallway.

"Eric, you really know how to jump ship." Laney walked out of the office and nearly rammed into Ford, who'd followed Eric into the house. Daniel brought up the rear of their three-car train.

Laney grasped Ford's arms to steady herself, and for the second time that day, Ford's hands were at her waist.

"We've got to stop running into each other like this." Ford's deep voice was even, but when their eyes connected, something flashed across his face that made Laney's stomach bubble. The entryway became peculiarly warm, and when Laney sucked in a gasp, the yummy scent of orange and cloves had her wishing she could sink into his chest and stay a while.

Ford dropped his hands, and the spell was broken.

Laney took a step back. "Exactly my point. If Eric hadn't left me to fetch the tree on my own, I wouldn't keep putting myself in these...these *positions* with you."

Ford's lips quirked. Laney glanced away because her face was already impossibly hot. She wrinkled her brow at Eric, who was looking between her and Ford with a curious expression.

"No one forced you to get the tree by yourself," Eric countered.

"That's neither here nor there," Laney said loftily.

Eric broke into a grin before pulling her into a bear hug. "I sure miss your snark when you're in Madison."

Laney shook her head into Eric's shoulder. "Whatever. Come on. Everyone else is already here."

Eric led the way and walked to the kitchen, immediately wrenching open the refrigerator. "It's looking a little bare in here, sis."

Laney felt Ford behind her, and a fresh wave of embarrassment crested in her chest. She wasn't as much of a cook as her mother. She had always planned to be, but up until this point, life had gotten in the way. Baking she could do. She made a mean kettle of hot cocoa. But beyond that, she didn't have much prowess in the kitchen. It was stupid to be self-conscious about it, but here she was.

"I-I thought we could just order pizza. And Isabel brought Christmas cookies."

"Sounds good to me." Eric ambled into the living room.

Laney closed her eyes briefly before glancing over her shoulder.

Ford's intense gaze licked her skin. He was closer than she expected him to be. He must have taken a step toward her while she wasn't paying attention. She caught another whiff of whatever citrus and spice cologne or aftershave he wore, and her mouth went dry.

"You know it's okay that you can't cook, right?"

She took a deep breath. "Of course. It's not like we live in the 1950s. I'm certainly no housewife—not that there's anything wrong with that," she hurried to add.

Ford chuckled as his eyes homed in on her. "No, you certainly aren't. And no, there isn't. It just seemed like maybe you felt bad about not being able to cook. You realize you don't have to be good at everything, don't you?"

Laney broke eye contact. *How* was he so in tune with her?

And why did holding his gaze make the bubbles floating around her stomach feel like they were now fizzing and popping?

"We both know I'm not all that good at getting a Christmas tree into my house on my own, so there's that. Clearly I'm not good at everything." She tried to keep her voice airy and joking, but Ford reached out and touched her arm, sending a tremor through her entire body.

"I mean it, Laney. Give yourself a break. No one expects you to be perfect, and no one expects you to be able to do everything on your own. I should have said this a long time ago, but I'm sorry if the way I treated you in high school ever made you feel like you had more to prove. You don't. You are enough. Just as you are."

Laney was so stunned by Ford's words that stupid tears sprung up in the backs of her eyes. She looked down to regain her composure.

Her gaze settled on his strong hand resting on her arm, and she found herself wondering how it would feel to lock her fingers with his. It had been a whole year since she'd held a man's hand. It was one of her favorite things about being in a relationship—that feeling of partnership. Nothing over the top, but an outward sign of connection between two people who cared about each other.

She missed it. Maybe that was silly of her, but the sweetness of Ford's gesture just now and the weight he put behind his words, like he meant his apology and was imploring her to believe him, made Laney's heart crack open a fraction. Just enough that she was contemplating holding Ford's hand.

In the middle of the farmhouse kitchen.

For the love.

She cleared her vision and met his gaze. Gosh, he had nice eyes. She hadn't noticed it before, but flecks of gold were sprinkled in the pools of dark green, like tinsel against a Christmas tree.

Pull yourself together, Laney. Now is no time to wax poetic.

"Fine. I hear you." She pitched a brow. "But you know I handled you just fine in high school."

Chapter 16

FORD WAS RELIEVED AT the reappearance of Laney's sharp tongue. He was afraid she was going to let Eric's offhand comment about her kitchen skills ruin her night.

It was ridiculous, but the Laney he knew was just enough of a perfectionist and just hard enough on herself that it might.

The more time he spent with her, the more he wondered if she hadn't let on to how much losing in the November election had messed with her. That, or whether there was something else driving her intense independent streak. Ford used to take the aura of unwavering confidence that surrounded Laney for granted, but lately, there seemed to be a chink in her armor. He didn't like seeing her off her game. Ford thought about their conversation earlier in the day.

That's what friends do, she had said about sharing their feelings. Laney needed a good friend right now, someone who she would eventually open herself up to. He could be that for her.

They wandered into the family room, and Ford sat down on the overstuffed leather couch while Laney collected everyone's pizza preferences before calling in the order for delivery.

"Alright." Laney hung up. "Pizza should be here in an hour. In the meantime, there are cookies. I can't thank you guys enough for coming to help me out tonight."

Julia opened another one of the containers from the basement. "Your parents' ornaments are gorgeous."

"Are all those boxes ornaments?" Amanda asked.

Eric shook his head. "No. These are decorations Mom puts all over the house. Not a single room is left untouched."

Isabel nibbled her lip and shot Julia a look. "Are you thinking what I'm thinking?"

Laney sat down on the couch next to Ford, her gaze darting from Isabel to Julia. "What are you thinking?"

"They want to deck the entirety of your halls," Ford guessed.

Isabel grinned at him. "My brother knows me well. What do you say, Laney?"

"I mean, I guess—if you guys want to."

Isabel and Julia pounced on the boxes and started unpacking decorations.

When Ford glanced at Laney, he noticed her face held the trace of a grimace. He dropped his voice so only Laney could hear him. "What is it?"

"Nothing." Laney didn't meet his eye.

Ford wanted to reach out and use his fingers to tip her chin up to him, but he didn't do that because...*friends.*

Instead, he said, "I can tell Isabel to stop."

"No, please don't. It's sweet." She shot him a rueful grin. "I wish I could have done it all on my own, but I guess I just didn't have the gumption. I don't want to get my hopes up that the twins will be in the clear by Christmas and my parents will be able to come home."

"You're worried about them." Of course she was. Ford felt foolish for not thinking of it before. For as assertive and independent as Laney was, everything she did was always done for others. Her heart was as big as her perfectionist tendency.

"Yeah," she said, almost sounding sheepish. "I check in every day, and they keep saying things are stable, but I guess I expected more progress at this point. It's hard to get the full picture from Mom and Dad over the phone, and I haven't talked directly to Eliot or Carly other than through quick text messages."

Ford wished he could guarantee everything would be okay, but that wasn't possible. He thought for a moment. "You know what I think?"

"What?"

"We should bedazzle the crap out of your parents' house and send them a bunch of pictures. You never know, it could be the morale boost they need. Hopefully, they'll get home to enjoy our decorations in person, but if not, at least you will. In the meantime, you're providing all these fools with a good time. That's something."

Ford and Laney looked out over the room. Eric had donned a stocking cap, cranked up the holiday hits, and was currently singing along to "Last Christmas"—the iconic Wham! version, to be exact—at the top of his lungs. Amanda wore garland around her neck as she and Julia tackled the staircase leading to the bedrooms. Isabel and Daniel sat on the floor, examining ornaments. Daniel held two bulbs up in front of his face, making bug eyes and eliciting a giggle from Isabel.

"Did you spike the hot cocoa?"

Ford's joke was rewarded with a full-on laugh from Laney.

"No. But I'm glad they're having fun, and I have an idea." She stood abruptly and went to the kitchen, banging open cupboard doors.

Ford followed and hoped she wasn't going to attempt to become a culinary master in one night.

"Bingo!" Laney held up a bag of popcorn, a victorious smile on her face. "Let's get popping and stringing!"

·♥·♥·♥·♥·♥·

An hour later, the popcorn garland was draped expertly around the tree, and almost all the ornaments were in place. When the doorbell rang, Laney hurried to meet the pizza delivery guy, and Ford took a moment to assess the room.

Samson had clipped the bottom branches off the tree, and Laney had spread out a plaid tree skirt. Isabel scooped up the pine remnants, and after asking Laney for a couple vases, she'd somehow fashioned exquisite mantel décor from the discarded boughs. They'd placed candles in all the windows and strung greenery around the banister.

Isabel was currently adding cranberry-red beads to the garland. Amanda was tacking up twinkle lights around the island in the kitchen while Seth poured himself another mug of cocoa.

The tree stood, sparkling with old-fashioned bulbs in an array of colors, and all the family's ornaments—from the McGregor siblings' handmade elementary school projects to the Green Bay Packers Super Bowl victory memorial orb—hung with pride.

Because Laney had picked the tallest tree on the farm, they'd needed a ladder in order for her to place the star. Ford braced it for her as she climbed up, and after she got the star in place, she'd stepped carefully back down. To ensure her feet landed on solid ground, he'd settled his hand on the small of her back as she eased to the floor.

"Thanks," she'd said, and it sounded breathless to his ear, but Ford told himself he was imagining things.

They'd paused together, staring up at the star, and Ford had made another wish.

From there, he had helped Laney set up the nativity scene. She told him the Fontanini set was her mother's favorite decoration of them all. When Ford went to place the baby Jesus figurine in the manger, Laney had snatched it from his hands.

"Not yet! We wait until Christmas to add Him to the scene." She'd cradled the little figure before stashing it behind the stable. "When we were younger, Eric and Eliot used to think it was hilarious to hide baby Jesus. Mom would always find him on the back of one of the camels or in some other obscure place around the living room."

Speaking of Eric...

He came bounding down the stairs. "I got the lights strung up in Mom and Dad's room. I'm starving."

"Then you're in luck." Laney reappeared and set two extra-large pizza boxes on the island.

Eric helped himself to a piece, and everyone else followed his lead. They all took their seats back on the couch where they'd begun the night and dug into the cheese and carbs.

"It's looking good in here," Julia said around a bite.

Laney swallowed. "It looks amazing, actually. I'm so grateful."

"I've got another idea." Isabel sat up straighter from her spot on the floor at the base of the tree. "Let's go around and say one thing we're grateful for. I'll start. I'm thankful for Mapleton and the fact that I get to work and live here with the people I love."

Daniel squeezed her shoulder and smiled. "I'm thankful for the *Village Tattler* and the stories I get to write about our town."

"I'm thankful for the café."

"That's mine, too!" Amanda laughed at Julia. "We have the best customers."

"I guess that's mine, too," Seth said.

Samson was next. "I'm thankful for Melly."

The whole room chuckled. Ford doubted anyone was expecting Samson to bring up the middle-aged administrative assistant at the village offices.

"You guys laugh, but I'd be getting my butt kicked at work without her. We're shorthanded, and she's pulling more than her weight."

"Here's to Melly, then." Isabel glanced around. "What about you, Eric?"

"I'm grateful for Laney and the work she's done on the farm for Mom and Dad, and for Ford and the way he's helped." Eric lifted his mug. "Cheers, you two."

Laney held up her glass in acknowledgement, shooting Ford a quick sidelong look. She turned her smile on the rest of the room before he could fully capture the sentiment in her gaze.

"Ford," Isabel prompted.

Ford glanced around at the people gathered in the now fully decked-out room. A peppy Mariah Carey tune played in the background. Everyone's faces were shining, and their eyes were bright. His gaze locked on Laney's, and at the soft smile on her face, a little part of him unraveled. "I'm grateful for friends."

Chapter 17

LANEY

"THANKS AGAIN FOR COMING." Samson walked toward the door, holding it open for Laney as she rose from the chair opposite the desk in his office. When Samson had brought up Melly last night, it reminded Laney of her promise to swing into the municipal center and talk shop with him.

Truth be told, she needed a diversion to keep her mind off Ford and the way he kept surprising her, the way he kept making her want him.

Busying herself with non-Christmas-related (and non-Ford-related) business was just what she needed this morning.

"My pleasure. I don't know Ted Talbert super well," she said of the man elected to take her place in the assembly. "But my colleagues who were re-elected are committed to continuing the work we've begun."

Laney's chest tightened at the thought of being out of her job at the Capitol. She'd been so tied up with the farm she'd almost forgotten about the gaping hole in her life where her career used to be. She did have Sally's promise to put in a good word with Senator McClaren. Since it wasn't a given, that didn't exactly settle her, but at least it was something.

She and Samson walked out into the lobby where Melly had the Christmas carols queued up on the sound system. Giant, sparkly snowflakes hung from fishing line suspended from the ceiling tiles. It was no State Capitol in terms of its decorations, but the Mapleton administrative offices oozed warmth and holiday spirit.

"Where's Donna today?" Laney scanned the desk of the long-time village clerk. It sat dark and empty in the corner behind Melly's receptionist station.

"Didn't you hear?" Melly swiveled around in her chair as Laney and Samson approached. "She went and retired on us. Can you believe that?"

"The nerve of her, wanting to relax and enjoy her grandchildren after twenty years of public service." Samson chuckled.

"Oh, don't get me wrong, I'm happy for *her*," Melly said. "Just not for us. We're about to be swamped with folks turning in their property tax bills! Samson hasn't started the hiring process yet."

"Not true. I listed the opening on our website."

Melly grunted. "And told no one about it."

"I'm waiting to see if the right candidate comes along. I don't want to hire just anyone. I'd like to find someone local or perhaps someone with ties to Mapleton."

"Donna's shoes will be big ones to fill for whoever takes over," Laney said.

Somewhere in the back of her mind, she wondered if that person could be her. She turned the idea over. She hadn't thought about coming back to Mapleton. She'd made her life in Madison, and she'd been happy there. She would be happy there again—especially if the job with the senator panned out. But the idea of working in Mapleton didn't totally turn her off.

"You can say that again," Melly huffed.

Before they could continue the conversation, Marge Wilson scurried up to Melly's desk. "You will not believe this."

"What is it?" Melly turned to Marge, who served as the village's resident volunteer coordinator and all-around busybody. Marge knew everything that went on in Mapleton, and she was in charge of just about as much.

"Heritage Hall is closing. Out of the blue. Middle of the month."

Melly's face crumpled. "Heritage Hall? As in the place where we're holding the Merry Mapleton Ball on the twenty-second?"

Marge nodded, looking grim. "Listen to this." She held up her cell phone and hit the speaker button. "I got this voicemail not an hour ago."

Marge, hi. It's Callie from Heritage Hall. Listen, I have bad news, and I feel terrible you're hearing this over the phone, but Heritage Hall is closing its doors effective December 15. Ownership told all of us today, and I called you first thing. I am so sorry. If there's anything I can do, please let me know. I don't know much beyond it being a financial decision, whatever that means. I can't really believe it myself, but call me if you have any questions. I hope you can find another venue for the ball. Talk to you soon. Bye.

"What are we going to do?" Melly wailed after Marge silenced her phone. "There is no other venue around here that's big enough to hold the entire town. Can they just shut down like that with events still on the calendar? Wasn't there a New Year's Eve wedding booked there? That poor bride."

As Marge and Melly launched into a conversation about their options, Samson and Laney said their goodbyes.

By the time Laney made it back to the tree farm, a solution to Marge and Melly's problem had come to her. She whipped out her phone and shot a quick text to Samson before pulling up a new message to Sally.

Laney: The hall for our town's Christmas ball closed this week. I just offered the family barn. Where have I seen this before? <upside-down face emoji>

Bubbles popped up on the screen immediately.

Sally: You ARE living a Hallmark movie. I am HERE FOR IT.

Laney laughed.

Laney: I figured you'd appreciate this, even though it's not officially on the cliché list.

She glanced down when her phone vibrated twice with incoming texts.

Sally: You know me oh-so well.

Sally: Admit it. You are enjoying all of these Christmas tasks, potential future job aside.

Laney nibbled her lip. Was she? The tree-lighting ceremony hadn't been so bad. It was actually fun to hang out with old friends, and the town really was beautiful, all lit up and bursting with good cheer. Perhaps if she stayed busy—even if it was busy with Christmas things—she could keep herself from thinking about last Christmas and Dustin's betrayal. She tapped out a response.

Laney: Jury's out. (But I'm still counting on that referral!) Talk soon. <kissing face emoji>

Laney tucked her phone into the pocket of her purse and looked through her windshield at the old basketball court.

She climbed out of her car and wandered around the front of the barn, letting herself inside and reminiscing about the fun they used to have playing pickup games out back. Eric, for as much as he gave her a hard time, always included her with the guys.

On the far wall of the barn, a single door opened straight out to the court. Off to the side, her dad still had a barrel of sports equipment.

Laney reached inside and grabbed a basketball. She pressed it between her palms. Flat. She went to the shelf behind the cash register, which was stacked with her dad's tools, and retrieved the trusty old hand pump. She made quick work of inflating the ball and tested it on the plank floor of the barn.

"Good as new." Laney dribbled around. It had been a while, and she was rusty, but it felt good to have a basketball in her hands again, the bounce of the ball against the ground an extension of her heartbeat. She walked in circles, crossing over hands and dribbling between her legs, letting her mind wander. She'd reached the far side of the barn for the third time when a deep voice startled her.

"You know, there's a perfectly good court right outside."

Ford stood just inside the barn door, a crooked grin on his face and his jacket hanging open to reveal a plaid shirt stretched across his broad chest, and Laney dribbled the ball straight off her foot.

Chapter 18

Ford

"Hey!" Laney chased after the runaway ball.

"Sorry." Ford hadn't meant to sneak up on her. He was surprised to see her at all. "I wasn't expecting you."

Laney looked at him funny. "Who else would be here?"

"Eric, actually." They had made plans to discuss his prospective business venture before the tree farm opened. Eric said Laney was tied up for the morning, which was why Ford agreed to meet at the barn.

Laney scoffed. "Why would Eric be here? His lack of presence is the whole reason you got stuck being my assistant, remember?"

"How could I forget," Ford said dryly. His heart surged when Laney's lips ticked up. "Actually, we were just going to talk about some work stuff."

"What sort of work stuff?"

"Nothing major. Do you still play a lot? Basketball, I mean."

"No, actually." If Laney noticed his conversational U-turn, she didn't say anything. "This is the first time I've dribbled around in years. You?"

"I've fallen out of practice. Need an opponent, or are you just going to wear a hole in the barn's floor there?"

"You want to go now? I thought you were meeting Eric."

Ford shrugged. "He's not here yet, so why not? Unless you're scared."

Laney smirked and popped her hip out, holding the ball under her arm. "You know better." She glanced at the register. "I do have a tree farm to run."

"Excuses, excuses. You don't open for another hour."

Laney didn't answer right away, but Ford knew she'd agree to play. She never backed down from a challenge.

"Alright, you're on." She bounced the ball with one hand and wedged open the back door with the other.

Ford followed her outside. They were both wearing jeans and a version of winter boots, so it wasn't going to be the prettiest game, but Ford didn't care.

Laney stopped at the arc of the three-point line and held the ball between her palms. "What are we playing up to?"

"First to twenty. Call your own fouls."

"Deal."

Laney bounced the ball to him to check it, he bounced it back, and then they were on.

Without hesitating, Laney drove to the basket. Ford matched her, shuffling in defense, but she pivoted and scored a reverse layup.

"You always were weaker on your left side," she taunted as Ford grabbed the rebound and dribbled back out to the top of the key.

"Watch it, McGregor." He checked the ball. When Laney tossed it back to him, he dribbled between his two hands for a bit, planning his move.

Laney faked a yawn. "There's no shot clock you have to run out, you know."

"Funny." Ford drew out a couple more dribbles, just to stick it to her, before he drove left. Laney jabbed for the ball, her momentum propelling her forward. He pulled up and shot a jump shot, which went swishing through the net.

"What's that you were saying about my left side?"

"Yeah, yeah." Laney's eyes gleamed as she snatched the ball.

·♥·♥·♥·♥·♥·

Twenty minutes later, they had shed their winter jackets. The score was 18-all.

"Next basket wins." Laney dribbled around the three-point arc.

Ford's lungs burned, but his body hummed with adrenaline. He smirked. "Don't miss, then."

"Wouldn't dream of it." Laney turned sideways, her face set as she started angling forward, protecting the ball from him as he tried to steal it away. Their bodies were pressed together, and Ford did everything he could to stop her from getting into a good position to take her shot. Laney was a lethal combination of strength and softness. He'd gotten up close and personal with her curves in the last thirty minutes, and it'd nearly brought him to his knees. She also smelled so good, which gave her an unfair advantage, but Ford wasn't about to complain.

She faked a spin left and then swiveled back to her right. Ford knew the second she got a step on him, and he couldn't make up the space. She threw up a layup, and the ball rattled around the rim before swishing through the net.

Laney held up her hands in victory, shooting him a wicked grin. "Winner, winner."

"I'd call for a rematch, but I don't think the result would be any different. How are you not exhausted?" Ford bent over, sucking in deep gulps of air. He couldn't even say he'd let her win, not when he was so clearly gassed.

Laney laughed, and Ford glanced up at the sound. Flyaway hair hung loose around her face. Her cheeks were flushed from exertion and the cold, and her eyes sparkled with mirth. Standing with the barn behind her, she took away any breath Ford had left.

"I may not play basketball as much anymore, but I keep to a strict running regimen. I'm not as out of shape as you," she teased.

A car horn honked, stopping Ford from making a reply. He stood upright and squinted into the sun.

Eric parked and jumped out of his truck. "Were you guys playing without me?"

"I was playing. I'm not sure what you'd call what Ford was doing."

"Hey!" Ford held his arms out to the side. "You only beat me by *one* basket."

Laney just laughed. "A win's a win." She glanced between Ford and Eric. "Who wants to tell me what Eric is doing here? We all know it's not to help out at the farm."

Eric rolled his eyes.

Ford couldn't help his chuckle. "I'm looking into starting my own real estate agency."

Laney whipped her head around. "What? That's amazing, Ford!"

"Nothing's finalized. I haven't passed the exam I need to take. I'm just tapping into Eric for his accounting expertise so I'm ready if I pass."

"You're going to pass." Laney said it as if it was a done deal, and Ford's chest expanded.

"Time will tell, I guess."

Laney stared at him for a minute and looked like she was about to say something else, but her phone rang from where it sat on top of her winter coat. She retrieved it, and her eyes went wide. "I-I should take this. Excuse me." She placed the phone to her ear. "Dustin, hi."

Laney's voice took on a tone Ford didn't recognize, and something about it made his insides curdle.

"Who's Dustin?" Ford asked when Eric joined him on the court. Together, they watched Laney walk into the barn.

"Her ex-boyfriend."

Ford glanced at Eric, whose trademark easy-going expression had turned to flint. Every muscle in Ford's body went rigid. He had no idea what Laney's history was with Dustin, but taking his cues from Eric, he sensed it wasn't good.

"Do we need to be concerned?" Ford tried and failed to keep his tone even.

Eric shot him a look and then shrugged. "Laney can handle herself. She's proven that. But it doesn't mean I don't have a few choice words for the guy."

Ford opened his mouth to ask for clarification, his pulse hammering in his ears at the thought of this Dustin character doing anything that would hurt Laney, but Eric spoke again.

"We should get to work. I don't have a ton of time, and I'd like to be out of here before tree farm patrons show up, or I'll get roped into conversation. You know Mapleton." He repeatedly brought his fingers to his thumb, miming chitter-chatter. "Let's meet in the farmhouse."

Eric strode back over to his vehicle, and Ford cast one last look toward where Laney had disappeared into the barn.

He was sure she had everything under control—she always did. But that familiar desire to care for her rose up from his toes and struck him just below the ribs, in the same part of his side that ached after their pick-up game, burrowing itself right under his heart.

Chapter 19

LANEY

ON SATURDAY EVENING, LANEY pulled up outside On Deck Café to take part in cookie-baking night. Julia had texted to remind her of the open invitation, and Laney talked to Eric about covering the farm with Ford's help, so she was able to join her girlfriends.

She'd also be able to check another item off Sally's Christmas Cliché list. *Bake and decorate Christmas cookies* was listed at number three.

Though Laney had given Sally a hard time about the list when they texted earlier in the day, she'd be lying if she said she wasn't looking forward to tonight. After her phone call with Dustin yesterday, she was ready to bury her muddled feelings in sugar, frosting, and sprinkles.

The café was fully decked out for the season. Walking through the doors was like slipping into a winter wonderland. The scent of fresh coffee grounds mixed with gingerbread soothed Laney's buzzing nerves. Julia and Amanda had strung a line of lights around the perimeter of the ceiling. Attached to the usual bell that hung over the door was a bunch of mistletoe, and Laney made a mental note to walk through the door solo from now until the Christmas season was over.

She took a step into the dining room. Patrons sipped their drinks at tables with holly-berry centerpieces. Some cozied up on the couch in front of the fire. Homemade stockings hung from the mantel, and warmth emitted from both the fireplace itself and from the smiles on the faces of all of Julia's guests. On Deck

Café was a special place, and within these four walls, Laney felt like nothing bad could touch her.

The tree Julia picked out from McGregor Farm was decorated in the corner by the fireplace. Laney crossed the room to check it out.

After a couple minutes, she looked up from where she was peering at a particularly beautiful porcelain angel ornament to see Julia walking toward her from behind the counter, wearing a festive green-and-red-checked apron. "I'm so glad you could make it."

"Me too. Your tree turned out stunning."

"Thank you! I asked everyone in town to contribute an ornament, so we have quite a spread."

Ornaments ranged from old-fashioned gold stars and candles to colorful, singing Disney characters. The result was a striking, if eclectic, tree.

"I love it."

"I should have told you to bring an ornament tonight." Julia palmed her forehead.

"It's okay. It's a good excuse to come back."

"I like the sound of that. Come on. Amanda is in the kitchen with Isabel and her friend, Grace."

Julia led Laney to the counter where two male baristas were working. Laney recognized Amanda's husband, Seth, behind the register, but the guy manning the drive-thru window was unfamiliar.

"That's Jacob. He's a new hire," Julia said, following Laney's gaze. "And he's single." Julia wagged her eyebrows, clearly mistaking Laney's curiosity for interest.

Laney held up her hands. "No, I—"

"Jacob." Julia cut her off and drew the man's attention.

Laney clamped her mouth shut and put a cordial smile on her face.

"Yeah, boss?" Jacob's gaze bounced from Julia to Laney.

"This is Laney McGregor, a classmate of mine who is back in town for the holidays. Laney, Jacob Veraton."

"Nice to meet you." Laney shook his hand.

"Likewise." Jacob clasped her hand a little longer than necessary, dropping his gaze in a quick and appreciative look up and down her body before locking his eyes with hers and giving her a good-natured smile.

Jacob was handsome in a drummer-of-a-rock-band way. If Sally were here, she'd be teaming up with Julia and pushing Laney directly into his tattooed arms. She tried to be open to the idea. After all, maybe Jacob could take her out on a holiday-themed date so she could check that item off the Christmas Cliché list.

Laney returned his smile and waited for a spark of anything to ignite. It didn't.

"Well, then," Julia said after a beat. "We'll be in the kitchen until the rest of the guys get here to talk about trivia night."

Seth nodded. "Smart of you to lure them here with the promise of freshly baked cookies."

"Not my first rodeo." Julia smirked and led Laney along.

When they entered the kitchen, Laney took off her jacket and stuffed her mittens and hat up a sleeve, stowing her winter gear on a coat hook. Christmas music poured from a Bluetooth speaker, and she greeted her friends over strains of Nat King Cole.

"I think you turned my new employee into a lovesick puppy." Julia tossed Laney an apron covered in snowmen as she joined the girls around the large kitchen island.

Laney slipped the apron over her head and knotted it behind her back. "That's very flattering, and I'm sure he's a great guy, but I'm not really interested."

Isabel's head popped up from where she manned the standing mixer. She was wearing a white-and-red ruffled apron, and somehow, she pulled it off. "Why's that?"

"It's just not the best time for me to start seriously dating right now—in between jobs and all that."

Laney lifted her shoulder as if it were no big deal, even as Dustin's voice played in her head: *I was a fool, Laney. I never should have let you go.*

Laney scoffed to herself. Let her go? She'd left. There was nothing Dustin could have done about it. Then or now. But that still didn't make it hurt any less.

Sure, she'd humor Sally and go out on a date for the Christmas Cliché challenge, but striking up an actual relationship made her more anxious than Rudolph on his first day of flying lessons.

Laney closed her eyes briefly when Ford's face flashed in her mind. For some reason, around him, the anxiety melted away.

"If you say so." Julia's unconvinced tone drew Laney's thoughts back to the kitchen. The café owner reached under the counter and pulled out a large mixing bowl and sifter. She pushed them across the island to Laney. "Isabel's handling the wet ingredients for the sugar cookies if you want to measure out the dry ingredients. I'll grab the flour for you."

Relieved to have something to occupy her focus that wasn't her relationship status, Laney scooped out heaping cups from the jar of flour Julia retrieved, carefully tapping them even with the back end of a butter knife and then smoothing them down before dumping perfect measurements into the bowl.

Across from her, Julia set out a rolling pin and a rainbow of sugar-sprinkle shakers before leaning against the counter and addressing Laney again. "You know, Samson and I started dating at probably the worst time for both of us. I was just out of a relationship, and he was new to town."

"Seth and I were new coworkers when we hit it off. Not ideal," Amanda piped up. "Though, it was a good thing we had an understanding boss." She winked at Julia.

"I convinced myself it wouldn't work with Daniel because of my job, but then I realized how dumb I was being and quickly made that right," Isabel put in. "Thank goodness." She held up her hand and stared at her engagement ring with a look of pure bliss before her eyes shot to Laney.

Laney swallowed hard. She understood what her friends were doing, but she hadn't expected cookie-decorating night to turn into *let's all shine a spotlight on Laney and her lack of a love life.*

"That's nice—for you."

Grace glanced up from where she was rolling peanut-butter balls between her hands. "If you haven't gathered, this is their nice way of telling you that you shouldn't let timing or circumstances dissuade you from taking a chance on love."

"Especially if you think you've found the right guy," Isabel added.

"O-kay." Laney stretched out the syllables. "I get that, but I don't know Jacob at all. I hardly see how I could know if he was the right guy."

"Who says we're talking about Jacob?" Julia asked the room.

They lapsed into a weighty silence with only the whir of the mixer filling the air.

"You and Ford seemed to have a nice time together at the tree-lighting ceremony," Amanda said after a minute, her voice nonchalant. "And when we decorated at your folks' house."

"We did." Laney wasn't going to lie. She could only pray that the heat creeping up her neck didn't turn her skin splotchy. They also had a *nice* time playing basketball. Even here in the kitchen, over twenty-four hours later, she could practically feel his body molded against hers as he played defense. Laney had never considered basketball to be a romantic sport, but somehow, going head to head with Ford behind the barn had her heart racing—and not just from physical exertion.

They worked side by side yesterday, trimming boughs at the back lot line after closing, and again today, staffing the farm until she'd left for the café. They'd talked and teased, and it was all so effortless. He hadn't pressed her about her conversation with

Dustin, and she'd never been more grateful to be able to talk to someone who wouldn't pity her. She doubted he had any idea how much it meant to her...just that he'd been there.

It didn't hurt that Ford was the opposite of Dustin in every way—loyal, trustworthy, kind.

"I tried to set Ford up with Grace," Isabel said offhandedly.

It was a good thing Laney had two years of political-poker-face practice under her belt, because she managed to keep her expression neutral when she looked to Grace. "I didn't realize you two—"

Grace waved at the air in front of her. "Oh no. There's nothing going on between Ford and me. We went out to dinner once, mostly because Isabel wouldn't get off either of our backs."

"Hey, now! I just want what's best for the people I love."

"I know, I know." Grace bumped Isabel's hip. "As smoking hot as he is, I can't see Ford as anything but a friend."

Isabel made a sour face. "Can we not talk about how attractive you find Ford?"

Grace lifted a delicate shoulder. "Well, he is. With that angular jaw and perpetual five o-clock shadow."

Amanda nodded. "You're right. He's like a brooding regency gentleman. He's always had a sort of mysterious, bad-boy air about him. Don't you think so, Laney?"

Laney's grip slipped on the utensil she was using, and she flung flour onto the counter. "Shoot. Um, yeah. I guess. Though, he's been less of the troublemaker I remember and actually really helpful on the farm. But I can't say I've ever thought much about Ford's looks."

She peered down to make sure her pants hadn't gone up in flames because...*liar, liar.*

"He's a good man, that brother of mine," Isabel said. "He's got a lot going for him other than his chiseled jawline."

"Yeah. About that." Laney dropped her voice and spoke directly to Isabel.

"What? His jawline?"

Laney flicked flour at her, and Isabel giggled. "Ford told me about starting his own agency."

"He did now?" A slow smile lit at Isabel's lips. "It's about time he got excited about his venture."

"That's just it. Honestly, I don't think he would have told me at all if Eric wouldn't have shown up to discuss finances."

"You know Ford. For all his messing around, he may as well be a closed book when it comes to real emotions surrounding stuff that actually matters. It's like bottling it all up is a defense mechanism of some sort."

"Yeah, but why? Especially with this. It's a big accomplishment. Isn't he proud?"

Isabel tapped her chin. "I think he is. He's just always been a little insecure. I think it'll take the right person for him to share his feelings with." She held Laney's gaze for a minute before smiling. "You ready with the dry ingredients?"

Just like that, talk turned to more general topics. They mixed cookies, snuck bites of dough, laughed, and discussed the upcoming town festivities.

The whole time, Laney couldn't get the girls' comments—and Ford and his chiseled jawline—out of her mind.

Chapter 20

FORD

FORD AND ERIC CLOSED the tree farm, grabbed a quick bite to eat, and talked through a couple work things before making the quick trek into town. They were meeting the rest of their friends at On Deck Café where Julia had summoned them for trivia-night prep. Ford had protested to Isabel, who'd demanded his presence, but when he and Eric walked through the door of the café and the smell of freshly baked cookies wafted out from the kitchen, he was grateful he hadn't put up too big a fight.

Laney was also here, so...

"Hey, guys." Samson greeted them from where he stood next to Seth and Daniel in front of the fireplace. Ford and Eric joined them, and they all shook hands. "Amanda just popped her head out and said the last batch of cookies is coming out of the oven as we speak, so they shouldn't be too much longer."

Sure enough, Ford heard laughter, and then Laney emerged from the kitchen with Grace. Ford's gaze immediately settled on Laney. She looked relaxed and comfortable, like she'd known Grace for years. Isabel's assistant was beautiful with her Southern California blonde hair and blue eyes, and Grace couldn't be nicer. But Ford didn't think he'd ever see her as anything but a little sister.

Laney, on the other hand? There was nothing sibling-like about his feelings where she was concerned. The woman turned Ford's world on its head. Tonight, her hair was pulled back into a simple ponytail, and her face shimmered in the twinkly lights of the café.

She looked effortlessly stunning in an olive-colored knit sweater and dark-wash blue jeans.

"Hey, guys!" Laney smiled as she and Grace joined them by the fireplace. "How did everything go at the farm?"

Eric gave her a thumbs up. "Smooth sailing."

"That's a relief. I wasn't sure if you remembered how to run things. The only reason I felt okay leaving it was because I knew Ford would be there."

"Hardy-har-har, sis. Good one." Eric tugged on Laney's ponytail, and she swatted his hand away.

Even though Laney was only teasing Eric, Ford couldn't help but puff up at the thought of Laney believing in him. He liked being someone she could depend on.

Something seemed to have shifted and settled between them over the course of the past two days, like the foundation of a house as gravity tugs it to its final resting place—not far enough that the structure becomes weak or damaged, but enough that it becomes solid.

Just where it's supposed to be.

After Laney had hung up with Dustin, she hadn't brought up the phone call or what had transpired, and Ford didn't pry. They'd set to work as before. Ford teased her and tried to make her laugh, and Laney ran her mouth with a string of comebacks.

Ford was surprised at how easy it was to be around Laney doing normal, everyday things. In the past, he'd assumed that if he wasn't pulling pranks or goofing off, they wouldn't have found any common ground. But the longer he spent in her presence, the more he felt like maybe he wasn't as out of place there as he'd assumed he would be.

Julia emerged from the kitchen with Amanda and a platter of cookies. There were spritzes decorated with red and green sprinkles, oversized peanut-butter balls, traditional sugar cookies frosted and sprinkled in a kaleidoscopic of hues, and a pile of ginger snaps. Everyone took one and found a seat around the fireplace, and they got down to business.

·❤·❤·❤·❤·❤·

After Julia gave them their homework (*"Watch as many Christmas movies as possible between now and the event!"*), and Isabel announced their team apparel (*"Ugly Christmas sweaters, of course!"*), and Laney came up with a team name, which had them all rolling, the official trivia-planning session concluded. The group disbanded, striking up individual conversations amongst themselves.

Ford's phone vibrated in his pocket, and he excused himself from where he was chatting with Laney and Eric to check his messages. Vince Vos had texted him.

Vince was a couple years older than Ford, but the two had bonded over the past year.

"Everything okay?" Laney asked when he stowed his phone.

"Yeah. Actually, I have a proposition for you."

Laney angled her head, and a mixture of skepticism and intrigue pooled in her eyes. They were more golden than brown in the evening light of the café, like melted butterscotch. "What kind of proposition are we talking about?"

"You know me," Ford chuckled. "A good, clean proposition. Vince Vos needs help. He was supposed to be St. Nick for his two nieces tomorrow night."

"Kristy and Ashton's kids?"

"Yep. They have a tradition where St. Nick leaves goodies in shoes they set out on their front porch on the eve of the Feast of St. Nicholas."

Laney furrowed her brow. "Really?"

"It's a Dutch pastime or something. I didn't ask a lot of questions." Ford shrugged, and Laney giggled. He got so lost in the sound he lost his train of thought, but then he caught Eric staring at him, and he cleared his throat. "Anyway, Vince forgot about a commitment he made at the high school, so he wants me to play St. Nick."

"Now we're talkin'." Eric slapped him on the back. "You could really pull off a white beard, man, and red is definitely your color."

Laney clamped her hand over her smile.

Ford's neck flamed. "Actually, that's the thing. I wouldn't be seen, or at least I better not be. The tradition holds that St. Nick knocks on the door after dropping off the goodies and then disappears by the time the kids get to the porch to find the treats."

"That's so cool." Laney's creamy eyes glowed.

"If you aren't busy and you're still trying to take in some of the holiday happenings around town, you could lend me a hand. This is a unique opportunity, after all."

"When you put it like that, how could I resist?" The charmed quality of Laney's smile sent a jolt down Ford's backbone. She swung her gaze to Eric. "You can close down the farm to give us enough time to get over to Kristy and Ashton's, right?"

Eric overemphasized his exhale. "If I must."

The three talked logistics for a couple of minutes before saying their goodbyes. Laney went into the kitchen to grab her cookies, and Ford and Eric turned toward the door.

As soon as Laney was out of earshot, Eric leveled Ford with an incredulous look. "St. Nick, huh?"

"What?" Ford slipped on his jacket. "Vince needed the help. I can show you the text if you don't believe me."

"I believe you. What I can't believe is how you've somehow gotten Laney to go along with you. When she arrived home at Thanksgiving, she had all but sworn off Christmas *and* men. It's interesting, is all. Very interesting."

Ford had the door halfway open and was about to ask Eric to clarify when Julia yelled behind him. "Ford! Eric! Wait. Take some of these cookies. We made too many."

Ford stopped and turned to see Julia gesturing to Laney, who hurried their way with a plateful of colorful sweet treats in each hand. She passed off the first one to Eric, who retraced his steps into the café to where Daniel and Isabel had flagged him over to the fireplace area.

Laney handed the second plate to Ford.

"Hey, you two!" Julia pointed upward. "You know the rules."

Ford glanced above their heads.

Mistletoe.

Next to him, Laney stared up at the Achilles heel of all non-couples at Christmastime, her face a shade paler than it had been.

"Chop, chop, you guys. It's bad luck not to kiss if you're standing under mistletoe," Julia said solemnly. "I will not test fate going into trivia night."

The rest of the room turned their attention to the door.

"Kiss. Kiss. Kiss. Kiss," Eric chanted, pumping his fist up and down.

Laney's pale face went bright red. When she met Ford's gaze, her eyes were as wide as the platter of cookies he held.

"We don't have to," he said under his breath. "It's a dumb tradition."

Laney blinked once. Twice. She gave an almost imperceptible shrug. "Yeah, but I don't want any bad luck."

Before Ford could register what was happening, she stood up on her tiptoes and placed a featherlight kiss right where the crease at the corner of his lips met his cheek.

Laney's lips were pressed against his skin for no more than a second, but in that second, something that had been floating around inside of him seemed to click into place. He forgot to breathe. Even his jaw went slack on a gasp.

Then, it was over. Laney rested back onto her heels, looking up at him through her eyelashes as, behind her, Eric grumbled about how that hardly counted as a real kiss, and Isabel, Grace, and Julia squealed for more.

Ford leveled them all with a stern look over Laney's shoulder. The last thing he wanted to do was make Laney uncomfortable. "That's enough, you mistletoe heathens. Our job here is done. We've repelled the holiday bad luck, at least for tonight, yes?"

The rest of the group voiced their agreement with varying degrees of enthusiasm.

When he glanced back down at her, Laney offered him a new kind of smile. This one held a hefty layer of respect, a sprinkling of trust, and a full serving of appreciation. "Thanks for that."

"Don't mention it. I'm a big believer in non-coerced consent."

She laughed outright, the low, lyrical sound warming the blood in his veins, making it feel like mulled cider.

What he left unsaid was that if he was going to kiss Laney again—deeper, for real—it wasn't going to be because some dead plant or their friends forced them into it. He would kiss her when he knew she wanted it as desperately as he did. And he would take his time.

Because that split second of lip-to-lip contact? It left him wanting more.

So much more.

Chapter 21

LANEY

"YOU'RE PANTING." FORD'S DEEP voice rumbled through the thin, night air.

Laney sucked in a breath and held it. She was crouched down behind him as they hid around the side of Ashton and Kristy Klink's house. She could blame the way her breath was coming in quick bursts on the adrenaline and excitement at their secret endeavor, but in reality, it had more to do with being pressed up against Ford's strong, warm body.

Again.

"Sorry," she murmured.

Ford chuckled, and Laney felt it more than she heard it—even through their dueling layers of cold weather gear.

"I'm just teasing you."

Laney released her breath and nudged him. "Well, stop. You're making me nervous."

In more ways than one. And also, don't stop.

Laney gave herself a mental shake. Tonight was not the time to turn into a pile of Christmas mush—*Chrismush?*—where Ford was concerned. The holiday belief system of two small children was hanging in the balance.

She readjusted her grip on the bag of goodies she was carrying, glancing down at the Lego set the Klinks had picked out for their daughter, Caroline, and the zoo animal board book for their newest addition, Georgia.

"I don't want to blow this," she whispered.

"We won't."

Ford's confidence was extremely appealing, as was being on this after-dark mission with him. Laney couldn't deny that she liked being on his team.

"How do you think we should play this?" she asked, directing her focus back to the task at hand. "Getting past the front window is going to be our major hurdle—both on the way to the porch and on the way back."

Ford nodded. Light poured out through the panes of glass that took up most of the front wall of the ranch-style home.

Laney was afraid that the instant they knocked, the girls would jump onto the couch under the window and spot them as they tried to make their getaway. "Our best bet might be to leave in the other direction and go around the back of the house to get back to your car so we don't have to cross in front again. It's a longer route, but we should be able to stay more hidden."

"Smart strategy."

Laney chuckled, feeling like a little kid. "You know me. Strategizing is sort of my MO."

"That's why I keep you around." Ford looked over his shoulder and winked. The man could pull off a wink.

Laney's skin tingled. She was a human-sized tuning fork, and every time she calmed herself down, Ford seemed to know the exact right note to strike. In this case—even if his praise was tongue in cheek—he'd hit upon her delight in being useful.

Ford glanced toward the front walkway. "You ready to do this?"

"Let's go."

They stepped out from the side of the house and ran in a bent-over position, ducking under the front window.

Ford led the way up the steps to the front porch. There, four single shoes were set out: two of the tiny, pastel-color variety; one black, men's business shoe; and a woman's running shoe.

It hit Laney all at once how adorable this was. It was pure and magical and everything the holiday season should be. A heady mix of nostalgia and a sensation she recognized as hope—something she hadn't felt in a long time—coursed through her and made Laney's hands shake. To think, she would have missed out on all of this if she'd had her way. Not only would Dustin have stolen the happiness from her memories of last Christmas, but from this one, too.

She blinked back the tears that tried to squeeze out of the corners of her eyes, but of course Ford noticed.

"You okay?" he mouthed, shooting her a look that was warm and kind.

Laney bobbed her head up and down, offering him a grateful smile.

Searching her eyes, Ford seemed to accept that she was, in fact, okay. He set about helping her retrieve the gifts from her paper bag. They worked side by side to place the treasures in the appropriate shoes, and when they were done, they sat back on their heels to admire their work. Ford glanced at her and back at the shoes before shooting her a thumbs-up. She could tell he was silently asking if she thought their mission was complete.

Laney straightened a folded pair of pajamas near the littlest shoe and turned back to Ford. "Looks good to me," she whispered. "You knock."

"Get ready to run," he said under his breath. They'd have to cross the driveway, cut around the side of the garage, and sneak behind the Klink's house to make it back to their parked car.

In one quick motion, Ford opened the storm door and pounded on the wooden front door with three sharp knocks. "Go!" he hissed.

Laney hopped off the porch, with Ford just behind her. Excited squeals from Caroline and Georgia rang out from inside the house, and little feet pounded the floor as the girls ran to the door. Hopefully, Kristy and Ashton took their time unlocking it.

Laney's legs churned against the snow-covered grass until she connected with the driveway's cement. She slid on a patch of ice but managed to keep her balance, propelling herself forward to the far side of the garage. Ford wasn't so lucky. She heard him go down behind her—a heavy thud followed by a suppressed curse. By the time she turned, Ford was already scrambling to find his footing.

The front door opened, and a strip of light from inside covered the front walkway. Ford and Laney dove as one around the corner of the garage. They landed next to each other in a heap on the ground.

The cold, wet snow soaked through her jeans, but Laney didn't risk moving. She glanced at Ford, who was similarly frozen in place, staring back at her.

Together, they listened to the elated voices of the youngest Klinks. Laney's heart swelled, and a smile broke on Ford's lips. It flooded his face like the streetlight on the road in front of them. Laney spotted a small white scar above his right eyebrow. She wanted to ask him about it, but she didn't dare speak.

After a couple of minutes, the quiet of the night was restored as the family made their way back inside.

Ford got to his feet first, wincing and rubbing his backside.

"Are you okay?" Laney whispered as she took his outstretched hand and let him help her stand up.

"Nothing hurts more than my pride."

Laney snorted. "Not all of us can be perfect."

Ford narrowed his eyes. "Watch it, Laney. I haven't forgotten about your snowball cheap shot, and I'm surrounded by a whole lot of ammunition right about now."

"You wouldn't dare."

Ford cast a glance toward the house. "You're right. But only because I refuse to be the one to spoil the magic of Christmas for Caroline and Georgia. Come on. Let's get out of here."

He reached for her glove-covered hand as if it was the most natural thing in the world and tugged Laney along around the back of the Klink property and toward his car.

Their St. Nick mission was officially accomplished, and Laney couldn't help but think about how Sally's mission for her to embrace Christmas was turning out to be a very good thing—and not just because of the promise of a job on the back end. In fact, when she was with Ford, the job with Senator McClaren was the last thing on Laney's mind.

Laney stumbled at the realization.

Ford stopped, giving her time to regain her balance. "You good?"

Was she? She should have been focused on rebuilding her career, which was in shambles. But with Ford by her side, it all seemed less bleak. Less significant, too. That was a whole different type of terrifying.

She pressed her lips together, forcing them into a closed-mouth smile. "Yep. Totally fine."

She made a move to continue their trek around the house, but Ford tugged on her hand. "I don't believe you."

Laney looked up into his Christmas-tree eyes, and the care she saw reflected back at her made her entire body sigh.

"You want to talk about it." Ford started rubbing his gloved thumb over the top of her wrist.

Laney's heart burned in her chest, and she squeezed his hand. Surprisingly, she *did* want to talk about it—to unload some of it—and there was no one she'd rather explain it to than him.

"I feel like I'm on a holiday teeter-totter," she tried to explain. The lines around Ford's eyes puckered, but he stayed quiet. "Moments like this are so good, you know? But then I feel like I'm yanked back to reality, which is me...jobless. I keep getting caught up in the happiness of the season, but it's going to fade once the calendar turns over, and then what?"

Chapter 22

FORD

THEN WHAT, INDEED.

Ford forced himself not to blink under Laney's direct gaze. His mind was racing as he worked to process everything she'd just said. It was frustrating to him that, in sharing this piece of herself, Laney was admitting that this wasn't real life—at least not for her.

"Maybe you could figure out a way to live in a Christmas version of *Groundhog's Day*," he suggested.

Laney turned her head, cough-laughing into the night.

"What?" he pressed on. "If anyone could do it, it would be you."

"Thanks for the vote of confidence." She faced him again, some of the tension in her face gone. But then she frowned. "I don't want to go around and around in circles, though. I've got to figure out a new direction. It's just hard not knowing what that'll be."

"Fair. You've always been a woman with a plan. It's one of the things I admired about you when we were younger—still do, actually."

Ford could barely believe he'd said the words. Apparently, he was the kind of guy who opened up and shared feelings now. Cool.

Cool, cool, cool.

Before he could panic about coming on too strong, Laney grabbed for his other hand and peered up at him, her searching eyes like cups of hot cocoa, all warm and sweet. The urge to kiss her swirled around like melted marshmallows in his stomach.

Focus, Ford.

"What if I don't figure it out?"

"You will." He pressed her hands, willing some of the heat that was streaking through him at her touch to spread back to her. "After all, if I can figure out my life after all my past misdeeds, then certainly you can."

This earned a chuckle, and Laney's shoulders relaxed. She flipped their hands so their gloved fingers were intertwined. "Honestly, I thought you'd just end up as a duck imitator for hire."

Ford rocked back on his heels. "You wound me, McGregor. Throwing high school back in my face like that. Low blow."

"What! I'm paying you a compliment. You were impressive with that duck call."

Ford leaned in to where Laney had angled her body toward him. They were sharing the same patch of cold, night air, the hint of cinnamon on Laney's breath tickling his senses, making him bold. "I can do more impressive things with my mouth these days."

Laney's eyes fell to his lips before rocketing back up to meet his gaze. "Oh yeah?"

Ford just nodded, refusing to break eye contact. The air shifted, charged with new energy.

"Prove it," Laney whispered.

Ford's heart shot to his throat, carrying his mouth forward. He was a fraction of an inch away from pressing his lips to Laney's when frantic barking broke the stillness of the night.

The two of them jumped apart. Laney's hooded eyes flew wide, and wordlessly, they took off in a jog in the direction of Ford's car.

No use hanging around for the neighbors to discover them lurking around the Klinks' house on the brink of a kiss that Ford was pretty sure would be life changing—*if* it ever happened.

"That did not go as planned," Ford murmured as they ran along. If he didn't know better, he would say someone had been spying on them and had intentionally interrupted their moment. For kicks and giggles. He wouldn't put it past the Mapleton faithful to make him work for it.

Laney snorted. "You should have seen your face."

She grinned at him, and despite being supremely exasperated at the disruption of their kiss, Ford grinned back. "You know what I want to know?"

Laney pulled to a halt outside his car door, eyeing him carefully. "What?"

"Who let the dogs out?"

They both dissolved into laughter, causing the canines to strike up their chorus again.

Chapter 23

LANEY

LANEY ARRIVED AT HAL'S Diner early for trivia night. It had been a long day on the farm after an equally long night spent surfing the internet, searching for anything she could find out about Senator McClaren and poring over other job prospects and options for her next career move. After sharing with Ford how she was unsettled at the absence of a plan for her future, Laney decided she could do something about it.

But after the near-kiss and the howling dogs heard 'round the world—or at least around Mapleton—the visions of Ford dancing in her head were all Laney could focus on. In the end, she had slammed the computer shut and flipped on *Elf*, deciding to take Julia's trivia night homework seriously. But not even Will Farrell cracking jokes in a skin-tight elf costume had been able to take her mind off Ford.

Now, Laney was intensely aware that she'd see him again in a matter of minutes. She felt like fireworks were coursing down her windpipe and invading her lungs. Her skin held a charge, and her whole body was snapping with electricity.

This out-of-control sensation was exactly what Laney had sworn to herself she would avoid after Dustin broke her heart, and she didn't know what to do about it. She could play it off as no big deal, but the truth was that the more time she and Ford were spending together and the more she was getting to know him, the more her heart was skating in Ford's direction.

She was terrified, and she wasn't above eating away her feelings. There was no better way to do that than with a delectable platter of cheesy, onion-y, potato-y, bacon-topped goodness. So, when Hal approached her table and set a heaping platter of loaded French fries down in front of her, Laney rubbed her hands together. "Thanks for this, Hal."

"My pleasure. Consider it brain food. You guys will need it if you're going to take down the reigning champs."

Laney dug in, grabbing a napkin to keep the cheese from slopping onto her sweater. Not that it really would have mattered. At the farm, Laney had pulled the red-and-white number she was wearing out from the back of her mom's closet. It was…something. The striped sweatshirt was accented with three-dimensional peppermint orbs, and the whole look resembled a candy-cane explosion. It was as if King Kandy, from the iconic children's board game, *Candy Land*, had spewed his lunch all over her.

Laney's phone dinged, and she wiped her fingers before turning it over on the table to reveal a message from Sally.

Sally: Miss you! How's it going in Mapleton?

Laney snapped a selfie of herself in her sweater and sent it back.

Sally's response was immediate.

Sally: Good heavens…

Sally: …where can I get one?

Laney snorted and shoved another fry into her mouth.

Laney: This, my friend, is a one-of-a-kind Joan McGregor original. Only the best attire for Christmas Trivia Night.

Sally: Trivia night?! I'm so jealous.

Laney: It should be pretty cutthroat from what I hear. How are things with you?

Sally: Fine. Fine. Though, I am still waiting for a picture of Ford... Will he be there tonight?

Laney: <eye roll emoji> He's on the team, so yes.

Sally: No excuses, then. Take a picture of him and send it to me, or I'm going to think he doesn't exist.

Oh, Ford existed. He *definitely* existed. Laney started sweating beneath her sweater.

Laney: I can't just take a picture of him. I'm not a creeper.

Sally: Stop. I know you can work your phone with your eyes closed. Don't tell me you can't snap one covert picture.

Laney looked up from her phone as the door to the diner opened with a *whoosh*. She waved to Amanda and Seth who were followed closely by Julia and Samson. She typed a quick message back to Sally, promising to try her best, before she stashed her phone.

Soon, the entire team was assembled, with Ford and Eric rounding out the crew. As greetings were exchanged, Laney told herself to play it cool where Ford was concerned, even though she sort of wanted to jump his bones.

She cast a quick look at him as he slipped off his coat, and the fry she was chewing got caught in her throat. She coughed hard.

Amanda patted her on the back. "You okay there?"

"Yeah, sorry." Laney gestured in a circle at Ford's chest. "That look is something else, Ford."

He wore a green-and-red, color-blocked sweater. In each quadrant was a different elf. The sweater was clearly meant to be worn by a woman—or at least someone with a smaller stature. It only hung to Ford's mid-stomach. He'd paired it with a white turtleneck which accentuated his broad shoulders and narrow waist.

"What?" Ford looked down at his attire. "I thought it was perfect."

A hiccup of laughter escaped, and Laney held up her thumb and pointer finger in an A-okay sign. "Yep. Perfect."

"You're one to talk. The peppermint balls are a nice touch."

"I was going for candy-cane chic."

Ford's lips ticked up, and Laney marveled at how easy it was to banter with him. It was no wonder she was drawn to him...and slowly lowering the wall around her heart. How could she not?

Laney blinked and realized the entire table had gone quiet, listening to their exchange. Her face may as well have been a solar flare. She reached for another fry. "We should get a team picture, don't you think?"

"That's a great idea!" Julia glanced around and flagged over her dad, handing him her phone. "Here, everyone, crowd in."

The team smushed together around the table, showing off their ugly-Christmas-sweater finest. Somehow, Isabel managed to make wearing an old tree skirt poncho-style around her neck look like a fashion statement, but everyone else looked equally kitschy.

"Okay. A little closer. Ford scooch in." Mr. Derks made a waving motion with his hand. Laney's right side was pressed up against Ford's left, and she stilled when she felt his hand settle on her hip. She stopped herself from looking down at it but barely.

"Say cheese!"

Mr. Derks snapped the photo. "One more now." He held the phone up and took another photo. "There you go. That's as friendly as I'm going to be with *the competition* until the trivia night is over." He handed Julia's phone back with a good-natured grin and sauntered to his table.

Laney shifted her body to get a reprieve from being tucked next to Ford, but she immediately felt empty at the loss of contact.

"A photo-op, huh?" Ford crossed his arms, and his turtleneck rode up, revealing a narrow line of taut skin at his waist. "You getting sentimental on us?"

Laney tore her gaze away from Ford's beltline. If he only knew her motivation.

"Nah. You never know when I'm going to need some blackmail on you and Eric." She hooked her thumb in her brother's direction. His knitted snowman sweater was as terrible as Ford's. "Julia, can you send us that pic?"

"You bet."

Laney smirked at Ford as her phone vibrated. She sent off a quick message to Sally before placing her phone face down on the table. "What do we do now?"

As if responding to her question, Marge tapped the microphone on the temporary stage Hal had fashioned to the side of the bar. "Is this thing on?"

A squeak of feedback had those in attendance yelling, "Yes!"

"Okay. Sorry, sorry." Marge held up her hands. "Would everyone please take their seats? We're going to get started here in two minutes."

Chairs scraped across the floor, and feet shuffled as all the trivia contestants and spectators worked to find a spot in the at-capacity bar.

Laney scooted her chair in and ended up wedged between Eric, who settled into the open chair to Laney's left, and Ford, who Isabel pushed into the chair to Laney's right.

"Watch out, or my elves will steal your peppermints," Ford said.
Laney snorted.
"What?"
"That sounded a lot like innuendo."

Ford blanched, and Laney chuckled. She appreciated being able to gain the upper hand on him every once in a while, to feel a bit in control. But her laugh got caught in her throat, and fire and ice waged war in her stomach when he winked at her, his eyes darkening in the low-lit diner.

"Alright, folks. Welcome to the second annual Merry Mapleton Christmas Trivia Night." Marge, who was dressed in a light-up sweater complete with a battery pack attached to her hip, waited for the crowd to get out its applause and cheers before continuing. "Competing tonight are three teams. We told them the theme for team names this year was Christmas carols. I think you'll be delighted with what they came up with."

Laney shared a smirk with her teammates, doing her best to ignore the way the full length of her spine was still sparking due to Ford's flirting.

Marge went on. "To my right, we have *Olive the Other Reindeer.*" The crowd clapped as the team members waved to their fans. "To my left, give it up for your defending champs, *12 Drummers Drumming Up A(nother) Victory.*"

Laney rolled her eyes as the "old folks" stood up. Julia's mom and dad, Isabel and Ford's parents, and the rest of their teammates made a big show of bowing and raising the roof.

Isabel put two fingers in front of her eyes and then pointed them at her mom.

Julia bellowed a loud, "Boo!"

"Finally, in the back, we have—" Marge paused and took a deep breath, as if saying the name would be the death of her. "*Watch Us Roast Your Chestnuts.*"

Laney's entire team leapt to their feet and stomped, pounding the tabletop, whooping, and being generally obnoxious. Marge shook her head from across the bar, and Laney giggled as Amanda high-fived her across the table.

When Laney sat back in her chair, she inadvertently bumped into Ford.

"Ope, sorry." She rocked forward again.

"No worries." His words came out low and soft, tiptoeing across her skin. He casually draped his arm over the back of her chair. It gave them more space, shoulder to shoulder, but when his warm forearm grazed the back of her neck, it sent Laney's pulse screaming. Their eyes locked, and Laney had a hard time looking away. It was definitely time to accept that she didn't want to. She eased back and blew out a discreet breath, savoring the feel of Ford's strong arm against her shoulders. She was sure her cheeks were the color of cranberry sauce, but she didn't care. With the way Ford was looking at her, even in her ugly Christmas sweater, she felt gorgeous—and ready to kick some trivia butt.

"Okay. Okay. That'll do. Time to get down to business." Marge held up her hands and started explaining the rules. Each team had a white board. Marge would ask a question, and they'd have thirty seconds to deliberate and write down their answer. When time was up, they'd present it, and Marge would keep track of how many questions each team got correct.

"Are we ready to play?" Marge asked, yukking it up with the crowd.

Julia clenched the dry-erase marker in her hand. "I'm so nervous."

"Question number one." Marge glanced at her notecard. "Where is the National Christmas Tree located?"

Everyone squashed in and looked to Eric and Laney.

"Oh, I know this." Eric's eyebrows knitted. "At least, I used to."

"It's the Ellipse," Laney supplied. "It's right near the White House."

Eric snapped his fingers. "That's it."

Julia scribbled down the answer, and when Marge called time, she held up their board. They were the only team to get it right, and Laney couldn't hide a smug smile.

This was going to be fun.

Chapter 24

Ford

THE CROWD AT HAL'S was buzzing. Marge was in her element. Ford's parents were snuggled up and beaming. It was a good night made infinitely better because he spent the majority of it with his arm around Laney.

Ford was captivated, silently observing the way she pulled her top lip into her mouth when she concentrated, listening to the melodic sound of her voice as she reasoned out answers, and enjoying the vibration of the side of her body against his as they laughed together at the antics of the town and the other teams.

The score stood:

OLIVE THE OTHER REINDEER – 7
TWELVE DRUMMERS DRUMMING – 9
CHESTNUTS – 8

Their team had pulled to within one point of the old folks' team because Samson somehow knew that Kathleen Kelly was the character who said a line about things shaking out and putting up more twinkle lights in *You've Got Mail*.

"How?" Eric had asked, mouth agape.

Samson had seemed almost embarrassed. "Growing up, we had rom-com night every Friday when my dad was deployed."

"That is awesome." Isabel smacked Daniel's arm. "Let's institute that for weekly date night."

Ford smothered a laugh when Daniel looked physically pained. But now it all came down to this.

Marge held up a notecard and read out the final question. "What do the composers of holiday favorites 'Sleigh Ride,' 'Let it Snow,' 'Silver Bells,' and 'The Christmas Song' have in common?"

Laney groaned next to him. "I have no clue."

"Does anyone know who the composers are?" Daniel asked.

Everyone shook their heads.

"We should just guess, then," Julia said. "Give ourselves a shot. Maybe they all wore glasses? Or secretly hated Christmas?"

"Maybe they were Jewish." Ford tossed out the suggestion as a joke.

"Wouldn't that be something?" Julia scribbled it down. "We're going with it because if it's not right, we might get points for ingenuity."

"Time!" Marge shouted.

When the boards were raised, Ford saw that his parents' team had guessed that the composers were all originally from Germany. *Olive the Other Reindeer* hadn't come up with any response, cementing their third-place finish.

Marge's gaze flitted over to the white board Julia was holding, and her eyes widened. "Wow! We have a correct answer from the Chestnuts."

Ford's jaw dropped. The whole table looked at him. Nobody spoke until Julia let out a squeal. "We're tied!"

The diner erupted in cheers.

Laney poked Ford's side. "Nice going."

Ford relished the compliment and tipped his chin. "Lucky guess."

"Alright. Alright," Marge yelled into the microphone over the din. "I have a plan in place for a tie."

Of course she did.

"This will be a sudden-death round with a series of questions. First team to get one wrong is out, and the other team will be crowned our champion. If both teams answer incorrectly, play continues."

Marge waited for the teams to nod in understanding. Julia was gripping the marker so tightly Ford was afraid it was going to snap and start spewing ink across the table.

"Here we go." Marge paused, and Ford thought Julia was going to lose it. "In the 1964 classic *Rudolph the Red-Nosed Reindeer*, what was the name of Rudolph's faithful elf companion?"

"Hermey," Eric said without hesitation. "He wanted to be a dentist."

Julia jotted down the answer and held up the board when Marge called time.

"Both teams correct. Next question. How many reindeer are featured in the poem 'Twas the Night Before Christmas'?"

The entire table was quiet, and Ford glanced around to see everyone deep in thought.

"It's eight," Daniel said first. "There's no Rudolph mentioned in the original."

"Are you sure?" Julia bit her lip.

"He's right." Samson nodded.

Julia wrote down their answer, and once again, both teams had it correct. Isabel planted a giant kiss on Daniel's mouth, and he smiled and looked guiltily in Ford's direction.

Even as he mimed gagging, a reluctant smile itched at the corner of Ford's lips.

"Focus, you guys!" Amanda said from her seat next to Julia.

Ford snapped to attention and eyed Laney, who was giggling.

"Who played George Bailey in the Christmas classic *It's a Wonderful Life?*" Marge asked the room.

"Oh! Jimmy Stewart!" Isabel said a little too loudly.

"Shh," Julia scolded as she scrawled out the answer. "You'll give it away."

"Sorry. I just love that movie so much."

"Me too." Laney smiled at Isabel.

"Both correct. Again." Marge frowned, evidently thinking she should have stumped someone by this point. She shuffled the notecards left in her hands before seeming satisfied. "These are the tougher questions."

Everyone crowded around the table even closer.

The diner went silent as Marge's gaze darted down to the card. "How tall—plus or minus twenty-five feet—was the tallest cut Christmas tree?"

Their whole table—and three quarters of the rest of the people in the diner—turned to look at Laney, and by extension, Eric, since he was sitting right next to her. If the earlier questions in the round were any indication—and Ford's table knew they were—Eric would not be able to help them out here. Laney was their best bet.

"Do you have any idea?" Julia asked.

Laney's jaw was set. Ford could practically see the wheels in her head spinning, and he recognized the look in her eyes—it was the same determined glint that sparkled every time she wanted to win and knew victory was within her grasp. He remembered it from high school, and he'd seen it countless times on the tree farm as she coordinated sales and kept patrons happy.

"I can't remember exactly." Laney pressed her palms into the table. "I knew this at one point." She closed her eyes as if that would help her cull through her memory for the answer.

"Ten seconds!" Marge's call had the diner gasping, and Julia's grip tightened on the marker.

"We should make a guess."

Laney's eyes popped open. "Two hundred feet."

Julia wrote it down without hesitation, and Laney gulped next to Ford.

"Hey." He squeezed Laney's shoulder and spoke directly into her ear. He had to swallow when the vanilla scent of her skin invaded his lungs. "It's just a silly game. No worries either way, right?"

Laney shot him a look. "Of course."

She may have said the words, but her stiff posture told a completely different story. She wanted to be right, and he'd bet if she wasn't, she was going to beat herself up over it.

"Time! Show your answers."

At Marge's directive, Ford straightened in his seat. The diner held its collective breath.

Julia raised the team's board. Across the bar, Julia's mom revealed her team's answer.

Marge eyed the signs. "We have one guess of two hundred feet and one guess of two hundred fifty feet."

In Ford's periphery, Laney was working her jaw. Her hands were still pressed into the table, and her gaze was unblinking as she waited for Marge to go on.

"I can tell you we'll be able to declare a winner after this round."

An anxious thrill zinged around the bar. Laney sucked in a breath.

Marge cupped the notecard in her hand. "The tallest Christmas tree ever cut was"—someone let out a shriek of anticipation before Marge finally finished her sentence—"two hundred twenty-one feet."

Ford did the mental math. His gaze shot to Laney. Her answer was within twenty-five feet of two hundred twenty-one. A giant—and relieved—smile burst over her face.

"Which means"—Marge offered their team a surprisingly indulgent smile—"*Watch Us Roast Your Chestnuts* is this year's Merry Mapleton Christmas Trivia winner!"

Chaos ensued. Laney stood, shrieked, and wrapped her arms around his neck. Ford barely had time to process and appreciate the direct contact before she was grabbed and pulled in another direction.

Eric leapt up onto the table and started beating his chest. Julia screamed and jumped up and down. Amanda and Isabel hugged each other. Everyone laughed and accepted the praise from the spectators who hurried over to offer their congratulations.

Marge wove through the crowd and handed an obnoxiously decorated traveling trophy in the shape of a Christmas stocking to Julia who hoisted it up over her head.

The crowd around Laney cleared as everyone turned to get a better look at the trophy.

"Well played, McGregor." Ford bobbed his chin at her.

Laney's eyes shone. "I really did not want to fail in my area of expertise—not again, at least."

"Again?"

"If I would have followed up my failure to get re-elected with a failure to bring home the Christmas trivia title on a question about Christmas trees, I don't know if I could have looked myself in the mirror—or faced anyone in town, for that matter."

She offered him a lopsided smile, but Ford frowned. He was about to tell her that he certainly didn't see her as a failure—far from it—and she shouldn't see herself that way either.

But Laney's eye caught on something beyond him. "Oh! I need to corner Marge and get some details sorted out about using the barn for the Merry Mapleton Ball."

Ford clamped his mouth shut. "Right."

"I'll catch you later." Laney smiled at him before she hurried after Marge.

Ford turned and watched their exchange, his heart tugging in his chest to go where Laney went and to be the one to help her believe that, accolades and achievements aside, she was one hundred percent incredible...just by virtue of who she was.

Chapter 25

THE MORNING AFTER SECURING a trivia victory, Laney looked on as Marge and Melly did laps in her parents' barn. When Laney tracked her down after the trivia competition, Marge had insisted she needed to come and see the place in person to figure out a game plan.

Now, she tapped her finger against her chin. "It'll take some work to get it into party shape, but it'll definitely do the job. You're really saving the day, Laney."

Laney brushed off the compliment. "No big deal. I'm just happy to help. My parents are thrilled, too. I spoke with them earlier this morning."

"How are they doing?" Melly's face was all kind lines and doe eyes.

"They're good."

"And the babies?" Melly said it softly, as if she was afraid even her words might tip the scales in the wrong direction for Asher and Gwen.

Laney pulled her lips to the side. "They're okay. Still on oxygen and getting food through a tube, but the doctors keep saying every day they're getting bigger and stronger, and they're one day closer to being home."

A faraway look flashed in Melly's eyes. "My son was a little NICU warrior. Those were some of the longest, hardest weeks of my life."

Laney's heart constricted. She didn't like thinking about what Eliot and Carly were going through. She could only imagine the rollercoaster of emotions they were experiencing.

Melly patted Laney's arm, reading her thoughts. "Don't worry, dear. It's good Eliot and Carly have each other. I don't know how I would have gotten through without the unwavering support of my husband. I never realized how true it was what they say—*marry the person who you'll suffer well with*—until we were facing some of the bleakest days. We were fortunate. Our baby came home after just two weeks."

A large lump wedged itself in Laney's throat, blocking her airway and making her unable to speak. After Dustin cheated on her, she'd doubled down, clinging to her independence to avoid further hurt. Deep in her heart, she knew she didn't want to be alone forever. She wanted a teammate, a partner. Like Eliot and Carly had in each other.

An image of Ford materialized in her head. Would the two of them suffer well together?

"The babies are going to be just fine." Marge's brisk tone broke Laney out of her thoughts. When she glanced at the older woman, expecting to see her all-business face in place, Laney was surprised to see kindness in Marge's eyes, too. "So are you." Marge waited for Laney to nod and then went on. "Now, let's talk logistics."

Twenty minutes later, Laney waved goodbye to the women before turning to face the barn and the tree farm. She'd been assigned a lot of work ahead of the ball. She wasn't entirely sure how or when she'd get it all done, but she'd just have to figure it out—somehow.

The sound of a car approaching had her whirling around. Ford waved through his windshield as he parked in the spot that, in just a few short weeks, she'd started referring to as *his*.

He slid out of his car and walked toward her. A crinkly feeling went up her back as she involuntarily stepped his way. "I saw Marge and Melly driving out of here. What did they think of the barn?"

"They said it would work. You're looking at the new home of the Merry Mapleton Ball."

Ford glanced past her to the barn. "It'll be perfect."

"I hope so. Suddenly, I'm in charge of decorations and marketing. And parking. Marge is concerned we'll have a serious traffic jam if we don't figure out a plan. She's not wrong." Laney surveyed the side parking lot. "I swear if Marge ever ran for government office, everyone else would just concede because they would not be able to handle her."

Ford let out a low chuckle, which sent goosebumps galloping over Laney's skin. "I'm happy to help with anything you need. Why don't you let me coordinate the parking situation?"

Laney ran her hands up and down her arms to try to physically quell her body's reaction to this man, and his laugh, and his kindness, and his overwhelming presence. "I cannot keep dragging you into my messes. First the tree farm, now the ball. I'm certain you have a life of your own that you've been neglecting. I won't be able to live with myself if I'm the reason you're dropping balls elsewhere."

Ford shifted his gaze.

"See. I'm right, aren't I?" Laney put her hands on her hips and stared him down, waiting for him to share something with her. She didn't know what his life was like, really. They always seemed to focus on her or the farm. He downplayed or joked around about everything else.

"Yes and no. First of all, you're not dragging me into your messes. I'm volunteering myself. But I do need to start studying for my real estate brokerage exam, or I can kiss my own agency goodbye."

"When's your test?"

"The twentieth of December."

"Ford! And you've just been acting like my farmhand? You should be studying."

Ford narrowed his eyes at her—not in a vicious way, but in an *I-can-take-care-of-myself* way. She recognized his defensive posture because she'd often employed it herself.

"You're not forcing me into helping out around here. I'm choosing to. I'll get to studying eventually."

"Yes, you will, because I'm going to help you."

"Help me?"

"I'm a very good study buddy."

"Is that so?"

"Don't act like you're surprised. I wasn't our class's valedictorian for nothing, now was I?" Laney stuck up her nose when Ford just smirked. "So, let's say tomorrow night. If you insist on helping out on the farm, then we can study here when we're done."

"That's really not necessary, Laney."

"It sure is."

Ford didn't say anything, just studied her.

Laney crossed her arms. "I'm not going to take no for an answer."

"Of course you aren't. Fine."

When he relented, Laney suppressed a self-satisfied smile.

"I should warn you that the real estate and brokerage material is pretty dry."

Laney laughed out loud at that. "I've spent the last two years writing and reviewing congressional policy. Believe me, I know dry. I can handle it."

Chapter 26

Ford

"Kill me dead right now." Laney flung her forearm over her eyes.

"I'd rather not," Ford said blandly, earning him an amused whimper from Laney. He crossed his ankle over his knee. "I won't blame you if you want to back out of helping me now that you've seen the material."

"No, no. I signed myself up for this." Laney dropped her arm and made an exasperated face that Ford found incredibly endearing. "I'm no quitter. And it's the least I can do. Don't you think this stuff is excruciatingly dull, though? So many rules and regulations...it sort of puts my work in Congress to shame."

"I doubt that." Ford took a sip of the wine Laney poured for them.

After another long afternoon and evening on the tree farm, it was nice to be sitting inside the farmhouse.

In front of the crackling fire.

With Laney.

While the real estate content may have been mundane, Ford was more and more certain that sitting in front of a wall and watching paint dry would have been enjoyable as long as he and Laney were together.

He was actually pleased with how much of the exam material he already knew. Even the hour they'd spent going over it had made him feel better about his chances of passing when he sat for the test in two weeks. He was also man enough to admit that impressing Laney was a major bonus.

"Do you like your work?" Laney burrowed into the oversized cushions on the couch opposite of him.

Ford swallowed his wine and set his glass on the coffee table. "I do."

"What do you like most about it?"

"The cookies at the open houses."

Laney chucked a pillow at him. "Be serious!"

Ford laughed, but then he thought about seeing his clients run into a house they'd taken ownership of for the first time—the delight and pride in their eyes. He lifted his shoulder in a shrug. "I guess I like helping people achieve something that's theirs...that they've earned and worked for. Home is about people. I firmly believe that. But the physical place is special, too. It's the backdrop for all the good things in life, and to be able to play a part in helping someone find that is really fulfilling. I don't take it for granted."

Ford reached for his glass and took another sip of wine. When he looked up, Laney was staring at him with a searching look in her eyes.

"What?"

"Nothing." Laney blinked, as if waking from a slight trance. "It's just—" She paused. "That's a really beautiful reason to do what you do. Thanks for sharing it with me."

"It's nothing, really. All in a day's work. Anyway, we should get back to studying. These agency competencies and managerial duties aren't going to learn themselves."

Ford busied himself with shuffling the papers that were spread on the coffee table in front of him. Laney's gaze dug into him, and her attention made Ford squirm. He wasn't sure he'd ever explained why he loved his job to anyone—wasn't sure he'd ever put it into words for himself, either.

Something about Laney made him want to open up. Beyond teasing and bantering with her, he found himself inspired by Laney's hard work and her heart for others. He valued her insights and the way she took on the world. He wanted to share his passions and his dreams with her, to get her opinions and hear her thoughts. He trusted her and admired her.

He was scared senseless about putting himself out there, though. What if she didn't like what she saw when he let her in? What if she still assumed he was the same old Ford who couldn't take anything seriously? They seemed to have developed a more nuanced understanding of each other, and Ford guessed he should trust that, but it was still hard for him to believe anyone could think *he* was doing anything of importance, especially someone as successful as Laney.

Ford tabled the thought and pushed the practice test back in her direction, pointing to the first question. "You can start at the top."

♥ ♥ ♥ ♥ ♥

They were ten questions into the mock exam, Laney reading the questions off and Ford talking through his answers, when Laney's phone rang.

"Sorry. I'll just silence—" Laney stopped talking when she looked at the caller ID.

"Don't let me keep you from answering."

"Are you sure?" Laney winced. "I hate to be rude, but it's my mom."

"Answer it." Ford gestured to the phone, and Laney nodded, connecting the call.

"Mom! Hi!" Laney's smiling face fell like a deflating sponge cake. "Wait. What? Slow down."

She catapulted off the couch and started pacing. As she walked, she held her hand to her forehead, tugging on her bottom lip with her teeth. When she faced him, there was a terrified look in her eyes.

Ford stood, his whole body going cold.

Joan was doing most of the talking on the other end of the line, so he could only glean bits and pieces of what was going on. At one point, Laney repeated the words "necrotizing enterocolitis" and asked what that meant. A couple minutes of strained conversation later, Laney hung up. She wobbled on her feet for a moment before crumpling to the couch.

In two strides, Ford was across the room and at her side. "What's going on? What happened?"

She stared straight ahead but didn't look like she was seeing anything. "It's Gwen. They're rushing her into surgery." Laney's voice cracked on the last word, and she dropped her head into her hands.

Ford put his arm around her trembling shoulders. "I'm so sorry. What can I do?"

Laney only hesitated for a moment before she curved her body into his, resting her head against his chest. He held her while she cried, his own heart breaking with helplessness. In that moment, he'd do just about anything to spare Laney pain.

Eventually, she eased away from him, using her fingers to swipe under her lash lines and rubbing the black smudges of damp mascara on her jeans. "Sorry. I'm a mess."

Ford dipped his chin to draw her gaze. "You don't have to apologize to me, Laney. It's okay to not be okay right now."

Instead of responding, Laney stood and started pacing again. "I don't understand. Last I heard, the babies were doing well, but it sounds like Gwen took a turn. She was fussy earlier in the day, and then they noticed some swelling in her abdomen. An x-ray revealed that her intestine is perforated, so they need to do surgery to stop her from going septic. There are all sorts of risks. Mom said the surgery is only successful fifty percent of the time." Laney's voice gave out again, and she choked on a sob.

"Hey. Hey." Ford stood and opened his arms for her. She tucked into him, and he placed a hand on the back of her neck, stroking her hair and pressing her head snuggly into his shoulder. "Going to the worst-case scenario isn't going to help you or Gwen right now."

He felt her inhale a deep breath before she nodded against him. "You're right. I just feel so helpless."

"What else did your mom say?"

"Just that she'd be in touch. Eliot and Carly are giving her updates from the hospital, so she said she'd call me as soon as she heard something else from them. She wasn't sure how long that would take."

"Do you want me to stay here with you?" Ford wasn't going to take no for an answer. No way was he leaving her by herself to wait for some potentially devastating news. He hoped she wouldn't fight him on this.

Laney's shoulders rolled inward. "Would you mind? I don't want to be alone right now."

"Of course not. You're not alone. I'll be here as long as you need me to be." He held her gently, squeezing the muscles of her upper arms to make sure she felt his support.

Ford was desperate to do something—anything—to alleviate some of her worry and to help her share the load. "Is it okay with you if I let the church prayer chain know?"

Laney opened her mouth, then closed it and nodded. "That would be great. I told my mom I'd get a hold of Eric. I should do that now."

They split up to make their respective calls. Ford kept one eye on Laney as he phoned Marge. If anyone could activate the prayer warriors in the community, it was her.

After Laney got off the phone with Eric, they cleaned up Ford's forgotten study materials and settled back onto the couch.

Laney's whole body shook with nervous energy. "I don't know what to do with myself. There's no way I'm going to be able to sleep."

"We could watch a movie. It might help pass the time," Ford suggested.

Laney leaned forward and grabbed the remote off the coffee table. "Good idea. Something happy."

Eventually, she settled on *Home Alone*, and by the time Kevin McCallister was claiming he'd rather kiss a toilet seat than say sorry to Buzz, Laney had fallen asleep on Ford's shoulder.

Ford didn't dare move. He sat still, watching the steady rise and release of her chest. Her face was peaceful for the first time since her mom's phone call, but he could still make out the faint, white salt trail left by the tears that had trickled down her cheeks. His heart cracked open, and he had to look away.

Out the window, snow fell. The flakes were being kicked up and tossed around by the wind. The house groaned as it was buffeted by the squall, and the weight of it all pressed in on Ford.

His mind whirred as he considered Gwen's condition and what the next few hours—not to mention the days, weeks, and months ahead—might bring. He didn't know what would happen. No one did. But he knew he wanted to be here for Laney, no matter the outcome, to walk with her through the storm and stick around for the rainbow.

She let out a small sigh and pressed closer to him in her sleep. Ford shifted ever so slightly so he could wrap his free arm more snuggly around her, cradling her body like he longed to hold her heart. Tenderness for her leached from his soul and solidified what he already knew.

What he'd known for a long time.

He had fallen in love with Laney McGregor. All of her. Her tenacious work ethic. Her desire to serve. The way she could carry a crowd but also still manage to make him feel like he was the only person in the room with just one look. How they laughed and teased. The raw, real, messy feelings she held underneath her strong skin.

He'd been well on his way to loving Laney since they were teenagers. Back then, falling for her had felt a lot like lightning.

All crash and flash with a strong propensity to do serious damage—to burn or get burned.

Now, his love felt like falling snow. Delicate and strong. Blanketing everything that once was—not changing it so much as heightening it. Brightening it. Making his whole world glow.

Chapter 27

LANEY

LANEY TOOK THE STAIRS two at a time, stopping on the upstairs landing when her phone vibrated with a text message. It had been two days since Gwen's surgery. The little fighter was doing as well as could be expected, and to say Laney was relieved would have been the understatement of the century. The medical team was monitoring Gwen closely, so Laney held her breath every time her phone rang, praying that someone from Chicago wasn't calling with bad news.

Mom: All is well here. Thanks for checking in. You go enjoy your night now. Love you.

Laney's shoulders sagged with relief, and a smile spread over her face. She stowed her phone in her back pocket and ducked into her childhood bedroom, planning to do just as her mom instructed.

After they got the positive news about Gwen following her surgery, Laney had wept full-blown, crocodile tears. She was so overwhelmed with gratitude she couldn't have stopped the waterworks if she'd tried. Ford was there to see her break apart, and in an odd sort of way, she was glad he'd seen her like that—the furthest thing from her usual, put-together self.

She was even more glad he hadn't run in terror from her and her big emotions.

Instead, Ford had been a rock through it all, crashing at the farmhouse so she wouldn't have to be alone while she waited for updates the night of the surgery. He'd pulled extra weight on the tree farm the past two days, too, because Laney had been so preoccupied. Even now, he'd volunteered to close up for the night so Laney could get ready.

She was the one who suggested they see the lights on Candy Cane Lane as a sort of celebration. They'd made it through the first half of the tree farm season. Gwen was doing well. It was a good night for some fun.

Laney actually wanted to go and not just because *See Christmas lights* was number four on the Christmas Cliché list. The list hadn't factored into her festive suggestion at all.

Excitement rattled her ribcage at the thought of spending a night under the Christmas lights.

With Ford.

Because yes, Christmas lights were one thing, but taking in the sights with the man who had somehow wedged himself into her every thought was a completely other thing.

An elevated thing.

A thing she'd like to pursue.

Laney was tired of fighting her rising feelings for Ford—no matter what she had promised herself about men and Christmas. She wasn't going to bury her emotions anymore. After all, she was a woman who went after what she wanted.

She didn't know exactly where Ford stood where she was concerned, but Sally's response to Laney's message with the group photo attached rang out in her head.

Any man who can make elves look that good is a keeper. Also, he's totally into you.

How her friend could tell that from a still shot, Laney didn't pretend to know, but she hoped Sally was right.

She took a little extra time getting ready, pulling her hair back off her face into a high ponytail. She swiped on an extra coat of mascara and applied a matte lipstick just a tinge darker than her natural lip color. Laney glanced at her watch. It was pushing seven o'clock. Maybe it was the late lunch they'd inhaled in the barn or the jitters she felt at spending a whole night with Ford, but she had absolutely no appetite.

A knock sounded on the back door a second before she heard Ford's voice. "Laney?"

"Yeah. Come on in."

Downstairs, the outside door clicked shut, and Laney blew out a breath before heading to meet Ford. His back was to her as he kicked off his boots in the hall. He had the slow cooker of hot chocolate on his hip and the money bag tucked under his arm. He shifted to hold the crock firmly with both hands before looking up. When his eyes connected with hers, it was as if he was trying to capture her with the force of his gaze.

She turned away from him, leading the way into the kitchen so she could hide her blush and her smile. "Everything go okay out there?"

Ford cleared his throat, but his words still came out with a delicious sort of rasp. "The barn's locked and ready for tomorrow." He set the slow cooker on the island. "Here's the money."

Laney took it from him, and their fingers brushed. A shock jumped between them. "I'll go put it in the safe." It was her voice's turn to sound a little quivery.

Ford's gaze weighed heavily on her back as she retreated into her dad's office. When she returned, money free, he was staring up at the tree.

His features were soft, and he blinked an extended blink, holding his eyes closed for a moment before turning in her direction.

She was struck, all at once, and again, with how handsome Ford was. She itched to run her hands along his jawline and feel the coarseness of his beard under her fingers. She fidgeted with her sleeve. "My mom loved it." Laney motioned to the tree. "I sent her a bunch of pictures."

"I'm glad to hear that." Ford's low voice rolled over her.

Laney gulped. "I wanted to say thank you. Again."

She'd thanked him up and down the past couple of days.

Ford offered her a small smirk. "You don't have to keep saying it. You're going to give me a complex."

Laney chuckled at that. "Fine. Are you hungry?"

"Actually, no. But you should eat something if you want."

"I'm good, too."

"Maybe we could grab a bite at Hal's after we go through the lights." The way Ford said it was so casual, but a vein in his neck popped. He was nervous, and it was adorable that he wasn't as unaffected as he tried to appear.

"Sure, that'd be great." Laney pulled on her black peacoat and cinched the belt around her waist. She stopped at the hall mirror and positioned a wool headband over her ears before slinging her purse over her shoulder.

Ford drove them into town and pulled off to the side of the road a block before the light displays began. Cars were parked bumper to bumper, and the intersecting street ahead was blocked with large traffic cones. Every inch of the street deemed Candy Cane Lane seemed to be frosted in lights.

Laney undid her buckle and hopped out of the car before Ford could make it around to open her door. She shot him an exultant grin as she heard their names being called.

They turned to find Julia and Samson walking their way, a golden retriever trotting between them.

Julia hugged Laney. "I'm so glad you could make it out! This is perfect timing."

"It looks incredible around here. Who's this sweet boy?" Laney bent to scratch the golden behind the ears.

"The one and only Mr. Waffles. Hi, buddy." Ford crouched down and rubbed the dog on the back.

Mr. Waffles wiggled with glee. He tugged on his leash, knocking into Laney and sending her tipping into Ford.

He steadied her, and they both stood up, limbs slightly tangled. Ford's hand lingered on her elbow, and Mr. Waffles let out a happy woof. Laney caught Julia and Samson sharing a loaded look before Julia grinned back at her. "You'll have to excuse Mr. Waffles. He fancies himself a matchmaker."

"His track record is pretty good, actually." Samson toggled the leash and pulled his wife closer to his side.

Laney opened her mouth to ask a clarifying question but then whipped her head around when she heard clopping coming down the street behind her. Her jaw dropped. "Is that what I think it is?"

"It's an actual one-horse open sleigh," Julia squealed. "Farmer Johnson agreed to give rides down the street, but we kept it a secret."

Laney looked on in awe. She grew up on a farm, surrounded by other farms, so horses weren't a novelty to her, but she'd never seen one pulling a sleigh that was decked out with garland, a giant wreath, festive pillows, and flannel blankets.

When Farmer Johnson tugged on the reins and stopped right by them, Julia bounced with delight. "Would you two care to take the inaugural ride?"

Laney shot Ford a look to be sure he was on the same page. He had a boyish grin on his face, his enthusiasm mirroring hers. They chorused a resounding, "Yes!"

"Have fun, then!" Julia wiggled her fingers before she and Samson disappeared into the crowd.

Laney stepped forward and put her right foot onto the tread of the sleigh. She reached up with both hands to pull herself onto the bench, but before she could grab onto anything, Ford was at her side, his hand under hers. With a firm, warm grip, he guided her up into the sleigh.

Laney scooted into the seat, stunned. Her mind flashed to her favorite scene in the most recent *Pride and Prejudice* film, when Elizabeth Bennet's and Mr. Darcy's hands touch as he escorts her into the carriage. Darcy walks away, flexing his fingers, and it is the *swooniest* of moments. Laney glanced at Ford's hand. She couldn't tell if he was flexing his fingers beneath his glove, but she was helpless but to think that Amanda had been right in likening Ford to a regency gentleman, and she'd just been on the receiving end of her very own *Pride and Prejudice* moment.

Had Elizabeth Bennet felt like a million stars were burning in her head at Mr. Darcy's touch?

Because, yeah. That was happening.

"You okay?" Ford took his seat next to her.

Laney blinked away the dreamy aura that was clouding her vision. "Of course. This is incredible. You really didn't know about the sleigh?"

Ford lifted one of the fleece blankets and handed it to her. "I wish I could take credit, but no."

"We just have good luck, then." Laney made work of covering her legs.

"Speaking for myself, I'd say I've had some of that lately, yes."

She flashed him a smile, which slipped when Farmer Johnson clicked his tongue, loosening his grip on the reins, and they lurched forward. Laney toppled over into Ford's lap. This time, she couldn't even blame Mr. Waffles. She put her hand on his thigh to stop her fall, and the firm muscle beneath his jeans was suddenly taunting her.

Laney started sweating—legitimately sweating in the cold of December. She snatched her hand away, not wanting to be caught—*ahem*—lingering.

"Sorry," Laney squeaked.

"Don't be."

Laney opened her mouth, but nothing came out.

"Look." Ford's breath was hot against her cheek, and Laney's body temperature peaked.

She shuddered, turning her gaze to where he pointed ahead at the amazing light displays lining the street.

Chapter 28

FORD

THE LIGHTS OF CANDY Cane Lane were just as impressive as Ford remembered, but they couldn't hold a candle to the woman sitting next to him and the way she lit up the night with her smile.

Laney's head swiveled from the left side of the street to the right as the horse trotted forward. Lights glittered in every direction. Strands crisscrossed yards, spanning from houses to trees and back again like expertly woven spider webs. "It's like a feast for the eyes. I don't know where to look first."

The first house on the left had its roofline strung with alternating green and red lights. Oversized, lit-up ornaments glittered where they hung from the maple tree branches in the front yard, and a giant, mechanical train circled its trunk.

"Look at those kids!" Laney exclaimed.

Ford peered at the train more closely. Sure enough, little tikes were riding on each of the train cars. "Here I thought we had the best ride on the road."

"Don't tell Julia," Laney joked. "Although, I have to say, this is amazing. The last thing I thought I'd be up for this month was a sleigh ride. Wait until I tell Sally."

"Sally?"

"My best friend. She's, uh, really into Christmas. Before I left Madison, she was trying to rub some of her holiday cheer off on me." Laney shrugged, and Ford sensed there was more to the story. He started to ask, but Laney kept talking. "Anyway, she'll be thrilled when I tell her about this and all the holiday revelry we've gotten ourselves into."

"I hope it's been okay," he said, trying to mask the slight tremor of insecurity in his voice. Ford was having the time of his life this month. The season had never shone brighter, but he wasn't sure where Laney's head was at with it all.

Laney squeezed his forearm. "It's been more than okay."

Their gazes connected, and before Laney could pull her hand away, Ford covered it with his own. He held his breath when she glanced down. Her cheeks flushed, but she relaxed back into her seat, seemingly content to let him hold her close.

Across the street from the train house, there was a two-story brick colonial. The giant arborvitae trees that flanked the front door had been decorated to look like Christmas gnomes.

The owners had tied a red ribbon around the trees one third of the way up and draped white strands of fabric from the ribbon to make it look like a beard. A peach-colored ball was affixed to the center of the red ribbon, mimicking the gnome's nose. At the top of the tree, the homeowners had used more ribbon around the tip of the evergreen branches to mimic the puff on top of the gnome's stocking cap.

"How clever!" Laney's face was still etched with remnants of a giggle. "How do people come up with this sort of stuff?"

"Beats me. Julia does interview prospective home buyers who are looking at houses on Pine Street so she can make sure they're up to snuff for the Candy Cane Lane festivities."

Laney faced him in the sleigh. "Are you serious?"

Ford chuckled. "No."

Laney swatted him with her free hand.

"I wouldn't put it past Julia, though."

"She's something else. The way she put this all together. It's really cool for the community." Laney glanced out her side of the sleigh at a house that had music blaring from the front yard. The lights were blinking in time with the Jackson 5 version of "Santa Claus is Coming to Town."

They waved to people on the sidewalks who were marveling at the sleigh as it passed by. Laney called down a kind word and a greeting to every single person, and not for the first time did Ford wonder if Laney knew *she* was something else. He remained silent, letting her charm the residents of Mapleton from her perch. He gave her hand a slight press where he still held it against his arm, and she flashed a wide grin back at him.

They rode by a life-sized Nativity scene in one yard. The next house had different shades of blue lights swirling up the trunks of all the trees and their branches. Electric snowflakes hung from each window, making the entire yard look like an ice palace.

Farther down the street, a crowd had gathered in front of Julia and Samson's house. The property was dripping in lights. Julia and Samson had fastened icicle-like bars from the roofline and the tree branches on the two birch trees in their front yard. The lights skated down the bars at differing speeds, and the effect was truly spectacular.

"It looks like the scene in *Beauty and the Beast* when the beast transforms into the prince! It's so beautiful." Laney's voice came out in a whisper, as if speaking any louder would make the magic of the view disappear. She was mesmerized by the cascading lights, and Ford was mesmerized by her.

"I agree."

Laney turned her head slowly, and Ford didn't bother tearing his gaze from her face. She was looking at him with so much fire in her eyes that the lights around him blurred to a technicolored haze, and the only thing Ford could see was Laney. She slid toward him, placed her hand on his chest, and the next thing Ford knew, she pressed her mouth against his.

Laney was kissing him. *Him.*

One word popped into Ford's head—*finally*—before he lost himself to the wonder of the moment.

Laney's lips were cold and soft, and Ford wanted nothing more than to draw her into his arms, pull her down into the sleigh, use his body as a blanket, and kiss her for the rest of the night. Instead, he let his eyes fall closed and returned Laney's gentle kiss, every fiber in his body on high alert, drunk on the woman leaning into him. Laney shifted, reaching up to grab the lapels of his jacket, drawing him closer.

Ford lifted his hand to her jaw and cradled her head, savoring the way she pressed into his palm and willing the warmth of his gloved hand to steal the chill from her cheek. She shivered, and Ford instinctively tucked her closer to him. Her whole body seemed to moan with relief, and Ford felt like the Grinch the day his heart grew three sizes. He was almost certain his chest would burst.

All too soon, Laney pulled back. Her eyes popped open, and a surprised breath puffed from between her lips.

"Wow." Laney reached up and touched her mouth, her eyes dropping.

That was the word Ford had come up with, too. Kissing Laney in real life was better than anything he'd dreamed of.

"I-I'm sorry."

"For what?" Ford curved his head down and forced Laney's gaze to return to his.

"For, umm...*that*." Laney waved her hand in between them.

"I'm not." Ford certainly wasn't going to apologize that he returned her kiss.

"You're not?"

"Nope."

Laney stared at him, her jaw an inch unhinged. "That's it? Shouldn't we talk about what just happened? I mean, I kind of ambushed you."

A surge of amusement hit Ford at her obvious embarrassment, only because this was Laney, and she was always so in control. He liked that she kissed him without really thinking twice about it.

"Sure, we can talk about it. You definitely ambushed me. Took complete advantage. Quite frankly, how dare you?" Ford deadpanned.

Laney screwed up her mouth. "Hey, you kissed me back."

"I absolutely did. Really enjoyed it, too. I plan to do it again, if you'll let me."

Laney's eyes widened.

"Is that an issue?"

"Well, no. I guess not. I just—I don't know what I'm doing...what *we're* doing."

Ford studied her for a beat. She was all of a sudden totally in her head, and he wanted to get her back...next to him, in his arms, not freaking out. "Laney, did you like kissing me?"

Her cheeks flamed, and she narrowed her eyes at him.

"Be honest."

She crossed her arms over her chest. "You're enjoying this, aren't you?"

Ford's lips twitched. "Don't deflect. The question is, are *you*? Did you like kissing me?"

Ford didn't let his nerves show as he waited for her response. Finally, her face softened from its combative stance. "I did."

"That's settled, then." Ford marveled at the way Laney looked as she stared back at him. Her lips were parted and slightly swollen. Her cheeks were apple red. Her keen eyes were bright and flickering, reflecting the lights of the displays around them. It took everything in him not to kiss her again, but he'd let her get used to the idea first. Instead, he rested his arm around her shoulder and rearranged the blankets over their laps.

When she rested her head against him with no hesitation, Ford swore his heart struck up the "Hallelujah" chorus.

Chapter 29

LANEY

FORD MARSHALL KNEW HOW to kiss. Laney couldn't even appreciate the remaining decorative displays because her mind was so fixated on the man next to her. On his arm around her shoulder. On the rough rub of his beard against her skin.

She had melted the second their lips touched, and Laney wasn't sure how to get herself back to her normal functioning capacity. Her heart was knocking around inside her chest cavity with such force she feared for the neighboring organs, and her lungs kept pulling into deep gasps of Ford-scented, spicy air. Would they be able to function on normal, everyday oxygen, or would they go on strike, holding out for the good stuff?

Farmer Johnson steered the sleigh around the block, and they rode down the adjoining street in silence before coming back around the corner to where they'd started their ride.

When the sleigh came to a stop, Ford squeezed her shoulder, stood, and descended the sleigh step. He turned to her to help her dismount. Laney thought he was just going to offer her a hand, but then he grabbed her waist and lifted her down in one smooth motion. She stumbled on weak legs and had to place her palms on his chest to steady herself. Laney looked up at him through her eyelashes and bit her lip. Every part of her that Ford skimmed with his gaze seemed to illuminate until she was sure her skin was luminous. Laney instinctively leaned back into him and rose up on her tiptoes, which were curling in anticipation of another kiss.

"Hey, you two! How was it?!" Julia's voice sounded over Laney's shoulder, and Laney twirled around to see her friend walking toward them, holding hands with Samson, who was being yanked along by Mr. Waffles.

Laney's stomach dropped to her knees before soaring up into her esophagus at being caught pre-kiss, but she splashed a smile on her face and busied herself with greeting Mr. Waffles. "It was incredible!"

Ford snorted, almost imperceptibly, behind her, and Laney cast her gaze up to meet his. He was smirking. Of course he would take her words to mean *he* was incredible—or that his kiss was incredible. Laney should put him in his place, but she couldn't bring herself to do so. Not when she agreed with him. She settled for a roll of her eyes.

"Definitely a ride to remember," Ford said, not breaking eye contact with her. Laney thought she would certainly combust, but then Ford had mercy on her and looked toward their host. "Great idea, Julia."

"Glad you guys enjoyed it. We should probably head down that way and mingle. Get this guy inside before his paws get too cold." Mr. Waffles let out an appreciative bark. "Enjoy the rest of your night." Julia and Samson waved, and then they were off.

Laney and Ford stood alone on the sidewalk. Pleasure snaked through her as he nudged her shoulder. "You hungry?"

Laney shot him a jaunty look. "Starving."

Ford's eyes bugged, and she laughed. Two could play this game.

Hal's was half full, but they were able to get a seat in one of the booths that lined the diner's back wall. A waitress whom Ford called Sylvie took their drink orders and then left them alone.

Laney should have felt nervous or awkward, but she didn't. This was Ford. Being around him was fun and easy.

She clasped her hands on the worn wooden table. "So."

"So." Ford mimicked her pose.

"Has anyone ever told you you're an exceptional conversationalist?"

"All the time. Right after they commend me for my stellar wit and dashing good looks."

Laney laughed. "Modest, too."

"Naturally." Ford winked as Sylvie returned with their drinks.

"What can I get you guys?" She peered back and forth between them, and Laney had the sneaking suspicion they would soon be the talk of the town—if they weren't already. She *had* kissed Ford in an uncovered sleigh as it was rolling down a public street. It hadn't exactly been an act of discretion.

"Want to split a nacho platter?" Ford drew her attention.

Laney licked her lips, the plate of fries she devoured before the trivia contest still fresh in her memory. "That sounds great."

"Perfect. I'll have that out in a jiffy." Sylvie spun on her heel and bounced back through the dining area and behind the bar to put their order in. Sylvie smiled at Hal and nodded in the direction of their table. Hal caught Laney's eye and waved before turning and whispering something to Sylvie.

Laney swung her focus back to Ford, who was watching her closely.

"What is it?" he asked

"Nothing." She offered him a smile. Ford lifted a brow—not buying it—so she explained. "It's just weird. I've spent the past two years making sure everything I did was a perfectly presented front. Not a hair out of place so nothing would detract from my job or the work I was doing. I didn't want to give people anything to talk about. But I'd forgotten how much people talk in this town."

Ford's gaze roamed around the diner before settling on her again. "You're worried about being seen here with me."

He said it as a statement as opposed to a question. His voice was even, not a trace of hurt or bruised ego to be found.

"No, of course I'm not worried. I mean, I kissed you, remember?"

Ford finished sipping his drink. "Fact. And I kissed you back."

Laney stared at him for a second. "You know, you really need to stop doing that."

"What? Kissing you back?"

"No. Cutting yourself down. You do it all the time, and you shouldn't."

When Ford took another drink of his water instead of responding, Laney scowled, but her lips kept quirking up. "What am I going to do with you?"

"You could kiss me again." Ford grinned at her, and before she could press him on why he was always so self-deprecating, he tossed out a question of his own. "So, no romantic interests lately, huh?"

"Nope. Haven't dated in a while. You?"

Ford eased back in the booth. "Nah."

"What about Grace?"

"What about her?"

Laney ignored the embarrassment perched and waiting to take flight from the back of her throat. She put on her best blank face. "I know that you two dated. I'm curious about it, that's all."

Laney would be lying if she said she wasn't a little self-conscious. Grace was gorgeous in a regal sort of way that would perfectly complement Ford's Darcy-like qualities.

"To say we *dated*"—Ford used his fingers to make air quotes around the word—"is a stretch. We went out to dinner once at Isabel's behest."

Laney snorted. "Who uses the word *behest* these days?"

Ford shot her a serious look that only made her laugh harder. "Have you met Isabel? If anyone requires the use of a word like *behest*, it's her. She all but demanded that I take Grace out. Not that I complained too much. Grace is great."

Laney sat up a little straighter.

"She's cool, funny, and beautiful."

Laney broke eye contact.

"She's also like another sister to me." Ford paused, and Laney dragged her gaze back to his, forcing herself to remember that Ford wasn't Dustin. "I'm pretty sure Grace pictures me as a big-brother figure, too."

"A brooding big brother," Laney muttered before she could stop herself.

"Did you just call me brooding?"

"I—"

"Here we are!" Sylvie reached between them and settled their platter of nachos on the table. In that moment, she became Laney's new favorite person.

They dug in, and she was spared having to explain herself—or embarrass herself—any further.

"So, who's Dustin?" Ford asked after a couple bites. He sounded casual, but when Laney caught his eye, his gaze was anything but.

She paused with a chip halfway to her mouth and then cursed as a heap of gooey cheese and tomato fell back onto her plate. She made a fuss of scooping it up. "He's my ex."

Laney chomped down on her chip as Ford stared at her. When she didn't elaborate, he prompted her with another question. "When did you two break up?"

Laney swallowed a hard bite and winced. "Right around this time last year, actually."

Chapter 30

FORD

"OH." FORD SAT BACK. Eric's comment about how Laney had sworn off all things Christmas suddenly came into focus. Whatever had happened with Dustin, it obviously was bad enough that it initially made Laney reluctant to participate in this season's festivities. The part of Ford that was slowly finding its self-confidence hoped her holiday about-face was because of him. That she was comfortable enough with him to make new memories—better memories—to blot out whatever Dustin had put her through.

Dustin. Just the guy's name set Ford's teeth on edge.

"Yeah. He turned out to be a jerk." Laney shoved another chip in her mouth.

He would have liked to know more, but Ford sensed she wanted to change the subject, and he wasn't going to push her. Not tonight. He wanted her to feel like she could talk to him, unpressured.

"Is Eric all set to help you on the farm tomorrow?" Ford asked.

Laney swallowed and nodded. "Yep. He needs to put in his time. The slacker. I'm sure you'll appreciate having the day off duty."

Ford kept his face neutral, not willing to give away the fact that there was nowhere else he'd rather be than working the farm with her. He was afraid that he'd come on too strong by saying so. "I do have some of my own work to get done. I should study some more, too."

"I'll help you prep for your exam again one night this week."

"What are you? A sucker for punishment?"

Ford was secretly thrilled that maybe she was looking for ways to spend time with him. He could easily imagine sharing all the moments of his days—from the exciting to the ordinary—with Laney...for a lot of days to come. Somehow, in a matter of one sleigh-ride kiss, he'd gone from believing Laney was out of his league to imagining being in her life for a long time.

Laney chuckled. "I guess so."

"Actually." He wiped his mouth with a napkin before balling it up and tossing it onto his empty plate. "I was hoping to show you something work-related on Monday, if you're free?"

"I'm nothing but free other than for the tree farm. Can you show me in the morning?"

"Yeah, that'll work great."

"Are you going to give me a hint as to what this is?"

"No. It's not a huge deal, though."

Laney crossed her arms. "If that's the case, why won't you tell me?"

"Because it's an important life lesson to learn to wait for something good."

"Is that so?" She shot him a teasing look. "You know this because of all your experience waiting for something good, huh?"

Ford peered across the table at Laney. With her dark hair pulled off her face and her bangs clipped back, he had an unobstructed view of her sparkling eyes. They looked more golden than brown in the light of the diner. Yep. He'd say he had experience waiting for something. And that something was very, very good.

"I do."

Laney searched his face, staring hard at him. "I'll take your word for it. Will you come to the farm? Are you going to pick me up, or should I meet you somewhere?"

"Stop angling for information." Ford pointed his finger across the table at her. "Patience is a virtue."

Laney reached out and grabbed his finger, pulling it down. "I wasn't angling!"

Ford stared at her, relishing the feel of her skin on his. He took the chance to flip his hand over so he could hold hers. He used his thumb to trace small circles along her wrist as they sat there, eyes locked.

Laney groaned and relaxed in her seat. "Okay. Okay. Fine. I was. You really know how to pique a girl's interest."

"Here you go, guys." Sylvie appeared with the check. "Take your time and bring that to the register whenever you're ready." Her eyes dropped to where Ford still held Laney's hand, and Ford caught the smile on Sylvie's face as they thanked her and she retreated.

He had a strong feeling Laney was right about how fast word of their pseudo-date would spread through town. He wasn't sorry about it, though.

"You ready?" Ford asked.

When she nodded, Ford reluctantly released Laney's hand so she could stand and put her jacket on. He waited while she repositioned her wool headband, and then they walked to the counter. Laney insisted on splitting the bill, and Ford knew better than to argue with her about that.

They made the drive back to the farm in easy silence, and when they arrived, Ford walked Laney to the front door, trying to tamp down his disappointment that their night together was over.

She stopped on the top porch step and turned to face him. He was a step lower, which put their eyes level. "Thank you for coming with me to Candy Cane Lane." Laney set her hands gently on his shoulders. "And for the dinner company."

"I enjoyed it all." Ford placed his hands on her hips, drawing her even closer. Their noses were only inches from each other.

He wasn't sure how long they stood there, peering into each other's eyes. Time seemed to lurch ahead and come to a screeching stop all in the same moment. He was waiting for Laney to make the first move, but his resolve grew weaker and weaker by the second as Laney's gaze seared his skin. She looked so innocent, like she had no idea that being close to her like this was slowly turning every one of Ford's muscles to jelly. Finally, he couldn't take it anymore and bowed forward, his mouth a hair away from hers. "Are you trying to kill me?"

The corners of Laney's mouth hitched up. "Weren't you the one who just said good things were worth waiting for?"

She barely got the words out before Ford leaned in and nipped her lips with his. He moved his hands to the nape of her neck and drew her into a longer, deeper kiss. Ford savored the slight moan that traveled from her mouth to his as his senses were flooded with the vanilla smell of her hair and the salty taste of her lips.

He'd waited as long as he could.

When they broke apart, he dragged in a breath, and Laney's hooded eyes held a mischievous glint. "What?"

"I think you know what." Ford let his hands trail from where they were tangled in her hair back down to her waist. "You always did have to be the best, didn't you?"

Laney just chuckled, but when she blinked, she looked up at him a little shyly. "You know, I thought you were going to kiss me once before. A long time ago."

Ford froze in place before edging his forehead to rest against hers. "The history hallway after graduation?"

"Yes," Laney whispered. "Why didn't you?"

Ford closed his eyes. He didn't know how to tell her that the same reason he didn't kiss her back then was the reason he felt a little terrified kissing her now.

She had always been destined for big things, and he hadn't wanted to complicate that by kissing her senseless outside their political science classroom. He was a lot of things, but he wasn't a player, and he'd known the kiss wouldn't have amounted to anything. He hadn't been in a position to offer her anything more. He'd had no direction back then, so it would have been selfish, his own teenage hormones taking over. Because yeah. He'd wanted to kiss her.

Now that he had, he didn't know if he could live without kissing her every day for the rest of his life.

Dramatic? Maybe. But this was Laney. She was that amazing.

And that could be a problem. Because he was Ford. Not that amazing. He still wasn't sure he had anything to offer her.

None of this seemed like the right thing to say at the moment, so Ford settled on something a little less heavy. He opened his eyes to find her staring back at him with a vulnerable gaze. He brushed her nose with his. "Honestly, had I known what I was missing, I probably would have kissed you then and never stopped."

Laney's shy, uncertain smile quickly turned to a full-blown grin, illuminating her features. "For the record, you give as good as you get."

Ford's lungs seized up, and he wouldn't have been able to get another word out if he wanted to. Instead, he placed a kiss on Laney's lips in response, softer this time, and then he stepped back. "Goodnight, Laney."

"Goodnight, Ford." She held his gaze for a second longer before turning and opening the door.

Ford waited until he heard the lock turn before he walked back to his car—his mind and his heart full of Laney McGregor.

Past, present, and future.

Chapter 31

LANEY EXERCISED EVERY LAST ounce of her restraint in waiting until eight o'clock the next morning to call Sally.

When she'd closed the door on Ford the night before, Laney had let out an audible gasp. Who knew Candy Cane Lane would turn out to be so, so...incandescently romantic?

She'd been up with the sun after a night of replaying every moment with Ford like a slideshow in her mind. She kissed Ford. And then he kissed her—like, *really* kissed her. And they talked. And they teased. And—

Laney sighed.

It was all really good.

But now, as she sat at her parents' kitchen table, sipping coffee in the morning light, the doubt crept in. Laney felt a little like a runaway Christmas tree ornament, rolling across the hardwood floor, one wrong turn away from shattering. Fragile.

"Hello?" Sally sounded groggy.

"Did I wake you up?"

Laney heard rustling on the other end of the line. "It's fine. What's up?"

"I kissed Ford."

A long pause. "Did you now?" Sally was suddenly alert, and Laney could hear the smile in her voice.

"What the heck was I thinking, Sal?"

"You were probably thinking this man is gorgeous, and a good friend, and I'ma get me some of that. Tell me everything."

"Sally!" Laney tried to scold her, but she ended up laughing.

When Laney finished recounting the previous night, Sally sighed on the other end of the phone. "A sleigh? A legit sleigh? That is so dreamy! Don't be surprised if I steal your play-by-play and turn it into a show at the theater next year. I'm happy for you, Lane."

"Well, I'm freaking out!" Laney stood and started pacing. "Like, what do I do? We kissed, and it was great, but is it going to make things weird between us? I mean, do I kiss him every time I see him now, or what?" Laney stopped talking when Sally started laughing. "I'm glad to know you think this is so funny."

"Sorry. I'm sorry. It's just...well, listen to yourself. Laney. Take a breath! You need to chill out and enjoy this. You don't have to have a plan or know what's going to come next. Let things develop organically. You deserve to have a little fun. It's been a full year since you entertained the idea of anything that even hinted at romance. Instead, you've had your nose to the grindstone at the Capitol. I like to hear you've got your nose to the Ford-stone, if you know what I mean."

Laney could picture Sally's eyebrows wagging as she delivered her punch line, but she only groaned. "Fun or not, this can't possibly work."

"Not with that attitude."

"I'm serious! Even if I wanted it to work out with Ford—"

"Which you do."

"That's neither here nor there."

"But let's say you do. Humor me."

"Fine. How would it work? He lives here. I don't. I have no idea what my job situation looks like, but if you get me in with Ron's uncle and the senator wants me on his team, I could be in Washington D.C. or back in Madison. I don't even know what Ford wants out of this." Laney said the last line more quietly.

The truth was, she was scared. Scared of falling for Ford harder than he might fall for her. She'd been down that road.

"Sounds to me like he wants you."

"But what if this is just a Christmastime fling for him?" Laney hated the way her voice cracked.

"Would that be so bad? You said it yourself that you don't know where life is going to take you. What's the harm in having some fun with a decent guy while you're both in town for the next two weeks? I say go for it. Oh! You should bring him to the children's production here so I can meet him!"

Laney blew out a breath. "I don't know."

Could it be as black and white as Sally was suggesting? Could she enjoy her time from now until Christmas with Ford, regardless of the fact that the New Year would likely mean an end to their relationship?

If she could even call it a relationship.

"How'd you leave it with him?" Sally pressed.

"He's doing his own thing this weekend because Eric will be here to help out on the farm. But he's picking me up on Monday and showing me something. I don't know what it is. It's a surprise."

"Sounds juicy."

Laney rolled her eyes. "Keep your head out of the gutter."

"A girl can dream, can't she? But I mean it. Relax and go with this, Laney. I think it'll be good for you."

Laney plopped down on the family room couch and looked up at the giant Christmas tree. She closed her eyes out of habit and made a wish.

"Are you there?"

Sally's voice jarred Laney from her thoughts. "Yeah, I'm here. And you're right."

"Of course I am. Now bring him to Madison so I can meet him. I'm setting aside an extra ticket for him for the Friday-night show. Your tickets will be at will call when you get here."

"But—" Laney tried to interject. She hadn't even talked to Ford about taking a trip with her, and she had no idea if he was available.

"I won't take no for an answer. You at least have to invite him. I have a strong suspicion he'll say yes to coming along."

"Fine," Laney grumbled.

"Good. Keep me posted. Now, if you don't mind, I'm going to go back to bed to snuggle Ron."

"Eww, gross." Laney ended the call on Sally's laugh.

She closed her eyes. Ford's face popped up on the back of her eyelids as her friend's words replayed in her head.

Having fun with Ford definitely wouldn't be any problem for her. She enjoyed her time with him more than she could say. She liked the way he challenged her, always keeping her on her toes, but not in the same sort of brutal way as her job in politics. No, with Ford, she knew he wasn't out for blood. He never had been.

He was kind—she'd seen countless examples of it in the past couple of weeks—and she appreciated that about him, which is why she wasn't so certain she could just leave what they had in the "for kicks and giggles" category.

Then, there was the Christmas Cliché list to think about. What would Ford think when he found out that she'd been tasked with checking off a box next to *Go on a holiday-themed date*? Would he assume she'd just been using him for some sort of planned Christmas romance?

Laney breathed in a deep breath through her nose and blew it out her mouth. She repeated the action two more times, sorting through all the thoughts pinging around her mind as she did so. She blinked her eyes open on the final breath of the exercise. The only thing it had made clear to her was that she was well on her way to falling for Ford. She didn't know how she'd recover if it turned out that he wasn't falling along with her.

But what else could she do?

She was halfway down the side of the cliff already. She'd just have to figure out how to fly as she went along—or deal with the ground when she smacked into it.

Chapter 32

FORD

FORD PULLED INTO THE circle drive in front of the McGregor farmhouse at nine o'clock on Monday morning, just as he'd promised Laney. They'd texted back and forth over the weekend, and Ford had had to physically stop himself from driving to the farm to see her.

He had lost all semblance of his cool, and he really needed to pull himself together, or Laney was going to think he was out of his mind for her.

Maybe she wouldn't be wrong.

As he got everything organized this morning, he couldn't help second-guessing himself for suggesting this to Laney. He didn't want to back out, not after he made such a big deal out of it being a surprise. But he felt like it would probably be a letdown to her.

Ford wrenched the key out of the ignition and got out of his car. He strode toward the porch, trying with each step to trample the feelings of inadequacy that welled up inside of him.

The front door opened before Ford made it to the top step of the porch, and Laney stepped out. Her face looked as fresh as the dawn, and today, her hair hung down in loose curls.

"Hi!" Her voice was brighter than the sun reflecting off the snow.

Ford was so struck by her he couldn't say anything in return.

Laney met him on the steps. "I was watching for you. I guess I was anxious."

How was she so calm? He felt like a pre-teen standing next to his first crush.

Ford cleared his throat. "You ready?" He turned to go back down the stairs, but Laney put her hand on his bicep, forcing him to turn and face her. She placed a quick kiss on the scruff of his cheek.

"Now I am." She skipped down the remaining steps to his car.

Yep. Ford was a goner.

Laney went to open the passenger door, but she shot Ford a look over her shoulder when she pulled on the handle and it was locked. "You locked this on purpose, didn't you?"

Ford smothered a grin, feeling more like himself as they fell into their usual banter. He clicked the unlock button on his key fob and reached around her to open the door. "Maybe."

She shook her head at him, but she was beaming, and Ford enjoyed the small surge of triumph that swirled in his gut at both his nearness to Laney and her smile at his chivalry.

Ford climbed into the driver's seat and successfully deflected every one of Laney's questions about where he was taking her for the entire drive into Mapleton proper. He parked in the tiny lot behind the old barbershop.

Laney looked out the window. "Are we going to see the town tree?"

"Nope. This is the place I wanted to show you." Ford led the way down the alley and up the stairs to the building.

"The barbershop? My dad used to get his hair cut here when I was little."

"Pretty much everyone in town did. It's been empty for years."

A gust of wind blew up, sending fluttery flakes of fallen snow swirling down the street. Ford retrieved the key from the lockbox hanging from the handle and made quick work of getting them inside and out of the elements. The wind slammed the door closed behind him as he followed Laney. The old wood floors creaked beneath their boots.

"Hopefully, not for long, though," he added once they were ensconced in the antiquated room.

Laney spun toward him, two lines creasing between her eyes in silent question.

"I put in a provisional offer on this place just this morning."

Laney grabbed his forearm and squeezed. "Are you serious?"

"I'll make it official just as soon as I pass my brokerage exam. If all goes as planned, this'll be the home of my own real estate agency."

Laney released her hold on him and walked in a slow circle around the room, pausing to run her hand over the old barbershop chair that sat on a swivel in front of the large front window. She looked out onto the main thoroughfare running through town.

"What do you think?" He held his breath, but then she turned her bright, smiling face at him, and he relaxed.

"Ford, this is incredible. I'm so happy for you!" She crossed the room in quick steps and threw her arms around his neck.

Ford savored the press of her body against his and the way her hair tickled his cheek.

"Thanks," he said, breathing her in. "I know it's nothing major."

"What do you mean? This is a huge step for the business you're building."

Ford nodded. "It's still not much. At least by comparison..." He trailed off.

"I disagree. You offer a real service to the community, Ford. You're in the business of helping people find a home. What could be more important than that? And all that matters is that you're doing what you love."

Ford swallowed around the emotion suddenly clogging his throat. She'd really been listening to him the night he opened up to her about why he enjoyed his job. He wanted to believe she meant what she said today. "Thanks for saying that."

"It's the truth." She clapped her hands. "So, talk me through your plans here."

Ford explained Isabel's design ideas and his vision for the barbershop. Laney listened intently and asked questions. When he finished his spiel, she nudged his side.

"I love it. You know, you could crack a smile and be excited or something. This is so great!"

"I'm excited."

"Could have fooled me. It's okay to show it."

"Fine." Ford flashed an overdone smile in Laney's direction, eliciting a giggle.

"I take it back. You look funny when you smile like that."

Ford smiled more normally at that. He looked around the space. "Just remember this isn't a done deal yet."

Laney waved her hand back and forth. "It may as well be. You'll ace your exam, and as far as your agency name, how about Ford the River Realty?" She winked.

Ford barked. "I am *not* using an Oregon Trail pun as the name for my business."

"How about We Are Marshall Realty?"

"How about no."

Laney poked at his side, angling to tickle him, but Ford grabbed her finger and gave her a "watch it" look. She just laughed. "Oh, come on! Have a little fun."

Before Ford could say he was full of fun, Laney's phone sounded with an incoming text message alert. Ford released her hand—begrudgingly—so she could scroll through the message.

"It's Melly. She has some questions about the Merry Mapleton Ball."

"We can swing by the village offices now, if you want."

"You don't mind?" Laney looked up from her phone. "You don't have anything else you need to be doing?"

"Not at all. Let's go."

From the barbershop, the pair cut across the street and over to the brick municipal center building. The place was hopping, and they waved to several villagers who were coming and going.

Three people waited in line at the high counter in front of Melly's desk.

When everyone else cleared out after having their business taken care of, Melly finally noticed Ford and Laney. "Well, hello, you two."

"I got your text, and we were just across the street. Is now an okay time to chat about the ball?" Laney rested her clasped hands on the desk and glanced left and right. "You're swamped."

At Laney's proclamation, Ford looked more closely at Melly. The middle-aged woman's hair was shoved behind her ears. All sorts of papers were strewn across her desk. A quick glance at her computer screen revealed countless open tabs.

"Definitely swamped." Melly pushed her reading glasses up onto the top of her head and scooped up a couple of documents from the workspace in front of her. "But there looks to be a lull. Samson can come out to cover the front desk for me. This shouldn't take us long, though I should probably loop Marge in." Melly picked up the phone and placed a quick call. After hanging up, she said, "She'll be here in ten minutes. Can you wait?"

Laney checked her watch. "Sure. The tree farm doesn't open for another hour and a half."

They retreated to a nearby bench and settled into playing a game of Would You Rather? Ford was not surprised that, if given the choice, Laney would choose to live in a tree house rather than a cave, and she'd prefer to labor in extreme cold versus extreme heat.

When Marge bustled into the office, she blew by Ford and went straight to Laney, interrupting her answer to the question of whether she'd rather fall in love tomorrow or win the lottery next year. Ford would have liked to hear the answer to that, but Marge waited for no one.

"Laney, hi. Glad you're here. Much to discuss," Marge said. She turned to Melly, who was just finishing up with a customer. "You ready?"

Melly nodded. "Let me get Samson up here." She pressed the phone to her ear, and a minute later, Samson appeared.

"Hey, everyone." He strode to Melly's desk, and Melly moved to open the swinging door and let Laney and Ford into the back offices.

"We can meet in the conference room. Samson, I'll try to be quick," Melly called over her shoulder.

"No problem. I've got this."

Melly led the way down the hall and to a room with two tables pushed together surrounded by eight chairs.

Laney plopped her purse on the table. "You guys are busier than Santa's workshop the week before Christmas."

"We're missing Donna," Melly admitted. "Samson's a sweet boy. Good at his job. I'm glad he and I are in it together, but we're going to need to hire someone sooner rather than later, or we're both going to go crazy."

"What about you, Laney?" Marge sat down next to Laney. "You're out of a job, aren't you? Have you thought about applying for the village clerk position?" Her gaze cut to Ford. "Especially since maybe there's something else that may make sticking around town worth your while."

Ford had been watching Laney in his periphery. He, too, had been considering her for the village clerk job, but he'd chalked it up as wishful thinking. When Marge hinted at him as a reason Laney might stay in Mapleton, his heart rate spiked.

Melly pressed her open palm to her chest, as if the thought of working with Laney was the most perfect thing she'd ever heard.

Laney's face turned pink, and her mouth opened and shut like a fish. She was most likely trying to figure out a way to let them all down easy.

"Actually, I had a similar thought," she said after a moment.

Ford was barely able to suppress his gasp.

"I do have a few things in the works back in Madison, too. My friend, Sally, has a connection to Senator McClaren, and she's referring me for a position." Laney sounded almost apologetic, and he couldn't get a read on the look she gave him out of the corner of her eye before she turned her gaze back to Melly. "I'm sure you and Samson will find the right fit, though. Whether it's me or someone else. Should we talk about the ball? I don't want to keep you longer than we have to. I spoke to Isabel this weekend, and she's on board to help me tackle the majority of the decorations."

"Excellent. Excellent." Marge gave a brisk nod and began rattling off details.

Ford sat back and listened to the women chat, even as his thoughts were stuck on Laney and her job prospects. A position with a senator would be huge, and Laney would be perfect in the role. Ford's spirits sank, but he tried to console himself. She hadn't said the job here in town was completely off the table, just that she was keeping her options open. The fact that she was even considering working in Mapleton should have buoyed him. And there was always the option of a long-distance relationship.

But this was Laney McGregor. He knew better.

She had amassed an impressive resume, and she wasn't yet thirty. As much as she praised his future small-town business operation, he couldn't blame her if she had her eye on something bigger than staying here in Mapleton.

Something bigger than him, as well.

Chapter 33

LANEY

THE NEXT DAY, LANEY leaned up against the counter in the barn and enjoyed the view. Out the open door, Ford slammed the tailgate on a patron's truck. His shoulders were broad under his winter jacket. His jeans fit just right. Laney's mouth went a little dry, and she fought the urge to fan herself when Ford turned away from the truck with the last wisp of a smile on his ridiculously handsome face.

She had all but frozen yesterday when Marge hinted at a relationship between the two of them, half terrified that the comment would scare Ford away. But he'd shown up again this morning, ready to help with the farm.

Ford and his constancy were quickly becoming two things Laney believed she'd always be able to trust.

A group of four high-school-aged girls burst through the open barn door—an avalanche of giggles. Laney snapped to attention, silently scolding herself for getting lost in another daydream about Ford.

"Did you guys find everything you were looking for?" Laney peered at the teens, who wore matching red-and-white stocking caps. They all had on leggings and long-sleeved shirts, plus Mapleton Cross Country t-shirts and running shorts layered over the top.

One of the girls stepped forward. "We sure did. We cut down one of the Balsam Firs. That man out there said it was a $50 tree." She fished a wad of cash out of the pocket on the waistline of her shorts.

"Coach and Grandma Ruthie are going to love it."

Laney glanced up from where she was typing the total into the register. She wasn't sure who Coach was, or Grandma Ruthie, for that matter.

A second girl beamed. "It's going to make their Christmas."

"What are you all up to?" Laney paused with the cash in hand.

The girl who'd given Laney the money faced her again. "We're surprising our cross-country coach with a tree for her and her mom."

"Grandma Ruthie," one of the other girls supplied.

The ringleader nodded. "Coach lost her husband, and it's only her second Christmas without him. She moved in with her mom, and she's doing okay. But when we were doing some off-season jogs with her, she let on that she hasn't had the heart to get a real Christmas tree, since it was always her tradition with her husband. But she didn't sound too thrilled about using the dinky fake one Grandma Ruthie has. So, we decided to get one for Coach. We're going to bring it by their house and help them decorate it."

"We know nothing will replace Eli, Coach's late husband, but we want to do something," another teen added from the back of the group, and the girls' heads nodded as one.

Laney swallowed down the lump in her throat as she looked between the faces of the teenagers standing in front of her.

She shut the drawer of the register, walked out from behind the counter, and handed the cash back to the girl in charge, who looked at her funny.

"Did I give you too much?"

"That tree is on the house."

The girl's eyes widened. "Really?"

"Absolutely. What you're doing is a really good thing. The least I can do is provide the tree. Take your money and get a bite to eat or something."

The first girl in line stepped forward and hugged Laney. Soon, everyone else had piled on.

"That's so nice of you."

"It'll mean a lot to Coach!"

"And to Grandma Ruthie!"

"I can't wait to see her face!"

They all talked at once, and the warmth of their love for their coach swirled around the barn, giving the drafty old building an almost tangible warmth.

"Thank you so much," the ringleader said when the group hug ended.

"Don't mention it. I'm happy to help. You guys look adorable, by the way. Love the hats."

The girls grinned. "We wore them to make Coach and Grandma Ruthie smile when we deliver the tree. They're from last year's Santa Scamper."

"Santa Scamper?" Laney screwed up her face. She caught movement at the barn door, and Ford stepped inside. "What's that?"

"It's so fun! It's an annual thing. This year's race is on Thursday, actually. It's a mile-and-a-half run to benefit the local food pantry. All you have to do to join in is bring a non-perishable item to registration. You run the mile and a half through town, finish, and the yearly Santa Scamper hat is yours."

"Along with a coupon for free ice cream!" The girls laughed.

Laney leaned back against the counter. "I hadn't heard of it until now."

"You should come! We're hoping for a big turnout this year. We even advertised in Turner and Apple Creek."

"I might have to check it out."

"Do it! We'll see you there."

"Alright. I'll think about it." Laney waved goodbye, already excited at the prospect.

Chapter 34

FORD

FORD FOLLOWED THE TEENS out to the parking area to help them load up, and when he returned to the barn, he shot Laney a questioning look. "They said you gave them the tree for free?"

Laney shrugged. "They're doing an act of kindness. It was the least I could do."

"That's really nice of you."

"Actually, if you could just keep the free tree between you and me, I'd appreciate it."

Ford studied her for a minute. "I guess you probably don't want everyone to start demanding a free tree now, huh?"

"No, I just don't want other people to react like you did."

"How did I react?" Ford twisted his mouth to the side.

"You immediately praised me for my good deed."

"Sorry?" Did Laney not want him complimenting her?

"No, it's fine." Laney pressed her hands to her cheeks as if she was flustered. "I'm not explaining myself very well." She took a deep breath, dropping her arms. "Those girls were doing something really kind for their cross-country coach and her family. Giving them a free tree shouldn't overshadow what they set in motion. They deserve the credit, not me."

Ford's head flinched back. Not for the first time did Laney leave him in awe. She always worked hard for the common good, and that usually put her front and center, but at the heart of her efforts were other people. He shouldn't have been surprised that Laney didn't want any praise. She cared more about the action than the accolades.

"You…" He walked over to her and placed his hands on her shoulders. She looked at him, her eyebrows lifting. "…are something else." Ford placed a quick kiss on her nose, but a noise behind him had him dropping his hands and taking a step away from Laney. He cast a look to the door to find Isabel bustling into the barn, followed by Daniel.

Isabel stopped and blinked her gaze from Ford to Laney, undoubtedly taking in their proximity to each other. A knowing grin spread over her face.

Ford silently groaned. Next to him, Laney's face was as red as a holly berry.

"Hey, you two." Isabel walked farther into the barn. She and Laney exchanged hugs.

Ford reached around and shook hands with Daniel. "What are you guys doing here?"

"Do I need an excuse to come and see my brother and my friend?" Isabel pulled away from Laney and widened her eyes at him.

Ford just stared at her.

"Of course I don't." Isabel swished her hand through the air. "But I also wanted to peek at the barn. I'm trying to figure out how many couches I need to have on hand here for the ball."

"Couches?" What in the world was his sister going to do with couches?

"Laney and I decided to bring in some comfy seating for the ball. I'm getting a bunch of couches from my vendors. We'll cover them with drop cloths so they're protected from the food—"

"And the inevitable hot chocolate spills," Laney added.

"Right. That." Isabel pointed at Laney before walking around the room. "We'll need two over here, and another three along the far wall. We can bring in some stools, too. With the bar-height tables and chairs, that'll be plenty of seating. Hopefully, most everyone will be up and dancing anyway."

Ford's mind flashed to holding Laney in his arms and dancing around the barn. Frankly, there wasn't much he could think of that he'd like to do more. He hoped she'd be up for it after all the energy she'd be spending to prepare for the event.

"Marge and Melly are handling the food and beverages." Laney's ongoing conversation with Isabel drew Ford out of his fantasy. "Are you okay doing the big setup with your decor on the day of the event? We can't really spare the barn much before then."

"Absolutely. I'll plan to have my guys deliver couches then, and we can get the lighting situation sorted out at that point, too."

"Samson volunteered the use of the village's leftover stash of lights. Apparently, there is some excess from the streetlights and the gazebo."

"That should work." Isabel's eyes roved around the barn, taking in the space with her designer acumen. After only a moment, she swung her gaze to Ford and Laney. "Speaking of the gazebo, have you guys checked out the ice rink by the old mill site? It's such a cute little spot." Isabel smiled as Daniel placed his hand around her waist.

"We're planning to go for a skate tonight. If you two aren't busy, you should join us." Daniel flipped his gaze from Ford to Laney and back to Ford.

"I'd be up for that. What about you, Laney?"

He glanced down to find Laney chewing on her lip, and Ford checked his hopes. Did she not want to spend time with him?

After a moment's pause, she said, "I-I guess that would work."

"Yay! This will be so fun." Isabel bounced up and down, oblivious to Ford's doubts. "Why don't we meet at the rink at about seven? Does that give you enough time to close up here?"

Ford looked to Laney, giving her another chance to back out. Instead, to his immense relief, she nodded. "I don't think closing up a half hour early will rub anyone the wrong way. I'm sure my mom's got skates here I could use."

"I can run and grab mine if you can spare me for a minute here." Ford looked to Laney.

"If I must." Laney shot him a grin, and Ford's heart soared, the worry of where Laney stood with him melting away like snow in spring.

"It's a date!" Isabel hugged Laney again before pulling Ford down into a hug. "See you in an hour."

Chapter 35

LANEY

"It looks so different over here." Laney stared out over the expansive grounds where the village's old paper mill used to stand. Two years ago, when she was campaigning for her seat in the assembly, the developers were just getting started on the new properties. Every time she'd come back to Mapleton since then, Laney had tracked the progress.

From the looks of it now, the project was complete. Homes lined the curved, newly paved streets. While they didn't match the light displays over on Candy Cane Lane, they were tastefully decorated for the holidays. A bookstore glowed in the corner spot in the row of commercial properties that made up the ground floor of the multi-use complex in the center of the development.

"Betty's Book Nook," Laney read the sign above the door. "That place is darling."

Ford nodded. "Betty reminds me a lot of Julia. She's a little younger than us, but she had a dream to start her own business. The village has really taken to her."

The thought of the community support in Mapleton warmed Laney from the inside out. "I'll have to pop in there sometime soon." She shifted her gaze back to the residential properties. "These houses are adorable, too. They did a really nice job with them."

Ford agreed and pointed to his right. "I sold several of these homes. A lot of really great families moved into town."

Laney looked up at him. The pride Ford took in his work was etched on his face, reflecting off the white of the snow. He'd had the same sort of glint in his eyes when he showed her the old barbershop. He cared about the homes he sold and the people he matched them up with. Laney envied him that. Would she find pride in a job well done if she went to work with the senator? She could only hope.

Her mind bounced to the cheery village office with its oversized snowflakes hanging from the ceiling and matronly Melly behind the front desk. Laney couldn't deny that there was some appeal to the position there. But if she put her name in for the village clerk role, was she selling out on a political career? Didn't she owe it to herself to keep trying? If she didn't, wouldn't everyone consider her a failure? Then again, did she even *want* a political career? Laney wasn't sure about anything anymore.

"You ready to go?" Ford was staring at her, and Laney realized she was frowning. She cleared her face and smiled. She didn't want to get hung up on her job or what the future held tonight. She had enough to worry about, what with the fact that they were ice skating.

When she'd seen *Go ice skating* as number two on Sally's list for her, she'd thought to herself, *There's no way in you know where.* Yet, here she was. If that wasn't proof that she was doing this for reasons beyond the list, she didn't know what was. The biggest reason for her willingness to ice skate was staring at her with warm green and gold eyes, waiting on her response.

Laney slung her mom's white ice skates over her shoulder by the laces. "Uh-huh."

They followed a snow-plowed path to a clearing behind a circle of new houses. It appeared to be a common area for the properties. In the summer months, Laney imagined it as grassy space that would be perfect for pickup football games or neighborhood picnics. But now, it had been flooded and frozen to create a decent-sized ice rink. Lights were strung from poles around the icy surface, and benches and picnic tables with electric lanterns sitting in the middle of them had been positioned around the outskirts of the rink. The trunks of the small trees were wrapped in lights with lit-up snowflakes and oversized, shiny ornaments hanging from their branches. The whole scene looked like a magical Christmas fairy garden.

"I had no idea this was back here," Laney marveled.

"Me either. You much of an ice skater?" Ford's voice glistened with the hint of friendly competition.

He shot her a look, and Laney flushed under his gaze. He was probably expecting her to say yes, but she couldn't pretend. She may as well get out ahead of it.

"Actually, I'm pretty terrible at it. I've only gone skating once or twice in the past couple of years in Madison. And by *gone skating*, I mean *gone with friends and sat on the sidelines and watched*."

She almost hadn't agreed to ice skating because it would mean her making a fool of herself. It said something that the lure of getting to spend more time with Ford beat out her perfectionism.

"Seriously? What about when you were younger? Didn't your dad make a skating rink on the farm one winter?"

Laney's eyes widened. "I completely forgot about that! Gosh. I was pretty little. Probably only seven or eight, so I skated in boots. Skating did not become a tradition on the farm because Eliot and Eric decided to use the ice as an excuse to act out the type of checks they'd seen professional hockey players make. I'm pretty sure Eliot still has the scar on his chin from where he landed hard after Eric hit him. A trip to the emergency room and eight stitches later, let's just say, my mom was not thrilled. She put the kibosh on the ice rink real quick."

Ford chuckled. He placed his hand on the small of Laney's back, and a non-weather-related shiver pulsed through her veins. He guided her through a group of people milling around one of the picnic tables.

Ahead, Isabel tied off her skate and glanced up as they approached. "You made it!" She stood and held out her hands to balance. "You ready for this?"

"I was just telling Ford I'm not much of a skater." Laney sat down and unknotted the laces of her skates before slipping off her boots.

"It's a good thing you're here with Ford, then."

"Oh yeah?" Laney's brows peaked.

"Our parents had us playing hockey in Apple Creek through middle school." Isabel raised her shoulders as if it was no big deal.

Laney tipped her head to the side and tried to reconcile the graceful interior designer in front of her with a rough-and-tumble hockey player. She couldn't. On the other hand...

She turned her gaze to Ford. He she could definitely picture mixing it up on the rink. A slight tremor at the thought of him checking someone—or getting checked—ran up her spine.

"So, you're going to stop me from falling, then?" Laney asked him as he finished putting his skates on.

Ford was turned away from her, but she still managed to make out his barely audible, "Always."

Laney felt like someone had just run a live wire over her nerve endings, and every muscle in her body went weak.

"Hey, what about me?" Daniel stood and wobbled.

Isabel held a hand out to steady him. "Don't worry, babe. I've got you. We'll meet you guys on the ice." They walked toward the pond in the herky-jerky way the ice skates required.

Laney took a breath and mentally willed her pulse points to cool it with their pounding before she turned to Ford. "Hockey, huh? That's kind of hot."

"If I would have known hockey was what did it for you, I would have led with that."

Laney smirked. "Is that how you got your scar?"

"My scar?"

"Right here." Laney reached up and ran her gloved finger above his right eyebrow.

Ford stilled underneath Laney's touch, a mixture of tenderness and heat in his expression.

She pulled her hand back, and Ford blinked. "Right, uh, my scar. I wish it was a more impressive story." Ford rubbed at his close-cropped beard before reaching up and touching his brow. "I actually got this when I slid down the banister at my parents' house and careened into the edge of the wood molding around the front door."

Laney burst out laughing. "Seriously?"

Ford nodded sheepishly. "Not one of my smoothest moments. But I can be smooth, I promise."

Laney did not doubt Ford's smoothness. Not one bit. She took his hand and let him hoist her up. She shot him a smile, and he returned it with his customary grin.

Maybe it was his smile, or the way she felt completely safe when their hands connected, but another part of Laney's heart tethered itself to the man standing in front of her.

Even though she told herself she wasn't thinking about the future tonight, she couldn't help but imagine how Ford would fit in her life going forward—no matter what career path she chose. She'd like to believe they could make it work. She wanted that. She wanted *him*.

Chapter 36

FORD

"I FEEL LIKE A baby deer." Laney blew out an exasperated breath. "Okay. Let me try." She let go of Ford's hand and attempted to march forward as he'd instructed. She made it all of two paces before she lost her balance, her arms flailed like pinwheels, and she nearly fell over.

"Take it easy there, Bambi. Since there is no rail, you'll just have to hold onto me." Ford clamped his right arm around her waist and steadied her.

He smirked, and Laney shot him a look. "Don't look so smug."

"Can you blame me? I've got you in my arms. I'm pretty content." Being near to Laney was becoming an addiction he didn't think he wanted to quit.

"There are better ways to get me in your arms, I'll tell you that right now," Laney muttered, and it was Ford's turn to stumble because...yes, please.

She chuckled. "I think it would take me years to get good at this."

"That's not far off," Isabel said as she and Daniel skated up next to them, arm in arm. "Ford and I weren't really good until probably sixth grade, and we had been at it since third grade. It's a lot of work."

"Can you do any tricks?" Laney asked the question to both Ford and Isabel. "The Olympians make it look so easy."

"Isabel used to be able to do an axel," Ford said. "Not sure if she still can."

"Yeah, I don't know. I could try, but I might end up with a bruised tailbone." Isabel grimaced. "Probably not worth it. I'd like to be able to enjoy sitting down to dinner this holiday season."

"Fair enough. What about you Ford? Any tricks?" Laney turned her gaze on him.

"I can body check someone with the best of them, but that's about it."

Laney stilled for a brief second before shuffling her skates forward. "I'd like to see that," she mumbled.

Ford skated along next to Laney in silence for a minute—if what they were doing could really be called skating—and he tried to decide whether or not to invite her to one of his league games. They didn't play again until the New Year, and he didn't want to be presumptuous. Of course, he'd love to have her come and watch, but what would their status be once her parents were home? Would Laney be onto a new job in a different city? He didn't want to make things awkward.

Laney squeezed his arm. "Hey, I was wondering, and no pressure at all, but I wanted to ask—whoa!"

Her skates split out wide, and Ford grabbed her tighter, keeping her upright. "You were saying?"

"I was thinking about going back to Madison for a show on Friday. My best friend, Sally, runs the children's theater, and they're having their annual Christmas pageant. I've got an extra ticket. Would you want to join me?"

"Sure." Ford's mouth reacted before his mind could tell it to hedge the enthusiasm. He took a deep breath. "I mean, if *you're* sure."

"Yeah, I'd like for you to come with me." Laney blinked, a blush creeping over her already wind-chapped cheeks. "I know your test is coming up, so I don't want to take you away from studying if you need to do that. No hard feelings either way."

Study for an exam or spend a night with Laney? That was a no-brainer.

"I should be okay." Ford kept his voice casual. "My exam is on Monday. I can study the rest of the weekend. I'm feeling pretty good about the material, anyway."

"Yeah? Okay. Great." Laney slipped on the ice again, and Ford caught her. "Thanks," she said, a bit breathless.

Ford didn't respond, just pulled her closer.

"I'd be glad to help you study some more—only if you want me to," Laney went on. "I feel bad that I'm taking you away from hitting the books with all this Christmas business we're doing."

"Pretty sure I offered myself up for all this Christmas business, didn't I? Don't go and try to take credit."

Laney shot him a challenging look, her eyes shiny with eagerness. "In that case, you want to offer yourself up one more time and join me for the Santa Scamper? If I'm going to get the full Mapleton Christmas experience, I think I need to see you in one of those hats, which means we should participate in the race on Thursday night."

"Is that right?"

"Definitely."

"Why do I feel like this is a set-up for you to beat me in something else? You're the runner, not me."

"Oh, come on. It'll be fun. Besides, I'm here, aren't I? Ice skating...badly."

It hit Ford then that Laney's hesitation about coming to skate tonight was tied up in her lack of skills on the rink. She hated not being the best at something, and she wasn't used to being unsuccessful. But she'd been a good sport, and she *was* here, letting her guard down around him. In this case, no one had forced her hand. She wasn't floundering by herself at the tree farm or in the throes of nerves and worry about her niece. She chose to come tonight. Ford wanted to cheer. Instead, he leveled her with a playful scowl. He was going to say yes, but he liked their banter so much he was happy to stretch it out.

"How long is the race?"

"It's only a little over a mile. Besides, I bet you'll be cute in a Santa hat." Laney wiggled her eyebrows at him.

"Red is my color."

Laney laughed and wrapped both her arms around him in a hug.

Ford felt the squeeze in his heart.

Isabel and Daniel skated alongside them again. "You guys about ready to be done? I thought we could go to the café and grab a nightcap," Daniel said.

"Julia and Amanda are working," Isabel put in.

Laney tipped her chin up at him. "Sounds fun to me, but do you need to get going?"

Ford shook his head. "Nope. Let's go."

As they started for the benches, Ford debated the merits of scooping Laney into his arms and skating with her the rest of the way. It would definitely be faster, but now that he'd guessed her insecurities, he figured Laney might not like more attention being drawn to her obvious lack of ice-skating skill. So, they inched along.

Eventually, they made it to solid ground, changed out of their skates, and trekked back to the car. On the drive across town, Laney stared out the window, making small talk about the village tree, certain homes and their decorations, and the route of the Santa Scamper, which she pulled up on her phone to scope out.

Ford loved listening to Laney talk. He offered the occasional, "Uh-huh," in response to her statements and observations, but mostly, he was content to let her voice settle over him, with all the coziness of a down comforter on a winter's night.

When they arrived, Ford hopped out of the car and walked around the hood to open her door. A thrill shot through him when Laney didn't protest.

She entered the café's dining room first, but Ford tugged her backward and into his chest.

"Uff." Laney exhaled. "What was that for?"

Ford turned his gaze upward at the mistletoe before dipping his chin and drawing them together in a smooth, sweet kiss. The whole café disappeared, and Ford was only sure of the woman in front of him.

Laney flattened her palms against his back and pulled, silently telling him she wanted him to come closer. Ford willingly obliged. Their lips danced a slow dance, and his heart pounded out a steady rhythm named *Laney*.

He could have kissed her forever, but the sound of an exaggerated throat clearing brought Ford back to reality.

Laney pulled away from him, blinking her eyes wide as if she, too, just remembered that they weren't alone.

They turned to find Daniel and Isabel standing a few feet off, sly grins spread across both of their faces.

"What's that you're always telling us about getting a room?" Daniel said.

Chapter 37

Laney approached the registration table for the Mapleton Santa Scamper in the parking lot of Colony Elms Assisted Living Facility. She had a box of canned goods wedged under her arm and against her hip.

A young woman sitting behind the table beamed up at her. "You can set that right over there."

Laney added her box to the pile of nonperishable food items already collected. "It looks like it's a good turnout."

"The community is so generous. We couldn't believe how much food we gathered when we started this race two years ago." The woman held a pen to the paper in front of her. "Can I get your last name?"

"McGregor. Laney McGregor."

The woman's head whipped up. "You're Laney McGregor?"

Laney shifted, a wave of anxiety crashing into her when she noticed tears had sprung into the woman's eyes. Did she know this person? Had she offended her in some way?

"I'm Olivia Carlson. My team told me I have you to thank for the Christmas tree they brought to my mom's house."

Laney hid a sigh of relief and offered Olivia a kind smile. "That was all them. Your team loves you. I was so inspired by their thoughtfulness."

"They're a good group of girls, that's for sure." Olivia brushed at her nose. "You know, you try to coach these kids in real-life stuff. It doesn't matter who wins the race, but if we can train them to be good, considerate team players for life, well then, that's something. I just never thought they'd turn the lessons I've tried to impart on them back on me."

"I'd say you're doing a very good job with them. I'm so sorry for the loss of your husband."

Olivia dropped her gaze. "Thank you."

A handsome man with jet-black hair who looked vaguely familiar slung his arm around Olivia's shoulder and gave it a kind, friendly squeeze. Laney smiled at him as Olivia finished taking her information, handed her a bib with a number on it, and shared the instructions for the race: a quick jaunt down Mapleton Avenue.

Laney thanked her and walked toward the large group of runners congregating near the starting line. Her mind was on what Olivia had said about how she framed her work—to build the high schoolers up into productive, compassionate citizens. What Olivia was doing was so tangible, the results so apparent. Laney had seen first-hand how important the lessons were to her student athletes. The trickle-down effect was real.

Laney was lost in thought when she felt a hand on her shoulder. She jumped and whirled around. "Ford! You scared me."

He raised his eyebrows, and a mischievous twinkle lit his eye. "I can leave."

Laney grabbed his hand. "Oh, no you don't. I was afraid you weren't going to show." Ford had told her he had a five-thirty appointment with Josh and Peg Ellis, a newlywed couple whom he'd been showing houses to for the past month. "I thought maybe you made up your work thing to get out of running with me."

Ford palmed his face. "I should have."

Laney let the pleasure of being at his side blanket her with warmth from her nose to her toes. She motioned to his bib. "You're all registered, so there's no backing out now."

Ford squished up his features into a scowl, but she just laughed and tugged on his hand. They walked to the starting line, where a buzz of anticipation knocked around their fellow Scamper-ers like a pinball in a machine—a red and green, Christmas-themed machine.

Village president, Neil Schamburg, did a theatrical reading of the first half of *'Twas the Night Before Christmas* to kick off the race, and his voice boomed out over the crowd of runners. He was obviously fully recuperated from his bout with laryngitis earlier in the month, and his enthusiasm had Laney covering a laugh on several occasions.

When Neil got to the line "Now *dash away, dash away, dash away all*," cheers rang out, and the runners took off. Leading the charge was a group of eight people who each wore a reindeer headband, their cloth antlers affixed with jingle bells. They ran in formation, looking for all the world as if they were pulling Santa's sleigh.

"Glad to see Neil's voice recovered. That was...something," Ford said as they fell into step with the mass of runners.

Laney snickered, and they began making their way down Mapleton Avenue. Villagers lined the street, cheering them on. Some held festive signs, others rang jingle bells. Overhead, the streetlights shone, illuminating large Christmas wreaths, their red bows fluttering in the evening wind.

When they passed Hal's Diner, a group of carolers stood in front of the village tree, lit up like a lighthouse on the shore of the sea, a beacon in the dark night. The carolers were singing a rousing rendition of "Twelve Days of Christmas" on a loop. Laney decided that between tonight and the carols she had semi-participated in singing at the tree-lighting ceremony, she could check item number one off of Sally's Christmas Cliché list.

At the intersection between Mapleton Avenue and South Road, a massive display of lights and tinsel in the shape of angels blowing trumpets was strung between the light poles on either side of the street. It was one of Laney's favorite things about Christmas in Mapleton.

As a kid, she would wait with bated breath each year for the village to string up the *flying angel lights*, as her five-year-old self called them. There was something magical about their size and effect, as if they proclaimed a message of hope and goodwill over all of Mapleton.

When she and Ford ran under the angels, Laney was overcome with gratitude for this town, these people, the time she was able to spend here, and for the man currently jogging alongside her.

A lot had changed in a year.

Ford caught her looking up. "Everything alright?"

Laney swallowed and focused on her stride instead of meeting Ford's gaze. "Just thankful."

Ford didn't push her, maybe because he could tell she was raw with emotion. Or maybe because he was too out of breath to carry on much of a conversation. Either way, Laney was content to jog along, their warm breath puffing out into the cold night air. She savored every sight and every sound of the season, storing them away in her mind to last her until next year.

When they reached the café, the high school drumline was playing a barely discernible version of "The Little Drummer Boy." Laney and Ford crossed the finish line and were greeted by the boys' and girls' cross-country team members, each carrying a stack of stocking hats. Laney recognized several of the girls who had come to get a tree for Coach Carlson.

One of them handed Laney her complimentary Santa hat. "Glad to see you again!"

Laney smiled as she caught her breath. "Thanks for the invite. This was fun."

She turned to Ford, who was holding up his hands and looking at the hat he was being offered as if it had cooties. He shot her a "help me" look as a teenage boy standing nearby shoved a hat at him. "They're free, man. Everyone gets one."

"I'll take it." Laney swooped in and snatched the hat.

Ford put his hands on his hips.

"Look how fun these are!" Laney shoved her hat on her head and struck a pose.

Ford looked her up and down. "You somehow pull it off."

Laney's heartbeat—which had just slowed from the run—thumped again in response to Ford's words. She motioned with her finger for him to come closer and rose up on her toes like she wanted to kiss him.

She didn't have to pretend.

Ford took a tentative step in her direction, and she looped her arms around his neck. Laney licked her lips, and just when Ford tipped his chin down, she pulled the stocking cap over his head.

"There!" Laney stepped back and held out her hands with a flourish. "Now, we match." He looked adorable with the scowl on his face and the hat with the oversized, fuzzy puffball on top of his head. Ford rolled his eyes, and Laney did kiss him then—swift and firm.

"Laney? Laney McGregor?"

Chapter 38

FORD

LANEY DROPPED OUT OF the kiss and spun around at the sound of her name, her hand skimming down the side of his arm and the smile that so effortlessly swathed her face during their run falling with it.

Ford followed her line of sight to a middle-aged man he didn't recognize. The man strode in their direction with a smug grin on his face.

Laney had recovered and was now smiling in such a forced way Ford thought her face might crack. Gone was the carefree, joking woman who had shoved a gaudy stocking cap on his head not thirty seconds before. When she spoke, her voice was practiced.

"Ted. What a surprise." Laney held out her hand as Ford raced to place the name.

"I've heard such good things about Mapleton's Santa Scamper that when I saw it advertised over in Apple Creek, I figured I'd join in the fun and show my support. The good people of Mapleton are about to be my constituents now, aren't they?" Ted rocked back on his heels, shoved his hands in the pockets of his sweatpants, and flicked his gaze to Ford.

Right. Ted Talbert. The man who had taken Laney's seat in the assembly.

"Where are my manners?" Laney turned to Ford, a politician's smile on her face. If he didn't know her as well as he'd come to know her in the past month, he'd have thought everything was normal. But he could tell Laney was working very hard to keep her expression relaxed. If anyone was keeping track, let it be known this wasn't Ford's favorite version of Laney's smile. "Ford, this is Ted Talbert, assemblyman-elect for the third district. Ted, Ford Marshall. A local real estate agent."

"Nice to meet you." Ford endured the man's barefaced scrutiny. It was as if he were sizing Ford up for something. Ford's muscles clenched when Ted turned that same glare at Laney.

"Likewise. Well, Laney, I see you're enjoying your newfound time off."

"You can't beat Christmas in Mapleton." Laney's voice was even, though there was strain in her usual low tone. "Did you enjoy your run?"

"Oh, I didn't run."

Laney frowned. "I thought you said you came out for the race?"

"Sure. To mill around here at the finish line. Show my face. Say hi to some folks. You know."

Laney just blinked, and Ford couldn't help but think how different Ted's philosophy was from Laney's. If she was going to take in an event, she was going to be all in. Not come at the end for show.

"Okay, then." Laney angled her head toward the café. "We have some people who we're meeting, so if you'll excuse us."

"Sure. Sure. I won't keep you. I just wanted to say hi. Will I see you back at the Capitol in any capacity in the New Year, Laney?"

Laney, who had started to turn away from Ted, stilled. "I'm keeping my options open." She tossed her colleague a withering grin, tucked her arm into Ford's, and rotated toward On Deck Café.

Ford gave Ted one last look and let Laney lead him toward the coffee shop. He held the door for her, but he could tell the familiar jingle of bells overhead did little to brighten her mood.

"I'm just going to run to the restroom."

Laney fled down the hallway, and Ford walked slowly to the counter, scanning the packed dining room as he went. He waved to several friends and other village residents. Behind the bar, Seth and Nick were fixing drinks, and Amanda stood at the register.

She greeted him with a smile. "How was the run? Nice hat."

He'd forgotten all about it, and Ford grimaced. "Thanks. It was good. Can you help me out with something?"

·♥·♥·♥·♥·♥·

When Laney reappeared, Ford stood waiting for her where the hallway met the dining room. In his arms, he held Amanda's winter coat for Laney, and Seth's winter coat for himself.

Laney eyed the outerwear. "What's up?"

"It's pretty busy in here. I know we were going to get drinks, but I thought you might like some space. Want to walk through the park?" He held out Amanda's jacket for her. His goal was to give Laney a chance to breathe away from the watchful eye of the town, but if they went out in their running gear, they'd freeze.

Laney grabbed for the coat like it was a life jacket and she was on a sinking ship. "Yes, please. That would be great."

The café's outdoor seating area was dotted with a handful of red-and-white stocking caps worn by fellow runners, but Ford and Laney were able to make their way to the path that lined the village's baseball fields uninterrupted.

It was darker the farther they went into Sunrise Park. The lights from the café and street were too far away to provide much more than a dim haze in the distance. The trees overhead creaked in the December wind, their branches bare but for the layer of snow clinging to them, making them look like white-chocolate-coated pretzel sticks.

Laney blew out a big breath and tipped her head to the coal-colored sky. "Thank you for this."

"I had a feeling being surrounded by the town wasn't what you needed right now."

"You're right." Laney sounded small, and Ford peered over at her. Stress lines were etched on her face. She had her arms crossed and wrapped around herself. Ford longed to take her hand in his, but he wasn't sure what she was thinking or feeling, so he squeezed his hands to his sides and waited on her.

She caught him looking and hooked up the corner of her mouth, though the smile heaved under her effort, and even then, it didn't reach her eyes.

"I haven't seen Ted since we were both campaigning this past fall. I called and congratulated him over the phone on election night. I guess it caught me off guard to run into him here." Laney sighed. "That, and seeing him just makes me feel like even more of a failure. He's a reminder of all I no longer have. I couldn't keep my job, and now I've got nothing. I feel like I've peaked, and I'm not even thirty." She kicked a chunk of ice in front of her, sending it skittering down the path. "It doesn't help that Ted Talbert is sort of a braggart. Salt in the wound, and all that."

"He did seem full of himself." Ford wasn't sure how Ted beat Laney out. Laney was head and shoulders above Ted, in Ford's opinion. Then again, he wasn't entirely unbiased.

"Ted is full of himself." Laney offered him a droll grin. "He's also full of money, which helped him reach a lot of people on the campaign trail. He's a lawyer in Apple Creek. He ran on a platform that said his experience would be a benefit to the district. He claimed I was young and inexperienced, since prior to my position in the assembly all I'd done was work as a congressional aide and help out on my parents' farm."

The disgust over her loss to Ted rolled off of Laney in waves. Ford hated that she thought her best days were behind her. She was wrong about that.

"Losing to Ted doesn't take away from what you accomplished during your time in office. You realize that, right? You'll also have a lot of new opportunities to serve with different jobs moving forward."

"I guess. But I still feel like I have to prove myself. I want to find another job where I can make a difference. I had that, and I just want it back. I'm sure it'll all work out, but seeing Ted was a gut check. I've had a great time in Mapleton the past few weeks, but…" She trailed off. "I don't know."

But it's not good enough? But it's not reality?

Laney hadn't ever said as much, but Ford couldn't help but put those words in her mouth, even though he didn't want to believe them.

"What's the status of your job offer with the senator?"

"It's not technically a job offer yet." She wore an expression Ford couldn't place.

"But it's what you want?"

"It would allow me to keep working in public service and build on what I've done with my career to this point. Getting a job with a US Senator is very prestigious." Laney listed toward him, tucking her hand into the joint of his elbow. "It's all a big question mark right now, though."

Ford relished her touch, trying not to let the implication of her words drag him down. And when she rested her head against his bicep, Ford wished he could freeze time, or at least pause long enough to cement a mental picture of this moment, because he didn't know how much longer he'd get to experience Laney like this.

Where would he fit if she was working for the senator? Would he be wedged out of the equation? They hadn't talked about the future, but he wanted to support her no matter where she was or what job she pursued…if she'd let him.

Ford wrapped his hand around her waist, anchoring her to his side. He bent his chin and placed a kiss against her temple. "You'll do great things no matter what job you pursue. You have made a difference to a lot of people in the past two years—and to a lot of people in the past month."

"Thank you." Laney squeezed his arm. "I wish I could see into the future and know for certain it will all work out. Too bad life doesn't work that way." She let out a humorless laugh.

Ford held her tighter, willing his body heat to imbue her with the comfort she needed.

He, too, would love nothing more than to know the future—to know Laney would be in his life going forward—but he said nothing. He couldn't. Not when everything with their relationship was so uncertain and, unfortunately for him, likely temporary.

Chapter 39

LANEY

LANEY WAS FIDGETY AND unsettled as she steered her car along Hwy 151 and into Madison. As she approached Capitol Square, the streets were crowded with last-minute shoppers, and the day-old snow had turned into dirt-colored slush.

"Happy to be back?"

Though they'd passed the last several minutes in silence, she turned her head to see Ford watching her from where he sat in the passenger seat.

If someone would have told her a month ago, when she left town, that she'd be returning with a man from her childhood whom she now had some very adult feelings for, Laney would have asked if she was being punk'd.

As it was, Laney forced a smile, trying to shake off the anxiety that gripped her with an icy hand. Her unease was twofold.

First, she wasn't sure where Ford stood in regard to their relationship, or whatever it was she should call what was going on between them. There was *something* going on between them, but last night, after running into Ted, they'd started talking about the future, and Ford had clammed up. She would have liked for him to share how he was feeling about the potential of her moving away again after the holidays.

Sure, their chemistry was off the charts, but was that all it amounted to for him? Some heated kisses and a fun Christmas fling?

Laney didn't know what to think, and she wasn't sure she wanted to broach the subject with Ford again, because she didn't know what she wanted him to say.

Well, she did. But it scared her.

The whole thing made her feel foolish and exposed. If Ford didn't see what was happening between them as anything permanent, then Laney would do well to keep her guard up, no matter how hard she was falling. It would be better that way. Getting her heart pulverized at the holidays once was enough, *thankyouverymuch*.

But that brought to mind the second prong of her anxiety—her professional prospects.

Ahead, the Capitol stood, solid and strong. Since attending college in Madison, she'd always been in awe of the hustle and bustle of people, of education and civics intersecting in one town, under one roof. She loved being a part of it.

Laney waited for the blast of exhilaration to hit her at the sight of the majestic white-steepled edifice, reminiscent of the US Capitol Building. But today, the excitement didn't come. The sky was painted a winter gray that matched her mood, and the dome of the Capitol swelled ominously, as if packed full of the political failures of her past and the murkiness of her future.

She was saved from having to expand upon her noncommittal grunt of a response to Ford's question by the ringing of her phone through the car's Bluetooth speakers. Her breathing picked up when she saw her mom's name displayed on the caller ID screen. Gwen was continuing to hold stable, but Laney didn't take anything for granted. She clicked the button on her steering wheel.

"Hi, Mom. I'm in my car. You're on speaker with me and Ford."

"Oh, how nice!" Joan's voice echoed with delight. "Hi, Ford."

Before her mother could say something embarrassing or ask what they were doing in the car together, Laney jumped in. "What's up, Mom? How are the babies?"

"Well, I have good news and bad news."

"What is it?" Laney clenched the wheel.

"The babies are doing just fine, but your dad and I definitely won't be home for Christmas."

Laney flexed her fingers before loosening her grip. She'd expected that. Eliot and Carly needed them in Chicago. It was still a bummer, though. "That's okay, Mom. Eric and I will manage here."

"I know you will, but I feel terrible that you've been home this whole month and we haven't gotten to spend any quality time with you. Who knows where the New Year will take you?"

You can say that again.

Laney shot Ford a look out of the side of her eye. He was staring out the windshield with an unreadable expression on his face. She wished he'd drop a hint at what he was thinking. He must've sensed her staring because he swiveled his penetrating gaze in her direction.

She didn't want him to see the vulnerability she was sure was splayed across her features, so Laney faced straight ahead while conversing with her mom, pretending to focus hard on the road even though she knew the route by heart. "It's really fine, Mom. I'm so glad you and Dad have been able to help out there. You're definitely where you need to be."

"Hang on. You won't get rid of us that easily." Joan's voice turned conspiring.

Laney tapped her thumbs against the steering wheel. "What do you mean?"

Joan laughed. "We're going to make a quick trip home for the Merry Mapleton Ball before heading back to Chicago for Christmas Eve and Christmas Day."

"Really?"

"Really! Carly's parents are coming into town shortly. We promised Johnny we'd come back for Christmas so he can see both sets of grandparents, but Eliot and Carly will have some help with him beforehand, so we figured we'd take the chance to pop back up to the farm. We could hardly stand the thought of missing out on the entirety of the tree season, and seeing the barn all done up for the ball is going to be fabulous. We can't wait."

Laney and her mom talked logistics for another minute before Laney disconnected the call. She shifted in her seat, running her hands around the wheel before settling them back at ten and two. "Well." Laney worked her jaw. "That's great news."

She should have been thrilled. She *was* thrilled about Asher's and Gwen's progress and about seeing her parents. So, why did she feel even more anxious after her mom's call?

"Absolutely," Ford agreed. "Though, I'm afraid if you keep grinding your teeth like that, you won't have any left to eat with."

"What? Oh. Sorry." Laney relaxed her mouth and had to physically work to release the tightness in her shoulders. "Why am I being like this?"

"Like what?"

"I don't know. Seeing Ted and now my mom mentioning not knowing where I'm going to be in the New Year...it's all just unsettling."

Ford sat back in his seat, peering out the window. "I get it."

Laney shot him a look. Did he?

He turned and looked at her, his expression soft and kind. "You've got to figure out where you want to be, Laney, and then go for it. You'll do great things, whatever you choose to do. I've no doubt about that. But it's all up to you."

Laney glanced at him as she navigated the square and headed for the parking ramp off of State Street. "That's both terrifying and exhilarating."

"I can only imagine." Ford laughed and reached over the console to give her knee a squeeze. "If anyone can handle it, it's you."

Laney grinned at the windshield, but it was a smile meant for Ford. "Thank you for that. And for letting me work through this. I know I'm sort of a mess, but I really appreciate you bearing with me."

"Duck. Reindeer. Bear. I've got all your animal needs covered."

Laney erupted with laughter. How did Ford manage to do that? To know just where to poke her and how far to go in order to release some of the tension in her life. Her anxiety fled, and in its place, she felt light and happy.

Laney parked and grabbed for his hand as they left the parking structure. Together, they walked down a glistening State Street toward the theater.

"The show doesn't start for forty-five minutes, but Sally said we should come early."

Laney was sure Sally wanted to meet and interrogate Ford. She should have been worried, but she was just going with it. "Here we are!"

Above Madison Children's Theater, the old-fashioned marquee sign with slide-in letters read "Children's Nativity + Santa Meet and Greet" in bold, uppercase letters.

Ford pulled the large glass door open, and Laney stepped inside and onto the lush, ruby-red carpet in the theater's lobby. She took a deep breath, inhaling the scent of cranberries and velvet that was the trademark aroma at the theater at this time of year. Laney spotted Sally immediately. Her friend had her back turned to the front door. Sally looked chic in a black sheath dress with forest-green tights and black flats. Her attire was both practical for chasing and wrangling kids and dressy enough for the theater's big night.

"Come on. I'll introduce you to Sally." Laney hooked her hand into Ford's arm and was about to call out to her friend when Sally turned, and Laney caught sight of her face, awash with panic and confusion.

Laney unlatched herself from Ford and crossed the lobby in four quick strides. She could sense Ford keeping pace behind her.

"Hi." Laney grabbed Sally into a firm hug. When she pulled back, Laney studied Sally's stunned face. "What's wrong?"

"We just found out that the Santa we hired for the meet and greet after tonight's show isn't going to be able to make it." Sally started massaging her temples. "He's got the flu."

"Probably not something you want to pass to the kids a week before Christmas."

Sally grimaced. "I know. But I've got a hundred kids and their little siblings who are coming with their Christmas wishes to share with Santa, and I'm not going to have a man in a red suit. What am I going to do?"

Laney hugged Sally again. "There has to be someone else who can play Santa tonight. How did you find this guy originally?"

"I went through an agency. We've been using the same Santa for the past four years."

"Do they have anyone else they can send?"

Sally shook her head. "They're completely booked. Santas are in high demand the Friday before Christmas."

"Unsurprising," Ford muttered behind her. "I—"

"I'm so sorry." Laney swung her head around. "Where are my manners? Sally, this is Ford. Ford, this is my best friend, Sally Hennessey, the woman who keeps everything running around here."

"Clearly not very well." Sally turned to Ford. "I swear I'm usually much more organized. This is so ridiculous. Here I was, all excited to meet you so I could give you two a hard time about whatever this is." She waved her hand back and forth between Ford and Laney.

Laney stuck Sally with a murderous glare before turning to Ford, who looked amused. Laney shoved down a surge of attraction that, coupled with her embarrassment, was making her face feel hot. "You'll have to excuse Sally. Evidently, the Santa crisis has gone completely to her head."

Sally rolled her neck. "You are not kidding. What am I going to do?"

"There has to be someone else who can do it," Laney suggested, immediately going into problem-solving mode. "I mean, how hard can it be? Listening to Christmas wishes from a bunch of excited kids? What about Ron? Where is he, anyway?" Laney looked around the lobby, trying to spot Sally's husband.

"He's in the sound room, making sure the mic packs are okay. He can't be Santa. The kids know him too well. That's the same reason I can't ask one of their dads." Sally took off toward her office.

"Laney, I—" Ford started.

"Hang on a second. Let's just ride this out," Laney said, motioning for Ford to follow her.

Sally was prattling on as she strode down the hall. "Everyone is too familiar with each other. For a couple of these kids"—she glanced over her shoulder at them and dropped her voice—"this'll be their last Christmas as believers. They'll pick up on anything that's suspect, and I refuse to be the one to spoil the holiday for these families. I need someone completely new to them, but also someone I know and trust. I won't sit my kids on just anyone's lap."

"Good point." Laney followed Sally into the cramped office. It was sad to have to think that way, but that was the reality of the world they lived in.

Sally plopped into the chair behind her desk, sending a pile of papers fluttering to the ground.

"I'll do it."

Laney froze and turned slowly around to where Ford was leaning against the doorframe, holding up a hand as if to say *Pick me!*

"You will?"

Ford pushed himself upright. "Sure. It's like you said...how hard can it be?"

Sally squealed. "I really should protest. Say something about how you're here as a guest and I couldn't possibly take advantage of your kindness, but I'm in too much of a bind. Ford, you're hired, and I'm forever in your debt."

She stood up and crossed the small office toward him. "There's just one problem. I don't know if the white beard I have in the costume closet is going to cover up your natural facial hair."

Ford shrugged. "Got a razor? I can shave."

Laney winced and might have whimpered a little bit.

Check that. She definitely had. Ford shot her an amused grin, and Sally swung around, eyebrows wagging. "Suck it up, Lane. It's for a good cause."

Laney pouted. "Doesn't mean I have to like it."

"Didn't know you felt so strongly about this." Ford stroked the sides of his face.

"Don't let it go to your head."

"Too late."

Ford closed the distance between them—or maybe Laney did. She couldn't be sure. Their lips connected, and Laney reached up and dragged her fingers through his beard, giving it a slight tug.

"Good night." Sally whistled. She was fanning herself when Laney broke the kiss. "You two finished? Because unless you want to don a Mrs. Claus outfit, Laney, we're going to have to lock that down for now."

Laney held up her hands in defeat.

"Alright, good. Ford, let's get you to Ron. He'll find you a razor and stow you away so no one will spot you before the show and grow suspicious."

Ford turned to follow Sally out of the office. He tossed Laney a wink over his shoulder, and she took one last good look at his beard.

·♥·♥·♥·♥·♥·

After the last child had told Ford his grandest Christmas wishes and the theater was empty and quiet, Sally, Ron, Laney, and Ford plopped themselves in the center of the stage. Ron had ordered Ian's Pizza for the four of them, and they were devouring their mac-and-cheese-topped slices in celebration of a successful evening.

"I'm stuffed." Laney tossed the corner of her crust back into the now empty cardboard pizza box and glanced at Ford. She was still mourning the loss of his beard, but she had to admit that clean-shaven Ford was every bit as sexy as bearded Ford, especially since he kept flashing some impressive dimples in her direction. He had shed the plush Santa coat and was now rocking his white undershirt with the velour, oversized red pants. Laney wasn't sure how it was possible, but he was totally pulling it off.

"I never realized mac-and-cheese pizza was a thing, but I'm a believer. This was delicious. Thanks for inviting me." Ford turned his charming smile toward Sally.

"Are you kidding? Not sure what we would have done without you. So, thank *you*."

Ron nodded in agreement with Sally as he pushed himself up off the stage. "I'm going to do a final sweep of the building and check the security system."

"I can help." Ford hopped up, and he and Ron wandered down the theater's aisle, talking as if they were old friends.

Sally grabbed Laney's wrist the second they were out of earshot. "Okay. Your man? Literally my hero tonight."

Laney sighed happily. She wasn't shocked that Ford stepped up—not one bit. He'd proven over and over again this month that when he saw a need, he filled it. "He's one of the good ones."

Sally's eyes were wide. "That's an understatement. Are you going to lock that down, then, or what?"

Laney scooted closer to Sally. "I don't know. I don't know how seriously he's taking all this, and every time I stop to think about it, it freaks me out."

"How so?"

"Ford's default is to joke around and keep things light, if you haven't gathered that. He hasn't told me how he's feeling about me, like *really* feeling, one way or another. Then, there's the Christmas Cliché list. I haven't told him about it. What if he's mad or thinks I was leading him on?"

Sally tapped the side of her nose and made a *pfft* sound of disbelief. "Doubtful. Mark my words, that man would lasso the moon for you."

"You don't know that. You've spent all of four hours with him, and the majority of that time was spent listening to him play Santa."

"Call it dramatic intuition. Besides, he might have done me a favor with the Santa gig, but he was totally doing it all for you. Just tell him the truth. It'll be fine."

Laney groaned. "Maybe. But I wish he'd just tell me where he's at and put me out of my misery."

"Yeah, you seem *really* miserable."

"Oh, I'm not miserable. Spending time with Ford is the stuff dreams are made of. It's the thought of that all ending, or of being made a fool for falling for him, that's making me panicky."

"You could just talk to him. Tell him how *you're* feeling and where you're at. I know it's scary to put yourself out there after Dustin, but—"

"Ford's not Dustin."

Sally nodded, a smile crinkling her eyes. "And thank God for that."

"Amen." Laney nibbled on her lip. "You're right. I will talk to him. Though, I'll probably wait until after he's done with his big exam. I don't want to stress him out when his professional future is hanging in the balance."

"Speaking of professional futures. Do you still want us to talk to Senator McClaren for you? Or have present circumstances changed your mind?"

Laney shifted her jaw. She didn't know what she wanted, other than Ford. But testing the waters with the senator wouldn't hurt anything, and she didn't want to close that door prematurely.

She tipped her head back and forth. "I held up my end of the Christmas Cliché bargain, so it's only fair, right?"

Sally studied her before giving her a single nod. "If you're sure. I'll have Ron reach out, and I'll let you know what his uncle says."

Chapter 40

FORD

FORD WAS HALF TEMPTED to bring the Santa suit along to McGregor Farm on Sunday. He'd wear the thing forever if Laney would look at him the way she had on Friday night.

Eric had helped with the tree farm over the weekend, which was a good thing because Ford needed to spend the time studying. He would have been lying if he said he hadn't missed seeing Laney, sneaking glances and kisses and laughing with her in the barn. He was happy she had offered to help him go over his exam materials one last time. Even though he was feeling prepared, it gave him an excuse to see her.

It was six o'clock when he arrived at the farm, and the parking lot was barren. He spotted Eric hauling something into the house, and when Ford got out of his car, Laney emerged from the barn.

"Hey, stranger." She went into his open arms with a smile.

Ford pulled her close. "Hey yourself."

Laney sighed, and he felt the warmth of her breath against his exposed collarbone.

"If I didn't know any better, I'd say you missed me."

"Nah." Laney pulled back. "I do miss the beard, though."

She winked, and he laughed. "You are something else, Laney McGregor."

"I'll take that as a compliment." She grinned and whirled around when the storm door to the farm slammed shut. Her mom trotted down the steps.

"Ford. Hello!"

"Hi, Mrs. McGregor. Glad you made it home."

Laney's mom came over and patted his arm. "You're such a good boy. Laney tells me you have some studying to do. Shouldn't you two get to it instead of canoodling out here?"

Laney flattened her lips in exasperation. "We're working on it, Mom. Dad's in the barn."

She hooked her thumb, pointedly shooing her mom in that direction.

Joan laughed. "I can take a hint. I'll make myself scarce. Tomorrow's the test, Ford?"

He nodded. "First thing in the morning. It could take me up to three hours."

"You'll be great." Joan patted his shoulder again and left them for the barn.

They watched her go before Laney shot him a rueful grin.

"Good to have your parents back?" he asked.

She chuckled. "Not gonna lie, I didn't miss not having the chaperones while they were gone."

Ford smirked. "It's going to be fun to try to sneak a kiss from you with your parents at home."

"We'll have to see if you're smooth enough."

Ford was about to show her how smooth he was, but the barn doors creaked open again, and this time, both Joan and Jeff emerged. They were grinning as they crossed the clearing toward the house—as if they knew exactly what they were interrupting.

Laney looked heavenward before glancing back at him. "Don't mind them."

"I don't mind at all."

That made Laney smile for real, which was his favorite thing—better than rocky road ice cream and the warm breeze of spring, he decided.

"It really is good to have them back. I didn't realize how much this house missed them—how much I missed them—until they walked through that door this afternoon. It was like all was right in the world again. Here. Look at these pictures of Gwen and Asher." Laney held out her phone to him, swiping through pictures of her niece and nephew.

"They look great."

Laney stared down at the photo for a beat longer. "They are doing really well, thank God. I feel like I can breathe a little easier. They aren't completely out of the woods, but their forward progress is the best early Christmas gift." Laney clasped her cell phone in front of her chest, as if trying to hold the babies to her heart. "But enough about me. How are you doing? How's the studying been going? What can I do to help?"

Ford smiled to himself. This was quintessential Laney. She couldn't help but ooze on about her family, but she also wouldn't be distracted from the task at hand—helping him. It was nice to be on the receiving end of Laney's goodwill.

"I'm feeling pretty good about everything. Actually, I'm starting to get antsy sitting in front of my books and studying."

"In that case." Laney tapped her chin. "I have an idea. There's this spot I want to show you, and you can talk through what you know while we walk out there. It'll help you recall things and sort out what you need to review." She grabbed his hand and pulled him toward the trees. "Go ahead. Start boring me with all your real estate knowledge."

Ford launched into the material he'd pored over the past few days and information that he'd made it a point to hone over the course of the past several years. Laney asked clarifying questions as they walked along, forcing him to extrapolate and recall other facts.

Eventually, they walked straight through to the far side of the farm and popped out into a clearing. "We're almost there," Laney said as Ford paused to look around.

"I don't remember ever coming out this far."

"Dad didn't want us to come this way when we were growing up. There's a giant ravine back here with a steep drop-off that's part of my parents' acreage. He didn't want to take any chances."

"With Eric and Eliot around, I can see why he'd make that rule."

"Exactly. But I'm all grown up now, so he doesn't mind. Besides, it's one of the best views in all of Mapleton, if I do say so myself." Laney led him through a thicket of quaking aspen and pine trees threaded together with varieties of maples. Several paces in, the trees started thinning, and they came to a ledge. "Here we are." Laney made a grand gesture as they stepped together to the drop-off.

Before them was a thirty-foot decline. Ford could see the tops of the trees in the ravine. If he looked out beyond the wooded area, he could see the neat lines of the neighboring farm fields below. But it was the sky above them that made this spot extra special. It stretched on in every direction, up and down and all around. The view was stunning.

"I think it feels like we're on the top of the world out here. But also, like there's so much more out there, you know?" Laney said in a whisper.

She was right. The inky black of the night sky was covered with blazing stars, one on top of another, like gold stitches on a stocking. They looked close enough that Ford was tempted to reach out and try to grab one.

"This is amazing." He wasn't sure how he'd lived his entire life in Mapleton and not known such a spot existed. Here he considered himself an expert on Mapleton real estate!

"We actually aren't that far from the main road." Laney turned to the east and pointed behind them. "From the street, you can't see that this little clearing is tucked back in here. I think that's what makes it magical." She looked wistful as she peered out over the ravine and then tipped her head up to the sky. She breathed in deep.

"I haven't been out here since—" Laney cut herself off.

Ford waited, and when she didn't continue, he prodded, "Since?"

Laney stared straight ahead. "Since I showed this place to Dustin last Thanksgiving."

Ford felt a swift upsurge of jealousy in his gut, but he told his ego to take a hike. This was obviously a touchy subject for Laney. He, too, faced the ravine and spoke to the wide expanse in front of them. "Do you want to tell me about him?"

Laney heaved a shrug next to him. "I thought he was the one. We met in Madison. He works at the Capitol, too."

Ford held back a grimace. Having to see her ex-boyfriend at work every day couldn't have been pleasant.

Laney adjusted her footing. "He was a good guy—or at least I thought he was. We had a lot in common, being in politics and having gone to school at UW-Madison. Things were getting serious, and I brought him back to Mapleton for Thanksgiving last year. That was when I showed him this spot." She motioned to the ground in front of them.

Ford nodded for her to continue. He was standing pin-straight, bracing for the worst.

"We spent Christmas with his family in Milwaukee. I was as certain as a person could be that Dustin was going to propose. He seemed to be dropping hints about us taking the next step, and I'd caught him being secretive at the end of a couple phone calls, so I thought he was coordinating some big proposal or a huge surprise engagement party for me." Laney winced, shaking her head. "Looking back, I should have seen it coming."

Ford didn't like this. He didn't like it one bit. The thought of Laney getting hurt made his stomach indent in the most uncomfortable way, like someone had taken a baseball bat to it.

"As it turns out, he wasn't planning a proposal to me. He was reconnecting with his ex-girlfriend. His parents own a huge piece of property, and when I went looking for him on the day after Christmas last year, I found him in bed in the carriage house—with her. I thought I was going to be walking in to find him on one knee, proposing to me, and...yeah. That was *not* it."

Ford reached over and took Laney's upper arms into his hands, turning her to face him. "Laney, I am so sorry. That's terrible."

She offered him a grateful look before continuing. "He tried to talk to me, to explain himself. He said he felt so much pressure within our relationship, like he had to work too hard for us. Said it had always been easier with his ex."

"Sounds like he found you intimidating."

Ford imagined Dustin as one of those men who wasn't confident enough in himself to be proud of the woman he was with, instead needing to belittle his partner in order to build himself up—basically a deplorable excuse for a significant other.

If Ford got the chance, he would take care of Laney's heart, holding it up and protecting it like it was glass. He would never let his own insecurities affect the way he treated Laney.

Laney chuckled. "Maybe. I know now that a breakup was for the best. I'm not hung up on Dustin. But it still felt pretty crappy, especially since I spent over a year of my life with him. He called me the other week to tell me that he and his ex-girlfriend had broken up...again."

"Guess it wasn't as easy with her as he thought it would be, huh?" Ford couldn't help but scoff. Dustin's behavior grated on him. What did the guy think? That Laney would let him come crawling back? Welcome him, even? It was like Dustin didn't know her at all. Laney deserved a heck of a lot more than a man who only wanted her when it was convenient.

"Clearly not." Laney's voice was tinged with appreciation. "I'm mostly mad at myself for almost letting him steal the joy of this Christmas from me, just like he stole the joy from my memory of last Christmas. I thought if I avoided the holiday festivities, I could avoid being reminded of my massive failure in the relationship department."

"You didn't fail. He did."

She dipped her head. "Fortunately, between you and Sally, I wasn't able to put my steer-clear-of-all-things-holiday-related plan into place. I'm glad about that."

"Me too."

They stood in silence for a minute. Ford massaged the muscles in Laney's arms, and she dropped her head to her chest with what he hoped was a relieved sigh. She had been through a lot.

Ford wanted to ask her if she felt like she was less of a failure at relationships after spending time with him, but he couldn't seem to figure out how to ask the question without sounding presumptuous or like he was fishing for a compliment. The last thing he wanted was for his inquiry to come across as goofy or like he wasn't taking her experience seriously.

Eventually, Laney batted her lashes and met his gaze. "There's something else I have to tell you about."

"What's that?"

Laney looked decidedly uncomfortable as she pulled out a loose-leaf sheet of paper from her pocket. "Since I'm baring my soul to you tonight, you should see this, too."

Ford took the paper from her and unfolded it. "Operation Christmas Cliché." He read a list of Christmas items, several of them with slashes through them. He spotted places where Laney had added notes in the margins.

"Play St. Nick." He stared down at a record of their entire month. Ford glanced up at her. "What is this?"

Laney squished her eyes closed before cracking one open and giving him a guilty look. "Don't be mad."

"Why would I be mad?" Ford continued scanning the list. "Number 7: Go on a holiday-themed date."

"There. That one. That's why." Words spilled out of Laney's mouth in a rush. "Sally put me up to this. She said she wasn't going to let me go home for the holidays and stew, so she made me this list. She had me sign it and everything, as a promise that I'd live my Christmas vacation to the fullest. She made a deal that if I accomplished the Christmas Cliché list, she and Ron would talk to Senator McClaren on my behalf."

Ford nodded slowly. "I'd say you did well. You checked everything off."

"I know. That's just it," Laney all but wailed, her arms falling to her sides before she started flailing them about. "I wanted to show you this now because I didn't want you to find out later and see that I had this silly list and think the reason I struck up this...this..."—she motioned between the two of them—"whatever *this* is because of some arbitrary list or a job opportunity. Because it's not just because of the list. For me."

The look in her eye—a mixture of vulnerability and hope—made him feel like she had just struck a match and set his soul aflame. Ford bent down and pressed his lips to hers. Laney let out a squeak, and he tasted her gasp.

He was more a man of action than speeches, and he poured his heart into his kiss, working to show Laney how much he valued her with the gentle way his hands cupped her cheeks and how much he was in it for the long haul with the strong push of his mouth.

When she finally pulled away, Laney traced the clean lines of his jaw and searched his face. "So you're not mad?"

"No." Ford bent and kissed Laney's nose. "If I were to get mad at you and assume you had ill intentions with this list, wouldn't that make me the biggest cliché ever?"

Laney cocked her head back, a slow smile spreading across her face. "I guess you're right."

"I definitely am. Besides, I think this list is awesome. If I would have known about it, I would have thanked Sally for pushing you into it when I met her on Friday."

Laney turned them toward the ravine and rested her head on his shoulder. "Thank you." The words came out with a puff of her breath, white against the black night air. "I'm glad we came out here. I've been avoiding it." She squeezed his arm. "But it'll always be my favorite spot. Sometimes, when I've been in a bind, or stressed, or whatever, I picture myself standing right here and remember that, in the grand scheme of things, I'm just a small part of it all."

Ford looked down at her. Her eyes were fixed on a spot in the distance. A gust of biting wind blew up and tossed her hair around. She blinked and angled her head toward him, offering a small smile. "I wanted to share it with you. Maybe if you get stuck during your exam, you can picture yourself right here, and it'll provide you with some clarity."

Ford had a feeling he'd be picturing himself right here—with Laney by his side—for many days to come.

Chapter 49

LANEY

Ford: You left me hot cocoa?! <licking lips emoji>

Laney grinned at his text message. It was the morning of his exam, and she had snagged the spare key to his BMW from Isabel so she could leave a steaming thermos of the chocolatey goodness in the cup holder of his car for him to find...along with a good-luck note.

Laney: You like? <smiling face emoji>

Ford: Would have liked it more if you'd stuck around for a kiss instead of just taunting me with your lip print on the paper... <sad face emoji> <desperate face emoji>

Laney laughed out loud. She'd broken out the red lipstick for the grandest effect.

Laney: Didn't want to distract you. <angel face emoji>

Ford: Probably smart.

Laney: You know me. Always thinking! Seriously, though, good luck today. Not that you'll need it!

Ford: Thanks. You sure you don't want to sit for the exam with me? You probably know the material just as well as I do.

Laney: Nope. I would feel bad if I beat your score. <winking face emoji>

Ford: Always so confident.

Laney: Just keeping you on your toes. Let me know how it goes. You've got this, Ford. <kissing face emoji>

Laney clicked off her phone and slid it in her back pocket. She'd promised to walk her dad through what he'd missed on the farm this morning. Marge and Melly were stopping by a bit later to talk with her mom about the plans they had for the Merry Mapleton Ball.

She hurried to get ready, going through the motions of the routine she'd fallen into over the past month—worn jeans, oversized sweatshirt, and several layers of winter gear.

Her dad was already out tinkering in the barn when Laney joined him. It was a beautiful December day. The clouds were rolling in, causing the temperature to rise. While she appreciated a reprieve from the bitter cold, Laney was also grateful she had been able to show Ford the view from the ravine last night while the sky was still clear. As it turned out, the surroundings had paled in comparison to the magic of being in Ford's arms. A shiver went through her at the memory of how intensely he looked at her and how passionately he kissed her before they walked back to the farmhouse. Laney was pretty sure if she would have been standing closer to the ledge, they might have fallen over it.

"You okay, Laney? You're looking a little funny."

Laney blinked her thoughts back to the present. Her dad stood with a stocking cap askew on his head, shooting her a questioning gaze. She was sure her cheeks flamed, but she smiled. "Yep. All set."

They took off through the trees. Her dad took notes so he'd know what species to plant. By the time they made their way back to the barn, a gentle snow had started to fall.

"You know," her dad said, "I was so glad to be able to help Eliot and Carly out, but I missed this."

Laney looked up at him to find his eyes glistening. She imagined he was overcome with gratitude for the snow, the trees, the farm, and the life he had built for himself and their family.

That was what she wanted out of a job.

Something tugged at Laney's sternum, and she swallowed back the string of nerves that seemed to be lingering in her chest since her run-in with Ted Talbert, all tangled up like a badly kept strand of Christmas tree lights. She stood up straighter, shaking off her anxiety. She'd figure out what to do next. She always did. But it was almost Christmas. For now, she was going to leave the knotted mess of her professional life—and her feelings surrounding it—alone.

"The farm missed you, too, Dad." She put her arm around his waist, letting go only when he reached forward to open the barn door for her.

Marge, Melly, and Joan stood in the center of the barn when she and her dad entered.

"Oh good, Laney, you're here!" Her mom clapped her hands. "Marge and Melly were just telling me the plans. I think it sounds wonderful. Jeff,"—she turned to Laney's dad—"how would you feel about donating a couple of trees to the ball? I think we should put them up in each of the corners of the barn. Light them up and invite folks to bring a gift for the veterans' toy drive."

"Mom, that's such a good idea!"

"I suppose I could chop down a tree or two or four, if you needed them for the ball."

Laney rolled her eyes. "You *suppose*? More like you can't wait to get your hands on a saw and have at it."

"Guilty as charged. When do you need them?"

"The ball is the evening of the twenty-second. We're going to decorate all day before we go home and get ready." Melly glowed with anticipation. "Can't wait to show off my new dress," she added.

Laney, too, couldn't wait to see the entire town decked out for the holiday celebration. Though, Melly's comment reminded her that she still needed to figure out something to wear.

She half listened as Marge walked through how the evening would go. Her mind drifted to Ford, and she said a silent prayer that he'd have total recall on his exam.

"I'm going to go and get started on the cocoa," she said, catching her mom's eye.

Joan gave her a thumbs-up before leading Melly over to the counter with the register. Laney heard them discussing the appetizer spread they were planning as she left the barn.

Laney hummed the tune of Bing Crosby's "Hark! The Herald Angels Sing" and "It Came Upon a Midnight Clear" mashup as she got to work preparing the hot chocolate. Feeling particularly festive, she donned her hat from the Santa Scamper, stirred the cocoa, and arranged the tray of peppermint sticks, whipped cream, and other fixings to bring out. She walked to the barn, careful not to disturb the precious cargo.

Marge and Melly were saying their goodbyes to her mom and dad when Laney entered. She placed the tray down on the table, told the women she'd see them in a couple days for the ball, and hurried back into the farmhouse to retrieve the slow cooker full of cocoa. It was getting close to noon, and Laney wanted to be ready with warm drinks for their first guests of the day.

She hoisted the heavy slow cooker off the counter, taking care not to slosh any of the liquid chocolate over the edges. She used her elbow to open the door, turned and pushed against it with her back, and managed to make it out to the landing of the stairs without a single spill.

When she swung around to take the steps down to the barn, there was a man talking to her parents in the clearing. At the sound of the storm door clicking shut and sealing behind her, the trio faced her, and Laney nearly dropped the entire crock of cocoa.

The warm feelings of *peace on earth, goodwill to men* that she'd been swimming in all morning turned brittle cold.

"Dustin? What are you doing here?" Laney forced herself to move down the stairs, though her legs may as well have been snow blocks.

"Here, dear. Why don't you let me take that while you two catch up?" Joan grabbed the slow cooker from Laney's hands, eyes wary as she looked between Laney and Dustin.

"I've got some business to tend to with the trees." Her dad smiled, but it looked a little—*read: a lot*—forced.

When her parents left them standing there, Dustin smiled at her. "It's good to see you, Laney."

"I-I don't think I can say the same. What are you doing here?"

"I thought you'd have put two and two together." Dustin tucked his hands in the pockets of his coat and eyed her. It was a smarmy look, and it set Laney even further on edge.

What was going on? She'd spoken to Dustin three weeks ago, and he'd told her about his breakup with his ex. He'd been feeling her out, testing the waters where she was concerned, but she'd shut that down—or so she thought. She certainly hadn't expected to hear from him again, much less see him here, in the flesh, on her parents' farm.

"You're going to have to enlighten me, Dustin."

"I was passing through on business from my boss." Dustin paused, and Laney squinted her eyes. "Senator McClaren."

Laney's mouth dropped open before she could stop it.

Dustin nodded, looking all too pleased to have shocked her. "I joined his staff a couple months back. I thought you knew."

Laney waved her hand around her face. "Nope. No idea."

This was what she got for completely blocking Dustin on all social media platforms and leaving the room whenever his name came up. She was in the dark about his life, like a burnt-out Christmas lightbulb. If she'd had any clue Dustin was now affiliated with Senator McClaren, she wouldn't have asked Sally and Ron for the referral.

Dustin just laughed. "I'm going to try not to take that personally."

Laney gave a half-hearted chuckle before getting back to the point. "So, again, what are you doing on my parents' farm?"

"When Senator McClaren mentioned that he had a lead on another aide"—he pointed at her—"and it was you, I couldn't believe it. I knew you were here in Mapleton from Ted Talbert, so I volunteered to drive up and talk to you in person." Dustin grinned as if he expected Laney to be thrilled he was giving her this sort of special treatment.

To Laney, it didn't seem special. It felt suffocating.

"I'm not sure what to say. You'll have to forgive me. Of course I'm honored that Senator McClaren would consider me for his staff, but I wasn't expecting to hear anything until the New Year."

Dustin shook his head back and forth, looking self-righteous. "We don't really take days off at this level of politics. McClaren wants to meet with you personally to get an idea as to whether or not you'll be a good fit." Dustin paused as Joan scurried past them on the way back into the farmhouse.

Laney smiled at her mom, but her mouth fought the expression. She heard the storm door open and close and waited for Dustin to continue.

"The senator is mighty impressed by your resume. He wants you on his team." Dustin rocked back on his heels and shot her a grin. "On *our* team."

Laney sucked in a breath, standing up straighter. The compliment from Senator McClaren was a nice boost to her bruised self-esteem, but the thought of working with Dustin wasn't a welcome one.

"McClaren is in Madison, finishing up a few things before Christmas and New Year's Day." Dustin went on with his explanation. "He wants to be able to hit the ground running in January. It'll be a busy year with campaigning. I came to impart on you the seriousness of this offer and to get a time on the calendar in the next day or two for your interview."

Laney gulped. This was huge—a major career break. It was exactly what she wanted.

Wasn't it?

She hadn't imagined Dustin as part of the deal, that was for sure. She didn't know how to feel about him—or any of it. For one thing, Dustin's comment about how the senator's staff never took time off bothered her. She'd spent the past two years working herself to the bone, and where had it gotten her? Was that what she wanted to sign herself up for again?

"Uh, Laney? Anytime you want to—I don't know—show some excitement or gratitude, that would be nice. Not to toot my own horn or anything, but I did put a good word in for you." Dustin winked at her and took a step closer, placing a hand on her waist. "After all, we have a history, and nobody knows you quite like I do."

All Laney could hear was the blood rushing through her ears as she took a giant step back from him. "I don't know about that, Dustin."

Chapter 42

FORD

FORD TAPPED THE STEERING wheel in his car in time to Michael Buble's version of "Jingle Bells." He had passed his exam, and he was over the moon. He was sure that his face held the same type of permanent expression as one of those wooden nutcrackers. Except, instead of a stern, square, toothy look, his was a big, bold smile.

Ford checked the clock on his dash. It was five minutes to noon. He pulled onto South Road, and his finger tapping ramped up. He couldn't wait to see Laney. He thought about calling her as soon as the proctor handed him the print-out of his results with the giant word *Pass* typed across the top, but he decided against it. He wanted to see her reaction when he told her—maybe get a congratulatory kiss out of the deal—so he was driving to the farm.

His phone rang through his car's speakers.

"Hey, Iz," Ford greeted his sister.

"Well, what's the good news?"

"I passed."

Isabel squealed on the other end of the line, and Ford's smile grew.

"Ford, that is *incredible*. Congratulations!"

"Thank you."

"I bet you're relieved."

"It does feel good going into the holiday knowing I can take the steps I want to take in the New Year."

"This is so great. I can't wait to design the barbershop for you. Hey, maybe we could feature it on my show. It would be a neat way for me to demonstrate some range, you know, branching into designing office spaces. What do you think?"

Ford chuckled. "You know I'll take your help any way I can get it, Izzy—even if it comes with cameras attached."

Isabel squealed again. "What did Laney say?"

"I haven't told her yet. I'm on my way there now."

"She's going to be so happy for you, Ford." Isabel's tone turned inquisitive. "What's the deal with you two, anyway?"

"What do you mean?" Ford knew exactly what his sister meant.

"You've been nearly inseparable for the past month. Are you an official couple yet?"

"We haven't exactly talked about it. But I want to be...official, I mean."

Isabel squealed for the third time.

"Easy there, Iz. I don't know if she feels the same. I mean, she's Laney McGregor. I've sort of outkicked my coverage here. She's probably going to leave town. I don't know if she wants to do the whole long-distance thing."

"You need to tell her how you feel, Ford." Isabel's voice was firm.

"Not all of us have your way with words, Iz, or your success to fall back on."

"What does that have to do with anything?"

"I'm just saying that it's easy for you to say, 'Just talk about it,' but I'm not you. My life has been pretty modest compared to yours and compared to Laney's. It's hard to get out of the mindset that she deserves better than what I have to offer her."

Isabel was silent for a second, and Ford pictured her chewing on her cheek, weighing his words. He'd never opened up to Isabel about his insecurities before now.

When she spoke in response, her voice was quiet. "I can't make you believe in yourself, Ford, but I think you're a catch. You need to lay your feelings for Laney out on the table. Seriously—so she understands. Without you minimizing it all with sarcasm or jokes. Take it from me, clear communication will go a long way in figuring out how you can make this work."

Ford digested Isabel's advice. Even if it made him sweat, his sister was right. He needed to talk to Laney. Tell her how he felt. He pulled into the front circle drive. "Okay. I've got to go. I'm at the farm now."

"Keep me posted." Isabel's tone didn't allow room for any argument.

"Will do."

"Oh, and Ford?"

"Yeah?"

"I'm really happy for you. You make me proud."

Ford ended the call with a balloon of happiness filling his chest.

Since Laney's parents were home, he guessed maybe they were manning the farm and she was inside, so he hurried up the front steps of the house. His knock echoed through the quiet, midday air.

The door swung open, and Joan stood smiling at him. "Ford! How are you? How did your test go?"

"Really well, Mrs. McGregor."

Joan beamed and ushered him inside. "I knew it would. Laney will be so pleased."

"Is she here?" His eyes hungrily took in the empty kitchen and family room.

"She was out back last time I saw her. Go right ahead." Joan motioned to the rear door.

Ford forced himself not to speed-walk through the house. He opened the storm door to the backyard and spotted Laney immediately. She had her back to him and was talking to a man Ford didn't recognize. He walked down the steps and into the backyard. When the man reached out and put his hand on Laney's waist, the fire of adrenaline and excitement Ford felt about sharing his good news with Laney turned to white-hot ice and jealousy.

"I don't know about that, Dustin," Laney said, taking a step back.

Dustin? As in the man who cheated on her and broke Laney's heart last Christmas? Ford clenched his fists at his sides, his nails biting into his palms. He already didn't like the guy on principle, but now the way Dustin was smiling at Laney made Ford's blood boil.

"Come on, Laney. You know we make a good team." Dustin took a step toward her again, and Ford moved.

"You need to back off, man."

Laney spun around. "Ford!"

Dustin looked between Ford and Laney, his eyes narrowing. "Who's this now?"

"Dustin, this is Ford, a friend of mine from Mapleton. Ford, this is Dustin." Laney glanced down at the ground.

Ford willed Laney to meet his gaze so he could get a better read on the situation. She couldn't possibly want Dustin around here, could she? He hated seeing her look so timid, but if she didn't have the confidence to tell her ex to leave, then he would.

Ford crossed his arms over his chest. "I think you should go, Dustin."

Laney's head darted up. "No, Ford. It's fine."

"Is it? Because it looks like this guy doesn't know how to leave you alone."

Dustin smirked, and Ford fought the urge to deck him. "I'm pretty sure Laney doesn't want me to leave her alone. Not with the job opportunity I just gave to her."

Ford glowered at Dustin. Next to him, Laney's face paled slightly. What in the world was going on? Ford stared at her, waiting for her to say something—anything. When she did, he wished she hadn't.

"Ford, can you give us a second?"

That was the last thing he wanted to do. He didn't trust Dustin as far as he could throw him. He glared between them and relented. "I'll wait by the barn. Holler if you need anything."

Laney nodded, not meeting his eye.

Ford took his time walking away, catching some of Dustin and Laney's conversation.

"Really, Laney? A small-town guy? I figured you'd be more than ready to get out of Mapleton and get back to the real work in Madison. You always said there wasn't much for you in your hometown."

Ford's whole body went taut. Is that what Laney really thought of Mapleton? All this time, she'd been praising his work around town, and she'd seemed so sincere. She even said she was considering the village clerk position. Something wasn't adding up. Ford rubbed at the back of his neck as he walked on and told himself not to jump to conclusions.

"Dustin, you don't know the first thing about Mapleton or Ford," Laney said.

Ford exhaled when Laney defended him and their hometown. At least that was something.

"But that's beside the point," Laney went on. "If you're serious about Senator McClaren sending you here, then let's get something on the calendar for me to meet with him."

Ford stopped as he approached the barn. So, Dustin worked for the senator—the same senator whom Sally and Ron referred Laney to.

Laney and Dustin put their heads together over their phones, and Ford could no longer hear their conversation. He straightened the hot cocoa sign on the barn door before looking out over the trees and trying to relax his shoulders. He tensed again when Dustin's voice carried over to him.

"I'll see you at the senator's office tomorrow, then. I'm looking forward to it."

Laney's response was mumbled.

"If you are dating that guy, just keep in mind that your social life is about to shrink. It'll be even smaller than when you were a state rep. Here's an insider tip: make sure your boyfriend over there knows that his chances of seeing you are going to be few and far between. Most people aren't able to handle the rigorous schedule we keep."

If Ford hadn't wanted to punch Dustin before, he certainly did now. The worst part was that there was probably some truth to what the guy had told Laney. Ford just didn't want to believe it.

Across the clearing, Laney tugged her shoulders back. "You don't need to worry about me, Dustin. I'll figure it all out." She shot a look toward Ford, and he pretended to adjust the sign again, keeping one eye on the pair.

"I have to go. I'll see you in Madison." Laney's voice was level.

Dustin reached out as if to hug her, but Laney held her arm out, and Dustin had to settle for a handshake.

"Looking forward to working with you again, Laney." Dustin glanced in Ford's direction, and Ford didn't even try to hide his scowl.

Dustin gave him a slimy grin and sauntered off.

Laney watched as Dustin's car disappeared toward South Road, and Ford joined her in the clearing.

"That was Dustin." Laney still didn't face him.

"Your Dustin?"

"He's not my anything anymore, but yes. The same Dustin I used to date. He works for Senator McClaren now, and he came bearing interview news. I've been summoned to Madison. The senator wants to meet with me to see about joining his staff."

Ford crossed his arms. "So, you're going to take the job?"

"I don't know if there is a job to take yet."

"But you want it."

Laney shrugged.

Ford scowled. "I can't believe you want to work with Dustin."

Laney's expression hardened. "Are you jealous of him, Ford? Because I'll tell you right now, that ship has sailed, never to return."

"I'm not jealous. I just don't get it. Why would you want to do anything remotely associated with Dustin?"

Laney's mouth knotted. "This has nothing to do with Dustin and everything to do with me. This is an opportunity for me and my career, and I'd be remiss if I didn't see it through. I certainly don't need you riding in like a knight in shining armor, trying to protect me from Dustin. I can handle myself."

Her words felt like a slap across the face. Ford held up his hands. "Whoa. I know that, Laney."

"Do you? Because it felt like you were trying to take control when you got here. What happened to bearing with me while I figure this out?"

Ford frowned, his guard flying up faster than you could say *ho, ho, ho*. "Excuse me if I don't like the sight of you being towered over by another dude—especially a guy who you've told me hurt you in the past."

Laney put her hand up against her forehead. "What do you want me to do, Ford? Not go after this job?"

"I never said that."

"Well, it was all but implied."

"If that's what you think of me, then that's that." He made a move to step around her. His heart struggled to beat, fighting against the ice shards that seemed to take the place of all the blood in his veins.

"Wait." Laney grabbed his arm. "I don't like feeling like there's distance between us."

"But there's about to *be* distance, Laney." He gave a desiccated laugh. "You're about to put it there, and you don't want to let me in."

Laney stepped back and folded her arms. "That's not fair."

"Based on what you just said about being able to handle yourself, it's the truth."

Laney opened her mouth, undoubtedly to argue, but Ford stopped her with the shake of his head. "No. It's fine, Laney. I'm never going to stand in your way. I couldn't live with myself if I did. You should go. You'll be great. You always are."

"But what about...us?" Laney searched his face.

"I don't know." What was he supposed to say? He wanted her, wanted a partnership with her, but she'd blocked him out again. And if she wanted this position, she'd get it. Then, she'd be in Dustin's clutches and sucked into the whirlwind of working 24/7 for Senator McClaren. Where did that leave him? Them?

Ford looked away, surveying the tree farm. So many good memories had been made on these grounds this month. But that was all this would amount to—a memory.

All the self-doubt that Ford had tried to bury deep down bubbled to the surface. He'd known from the beginning he and Laney were on two different tracks. He'd been a fool to get caught up in dreams of a future with her.

"Maybe it's time to face the facts. We're orbiting in two separate spheres. You're about to go back to a high-profile job in the city, and I'm staying here, in small-town Mapleton. The more I think about it, the more I think we've been naïve this month. It never would have worked between us, Laney."

"Wait. What? You truly believe that?" She'd gone from stunned to angry.

"I hate to be a scrooge, but—" Ford felt himself spiraling and trying to make light of this, exactly like Isabel had just warned him not to do, but he couldn't help it. He let his eyes meet Laney's for a fraction of a second before he looked up and over her shoulder. He couldn't bring himself to say the words or meet her gaze. Call it self-preservation.

"Fine, then. I guess that's it." Laney threw up her hands and let them fall to her sides with a slap. "You know, Ford. Maybe you'd get a little farther if you faced how you felt and owned your accomplishments instead of just making jokes and blowing me off. Your behavior is annoying and childish."

That smarted. Ford didn't want her to jab at him about his emotions and feelings. "Whoa, so now I'm annoying and childish?"

"Your inability to open up and have any sort of pride in yourself is, yes."

"Well, excuse me for not wanting to share my feelings with someone who won't accept my help and can't see that I'm trying to support her. If we're being honest here, Laney, I think you should take a real hard look at why you're even pursuing this job with the senator in the first place."

Laney's hands went to her hips. "What's that supposed to mean?"

"I think you're afraid of saying no to this job and looking elsewhere because you're worried about what people will think. Worried it'll look like another mark of professional failure." Ford dragged in a breath. "You hate feeling like you've lost. But you know what, Laney? Your motivation is all wrong, and you're too proud to admit it. *That* is what I'd call childish."

"Ford!" Laney's face flushed.

"No. I need to go. You've got an interview to prep for, and I'll just be in your way."

Ford turned and strode around the side of the house, trying to stuff down his emotions with every step he took away from Laney.

When he sat down in the front seat of his car, he was almost too stunned to drive. He had been so *dang* happy when he arrived. Now, here he was—heart plowed over and left in a pile on the side of the road, frozen with the rest of the ice and snow.

Ford turned the key in the ignition, and Christmas music blasted through the speakers. He couldn't help but let out a morose laugh when he recognized the song that was playing—"Happy Xmas (War Is Over)" by John Lennon and Yoko Ono.

So this was Christmas...

What had he done?

Chapter 43

LANEY

SENATOR LARRY MCCLAREN'S HOUSE was set back from the road that ran along Lake Mendota.

House wasn't the right word, exactly. What Laney was dealing with was more of a complex. There were designated family rooms in one wing and separate business spaces in the opposite wing—the senator's personal and professional worlds coalescing in one sprawling building. Laney had gotten mighty acquainted with the facilities in the past day and a half, and she'd quickly had to come to terms with the fact that she wasn't in Mapleton anymore.

A twinge of regret rattled around in her ribcage, poking at her lungs and making it hurt to breathe. Laney straightened the jacket of her business suit as she leaned away from the oval table in the full-sized conference room and glanced at her watch. Preparations for the Merry Mapleton Ball should be in full swing. She couldn't help but feel like she should be there, even though she'd decided not to go.

After everything blew up in her face with Ford, Laney made her excuses to her parents, recruited Eric to help with the farm, and threw herself into prepping for her interview—or series of interviews, as it turned out.

Laney had been on the fence about what to do if a position with the senator presented itself, but she'd dug in her heels after Ford said she was being proud. Her decision to take this job had nothing to do with her fear of failure. She didn't have a fear of failure. She was just very good at not failing.

That was what she told herself as she left Mapleton behind.

Senator McClaren hired her on the spot. She'd spent the remainder of the day yesterday and all of today sitting in on meetings and familiarizing herself with the rest of the team.

The team the senator had assembled to handle his campaign was composed of people from all different backgrounds. Some were McClaren family friends. Some were colleagues. Some, like Laney, were recommended. She was holding her own in the group, which was satisfying.

"Alright, everyone. That'll do it for today. We'll reconvene on the second of January and go from there." The man serving as the senator's chief of staff closed his laptop and the meeting.

"Happy holidays to you all." Senator McClaren stood and glanced around the room, nodding to each of them before taking his leave.

Laney rose and gazed through the floor-to-ceiling windows that looked out over the icy lake water. She slipped on her black peacoat, saying goodbye to the woman who'd sat to her right. They had completed a full day of work, and it was only mid-afternoon. Everyone seemed pleased with their progress.

Dustin stood outside the door of the conference room, not having been involved in that particular seminar. She'd purposefully kept him at a distance the past forty-eight hours, but that didn't stop him from hitting her with his habitual salesman-like smile when she came into his view.

"How did it go?" He fell into step with her.

"Senator McClaren has pulled together a great group of advisors. I have no doubt the campaign will get off to a good start in the New Year." That was an honest answer. Laney had been impressed with the caliber of people in the room with her. She definitely could learn a thing or two from them, but...

"Everyone has spoken very highly of your contributions already." Dustin placed his hand on the small of her back and guided her around a corner and down the hallway toward the doors the senator's staff used. "I think McClaren is excited about what this campaign and reelection means. It's a great opportunity to really cement his place in the political landscape in D.C. He's not taking it lightly."

Laney took a step to the side, easing herself out from under Dustin's touch. Everything about him felt wrong. Forced. Out of sync. She wasn't sure how she hadn't noticed it when they were dating. Nothing about the two of them together was natural. Their conversation always seemed jilted. Dustin's politician's smile irked her. Even though she technically held a higher position than he did on the senator's team, she still felt like he was looking down at her, trying to make her fit into a box he'd assigned for her. To Dustin, it was all about controlling her.

Guilt gnawed its way on a scorching path up Laney's backbone. She was ashamed she'd accused Ford of being controlling when that was obviously not what he'd been doing.

"Are you going home now that your meetings are done for the year?" Dustin asked.

Laney's heart rose at the thought of Mapleton, but then her stomach flopped. She wasn't going back to Mapleton. Or Ford. "I'm meeting family in Chicago for the holidays on Christmas Eve."

Dustin placed a hand on her elbow, turning her toward him before she made it to the door.

Laney took a pointed step away, but he seemed to ignore her silent *back off* signal.

"That works out well, then. Let me take you out for a celebratory dinner. What do you say?"

Dustin looked quite pleased with the idea.

Laney was not.

"Dustin, no. I have no interest in going out on a date with you, now or ever."

"Come on, Laney. Why not?"

Laney took a breath. She shouldn't have to defend or explain herself if she wasn't interested, but she could tell Dustin wasn't going to let this go until she was clear.

"For starters, you cheated on me."

"A simple lapse in judgment. I've learned my lesson."

"I don't care how you want to define it or what you supposedly learned. I'm saying no now. Please respect that and leave me alone."

Dustin frowned. "I see. Is this about the guy in Mapleton? Dodge, or Chevy, or Ford, or whatever his name is?"

The sound of Ford's name made her heart skip a beat. Laney had worked for the past two days to keep thoughts of their final conversation from overtaking her. The truth was, with every passing minute, Laney was more and more certain she'd made a monumental mistake.

"Are you dating him?" Dustin sounded like a parent talking down to a misbehaving child.

"I'm not dating anyone." Laney spit out the words, a sour taste in her mouth at Dustin's patronizing tone and his arrogance at assuming he was above Ford.

"Then this is good. Come on. I understand what your schedule will be like. I won't give you a tough time about it. We already know we make a good match. You can stop playing hard to get now."

Laney didn't try to keep her temper in check any longer. "Dustin. I'll say it again. I do not want to date you." She punctuated each of the words. "A match of convenience is not what I'm looking for, nor is any type of relationship with you. Now or ever."

The crease between Dustin's brows deepened, and he stared at her for a couple seconds before looking away. "Suit yourself."

"Consider me suited."

Laney left the McClaren residence, keeping her shoulders back as she stomped across the small parking lot toward her car. The clicking of her heels was muffled in the light dusting of snow that had fallen since she arrived this morning, which was a shame because Laney would have liked to hear their pointed clicks—like nails in the coffin of any future interaction with Dustin.

The nerve of that man.

Laney was vibrating with annoyance and a deep desire to be wrapped in Ford's arms. She unlocked her car, tossed her briefcase in the backseat, and got behind the wheel before exhaling.

There was only one place to go from here.

She put the key in the ignition and drove downtown. She parked behind the children's theater and walked through the back door.

"Knock, knock." Laney poked her head into Sally's cramped office.

"Laney! What are you doing here?" Sally's face broke out into a grin, and she stood and hurried around her desk, wrapping Laney in a hug. "I thought you were in meetings all day."

"Just until three."

Sally released her and looked her over. "And? How'd it go? Can I just say again that I'm so sorry about Dustin? If Ron and I had known he was on Larry's staff, of course we'd have told you. I mean, that changes everything, doesn't it?"

Laney waved her off. "Not your fault. But yeah, not ideal." She told Sally about her most recent interaction with Dustin.

After sharing in her disgust and volunteering to drive to the McClaren residence and give Dustin a piece of her mind, Sally turned serious. "What are you going to do? Have you talked to Ford?"

Laney collapsed into the chair opposite Sally's desk. "No. Not since I left Mapleton. I don't know what to do, Sal. I don't want the job with the senator, but Ford doesn't want me."

Sally sat down and pressed her palms together, fingers tapping her lips. "I have thoughts. Lots of thoughts. First things first. Tell me about the job. Why don't you want it? Need I remind you that you *did* complete an entire Christmas Cliché list just to get an in with Senator McClaren? Is it Dustin? Or what changed?"

Laney puffed up her cheeks and blew out a breath. "It has nothing to do with Dustin. If I really wanted this position, I'd gladly do the job and run circles around him. You know that."

"That I do." Sally nodded solemnly. "But then what?"

Laney shrugged. "I don't know. It's a great gig. But the work we're going to be doing isn't really up my alley."

"How so?"

"I'm basically going to be tasked with raising money and generating buzz around the senator's campaign. I don't know what I was expecting, but this is not exactly what I had in mind."

Laney couldn't stop thinking about her dad and the joy he got from working the land and offering trees to the community.

About Coach Carlson and the student runners she worked with every day.

Julia at the café.

Melly and Samson at the village offices.

Isabel. Daniel.

And yes, Ford.

They were all doing what they loved and serving people in the process.

Sally studied her from across the desk. "You like getting your hands dirty. Doing the actual work. The job with Senator McClaren doesn't really give you the chance to do that. Am I getting this right?"

"Yes. Exactly." Laney crossed and uncrossed her legs. "Am I crazy, though? It's a really good job."

Sally tugged at one of her dangling earrings. "On paper, sure. But if it's not a good job for you, then it doesn't matter. Wouldn't you rather spend your time doing something that makes you happy—where you feel like you are actively helping others?"

Laney nodded slowly. Sally had drawn exactly the conclusion Laney herself had come to over the past two days. "You're right. This isn't what I want."

"A-ha! That is a great segue into the second issue on the table." Sally rested her elbows on the desk. "Ford. He's what you want."

Laney let her head fall back. "But he doesn't want me."

Sally scoffed. "Please. I saw him with you, Laney. The man has it bad."

Laney's eyes filled with tears. "I really like him, Sal. Like, *really* really. But he said we were on different paths, and he just let me come here without fighting for me to stay in Mapleton."

Sally rolled her eyes. "Oh no. You don't get to play that card. Admit it, you would have bristled if he tried to force you to stay, and based on what you told me about what happened, just before Ford let you go, you chastised him for trying to butt in with Dustin. If anything, this just shows that Ford understands that you have an independent streak as wide as Texas."

When Sally said it that way, Laney could see her point. She frowned. She'd programmed herself to fly solo after Dustin's infidelity last year. Seeing him again at the farm had brought that back out of her, and Ford had taken the brunt of her snap judgments and attitude issues.

Laney sighed, cringing at her own behavior. "You're right. But that doesn't mean I don't want to be pursued or, at the very least, have him tell me how he feels."

Sally held up her hand. "Maybe he hasn't told you how he feels with words, but think about it, Laney."

Laney's mind raced over the events of the past month. All the time she and Ford had spent together. His kindness in running the farm with her. The way he stepped up and anticipated what she needed. How he listened. The way he made her laugh. How he challenged her. The way he kissed her as if she was the most precious thing in the entire world.

Laney gulped.

Ford may not have told her how he felt about her, but he sure as heck showed her.

Chapter 44

FORD

THE CHRISTMAS MUSIC BLARING through the barn was giving Ford a massive headache. Though it was the absolute last thing he wanted to be doing, he'd been hard at work, prepping for the Merry Mapleton Ball since noon. It was now pushing four-thirty, and he was so ready to be done.

Marge stood like a general, barking orders and cross-checking her clipboard with Melly's.

Isabel was working with her crew to configure the couches she'd brought in and draped with cream-colored slipcovers.

Laney's parents coordinated the decorating of the Christmas trees in each corner of the barn.

They'd transformed the rustic space into a magical, elegant Christmas utopia. There might have been more lights looped around the rafters than there were on all of the trees lining Candy Cane Lane. It looked great, but everywhere Ford turned, he came face to face with reminders of Laney, and the fact that she wasn't here was killing him.

Eric poked his head into the loft. "You want some help with that?"

Ford was dropping paper snowflakes attached to fishing line through the rafters. "If you don't mind."

The kids from Mapleton Elementary School had cut out nearly a hundred white paper shapes to hang along the barn walls, but when Isabel saw them, she insisted the effect would be greater if they strung them up and hung them from the ceiling. She'd clapped her hands and said, "It'll be gorgeous and wintery and perfect."

"Let's divide and conquer." Eric climbed up the last step and joined him in the loft. He grabbed half the pile, sat down across from Ford, and began hole-punching the tips of the snowflakes.

"So, when are you going to move your office to Mapleton Avenue?"

"I'll officially take ownership of the barbershop mid-January. We'll start some renovation work then. Isabel has all sorts of ideas."

She'd dragged him there yesterday, insisting that he get out of his house and do something productive. To his sister's credit, she didn't mention Laney once, though Ford guessed that was her motivation for trying to keep him busy.

Eric chuckled. "That doesn't surprise me. Your sister is down there, following in Marge's footsteps. It's hard to believe she's only been back in Mapleton for a little over a year. She's already involved in so much of what goes on here."

"I'm glad she's back in town." Ford dropped another snowflake down through the floorboards.

"It sure was nice having my sister around for the past month," Eric said.

Ford didn't trust himself to speak, but he glanced at Eric, who was knotting off the fishing line.

Eric caught his look. "I'm guessing you thought it was nice, too."

"Really, man? You want to have this conversation?"

Eric rolled his eyes. "It's not like it was any secret that you two are...were...involved. You spent the entire last month together, and half the town saw you kiss in the sleigh. What gives?"

"It didn't work out." Ford tried to keep his voice nonchalant, but he couldn't hide the heaviness behind his words. With every minute that passed since his fight with Laney, he felt like he was slipping further and further into a forever winter.

Like he was destined to be cold until the end of time.

"Have you heard from her?" he asked Eric.

"She called on her way out of town. Made me swear I would be here to help set up for the ball. I think she felt bad that she was cutting out. I still don't understand why she had to leave when she did. It's Christmas. What could have been so pressing?"

"Her new job."

"I know, but it's not like her to abandon a prior commitment, and from what I've gathered, she's the one that made sure this ball would happen. Now she's just staying in Madison and skipping it? That's bonkers."

Ford focused on his snowflake, silently agonizing over the circumstances. When he looked up, Eric was staring at him.

"What?" Ford asked.

Eric shot him an exasperated look before tying off a snowflake and dropping it down through the space between the floorboards. "Maybe *you* should call her."

Ford shook his head. "She doesn't want anything to do with me."

"You sure about that? I mean, I'm not one to give relationship advice—"

"Then maybe don't." A scrape of heat crept up Ford's neck. Of all the people he expected to get a talking to about Laney, Eric was the last on his list.

"Hear me out." Eric waited to go on until Ford met his eye. "All I'm saying is that, to a third-party observer like myself, you and my sister were really good together."

Ford grunted, and Eric took it as an opportunity to continue.

"She needs someone who knows and supports her strengths but also brings her back down to earth and reminds her that she doesn't have to be perfect. That's you."

Ford sat back on his heels. That was exactly who he wanted to be for Laney. Who would have thought goofy, carefree Eric would be able to cut to the heart of the matter so succinctly?

"Laney is stubborn, and so are you. She told me she was okay when I asked about you two, but I don't think she's fine at all. One of you is going to have to bend here—to lay it all out there—if you want to make this work, which I think you do, or there is no way we would still be having this conversation."

Eric tied a snowflake off with a flourish, evidently satisfied with his advice, and they lapsed into silence.

Ford had replayed his last encounter with Laney countless times in the past two days. The more he thought about it—and now hearing Eric's take—the more he became certain that neither he nor Laney had been in a good headspace when they'd had their argument. He'd acted like a petulant child and brought her down with him. He'd jumped to conclusions and pushed Laney away when, really, he wanted to hold onto her for dear life.

"Two hours until guests start arriving, people!" Marge's voice bellowed from below. "Let's finish up so you all can go home and get ready for the evening's festivities."

Shrieks rang out, and a flurry of activity ensued.

Ford stood, his abrupt movement sending the few remaining paper snowflakes flying. He knew what he needed to do. It was what he should have done on Monday the second he drove away from the farm and felt his stomach bottom out. Nothing about leaving Laney was right. "I have to go. Can you handle the rest of this?"

Eric gave him a salute. "Sure thing, man. Care to share what you're up to?"

"You really want me to spell it out?"

Eric smirked. "Humor me. I have a feeling I'm going to take credit for this down the road, anyway."

"Fine. I'm going to try to win your sister back by telling her how I feel and then kissing her senseless." Ford dragged in an unsteady breath. "If she'll let me."

"Could have spared me the kissing comment." Eric made a gagging face. "It's a good thing I approve. Now go!"

Ford scurried down the ladder as fast as his feet would go. He searched the barn until he found his sister. "Isabel!"

"Hey, Ford. It looks great!" Isabel motioned to the rafters where Eric dropped down another snowflake and waved at them.

"Thanks. Look. I've got something I need to do—"

The ringing of Isabel's cell phone cut him off.

Isabel glanced at the caller ID and held up her finger. "Hold on one second." She answered the call and turned her back on Ford. "Hi! Yes! Doing pretty well. How are you? Okay. What do you need?" Isabel began walking away from him.

Ford ground his teeth together as he listened to his sister chat with whomever it was that was calling, as if she had all the time in the world. In her defense, Isabel had no idea that Ford's entire life may as well have been hanging in the balance. He only hoped he wasn't too late. He started across the barn, trailing Isabel, but Melly intercepted him.

"Thanks so much for all your help, Ford. I'm so excited about how this is all coming together. I wish Laney could be here to see it."

A hoarse sound escaped Ford's throat. "Excuse me, Melly." He side-stepped her and hurried after Isabel.

She was hanging up her phone when he exited the barn. She turned and beamed at him. "Sorry about that! You need to hurry home and get back here so you can help with the parking situation like we talked about."

"Yeah. That's just it, Izzy. I can't."

Isabel's face fell. "What do you mean? We're counting on you. Marge was right. We're going to have serious issues if we don't have someone out here corralling the cars."

"I know, but I'm driving to Madison."

Isabel's eyes bugged out, and her lips curled up. "You are? Well, now, that is excellent news. I haven't wanted to force your hand, but I've been thinking you need to do something about Laney. Thank goodness you've finally come to your senses. I was beginning to think you were more stupid than I thought." She patted his arm.

"Gee...thanks. Look. I'm going to go."

"No!" Isabel held up her hand. "You can't go *now*."

"What are you talking about? You better believe I can. My car is right over there. I'm leaving." Ford made a move to cut across the clearing, but Isabel snaked out an arm and grabbed him.

"Listen, Ford. I am all for you reconciling with Laney, but it doesn't have to happen tonight."

"How can you say that? I might have ruined the best thing that ever happened to me." Ford felt a chill of anxiety sweep through him. "I've got to see if I can fix it."

Isabel's voice softened. "You will fix it, Ford. But you can't right now. I talked to Mr. and Mrs. McGregor when we were setting up the trees."

Ford stilled. "And?" Maybe Laney was coming here. Hope sprouted in Ford's chest but was quickly choked out when Isabel continued.

"They told me they spoke with Laney earlier today and asked her to come back tonight. She was going to try to, but then a last-minute work meeting got scheduled for dinnertime. They got the text while we were hanging ornaments. She's tied up until tomorrow. Even if you did drive to Madison, you wouldn't be able to see her now anyway. Don't you think it would be better if you had this conversation after a good night of sleep?"

"No. I think it would be better to have the conversation now." Ford scrubbed his face with his hand. When he looked back at Isabel, she was eyeing him with sympathy.

"It's going to work out, Ford. Just stay here tonight. Help with the ball. Enjoy yourself. You can go drive into Madison tomorrow with a clear head and a whole day to woo Laney."

Ford deflated like a punctured tire. He had amped himself all up to see Laney in a matter of hours, and now putting it off until the morning felt like a cruel form of torture.

"Okay?" Isabel leaned toward him, drawing his eyes to hers. "Can I count on you to be the parking master tonight?"

Ford blew out a breath. "Yeah. I guess so."

Isabel gave his arm a quick squeeze. "You better go and put your suit on. If you get back here by six-thirty, that should be plenty of time to help with the arrival of the first guests."

Ford nodded absently and walked to his car. He was still wound up, but Isabel was right. There was nothing he could do tonight, no matter how badly he wanted to.

When Ford parked at the farm an hour later, a light snow was falling, and the McGregors had turned on the string of bulb lights that ran along the entrance to the tree farm. Ford took in the charming scene before he poked his head into the barn and waved to Isabel. "Just wanted to let you know I'm here."

"You're the best!" Isabel hurried over and hugged him. "Here. Wear this over your jacket." She reached over to a hook, retrieved a reflective vest, and handed it to him.

"Goodie." Ford put it on as Laney's dad walked into the barn.

"Ah, Ford. I hear you're handling the parking."

"Yes, sir." Ford shook Jeff's hand.

"I know you've seen how it works over the past month, but from the sounds of things, we're going to have more traffic than on a typical tree farm day. Feel free to direct the overflow cars into the circle drive out front."

"I'll move my car up front now to clear room for others." Isabel rushed out of the barn, the train of her gold-sequined gown dragging behind her.

Marge scampered over to him. "Let us know if you need anything or if there are any issues out there. I'd expect our first guests to begin arriving any minute." She shooed him out into the cold.

Ford walked to the break in the driveway where the gravel drive angled into the larger lot. Isabel walked past him, going the opposite direction.

"All set!" She glowed with happiness, and Ford wished he could return her good cheer, but he couldn't stop thinking about how Laney should have been here.

A steady stream of cars started to arrive, taking his attention. He pointed them this way and that, making sure everyone had a place and no one was blocked in. Eventually, the traffic slowed to a trickle, and the noise emanating from the barn increased. Ford checked his watch. It was quarter after seven.

"Hey, Ford?" From the barn, Isabel was waving at him with one hand and clutching a fur shawl around her bare shoulders with the other. "I have a check for the fundraiser from my TV network in my purse, which I left in my car. Can you go around to the front and grab it for me?" She tossed him her keys.

Ford snatched them out of the air. "Sure. Get back inside before you catch pneumonia."

Isabel nodded and disappeared into the din.

Ford peeled off the orange vest and stowed it in his own car. He took his time strolling down the dark gravel drive and around the farmhouse. The night air was peaceful, and it hung heavy with a winter chill. Ford looked up into the cloudy sky as a fresh batch of big, fat snowflakes started falling.

When he made it to the front yard, his gaze landed on a giant evergreen tree strung with lights. A lit star shone bright from the peak. He paused with his face turned upward, thinking about all that had transpired over the past month. His heart yearned to be with Laney, and the thought of waiting even twelve more hours to see her was almost unbearable. Ford closed his eyes and made a wish.

When he blinked his eyes open, Ford stood for a moment longer, staring at the tree, before he turned and found Isabel's car parked on the curved driveway. He hit the unlock button on her key and opened the door. Sure enough, her purse sat on the passenger seat. Ford nudged the clasp open and grabbed the check, slipping it into the pocket of his suit coat. As Ford stowed the purse under the passenger seat, he heard the front door of the farmhouse open behind him.

He straightened up, slammed the door, and turned at the noise. What he saw knocked the air from his lungs. Ford blinked. Blinked again. Only then was he certain he wasn't imagining things. His Christmas-tree-star wish glowed before him.

Laney stood just outside the front door, a vision in a long red dress with her hair pulled back and gold earrings dangling down to her collar bone.

"Hi," she whispered.

It had only been two days since he'd seen her, but he felt like it had been two years. Ford drank in every detail of her face—the curve of her cheek and the line of her neck. He tried to form words, but his mouth failed him. All he could do was echo her greeting.

"Hi." His voice was gravely, so he cleared his throat. "You look"—Ford gulped—"breathtaking."

Chapter 45

LANEY

LANEY'S HEART THUDDED SO hard she was sure Ford could see it beating out of her chest.

His gaze was like a warm caress, and it caused heat to flood her cheeks. He took a step in her direction. Then another. And another. The whole time not taking his eyes from her. Laney didn't feel the cold. She didn't register the snow, even as it started falling harder.

The entire night rolled into a tunnel between her and Ford.

She wanted to scream at him to get over here. To come hug her and hold her and tell her he loved her, too. But she didn't do that. She waited, deciding it was a good sign that he was walking toward her and not away like he had on Monday.

She drew in a breath, summoning her courage, as he came to a stop a foot in front of her. "Look, Ford—"

"Laney, there's something—"

"You go ahead." Laney smiled up at him through her lashes, pressing her lips together and praying that what he had to say wouldn't crush her heart.

Ford's evergreen eyes bore into her. "I was a fool, Laney. You were right. I was childish and immature. I didn't give you a chance"—he paused—"didn't give us a chance to talk through anything before I overreacted. I didn't tell you how I feel. I'm sorry." He stared at her and then quickly took off his jacket and draped it over her shoulders. It was only then Laney realized she was shaking. "I was going to drive to Madison. Tonight, actually. To see you."

Laney's heart dropped into her stomach before soaring back into her chest. "You were?" She inhaled Ford's scent, letting the heady mixture of orange and cloves that she'd forever associate with him go straight to her head and kindle a fire in her heart.

He nodded once. "I was. Isabel demanded that I stay and help with the parking here, like I'd promised. She told me you had a work meeting, so I wouldn't be able to see you anyway. I'm guessing she knows you're here." Ford rolled his eyes, and Laney let a giggle escape. But she turned serious when Ford grabbed for her hands. She didn't want to miss a word he said.

"It's been killing me to be away from you."

Laney swallowed hard. "I've missed you, too."

Ford dropped her hands and reached up to cup her cheeks. Laney's eyes fell closed at the feel of his skin on hers, but she forced them open when he started talking again. "I am not good at sharing my feelings, Laney. But for you, I'm going to try. Please hear me out." Ford took a deep breath. "I have always admired your fiery spirit, and your compassionate heart, and the way you go after what you want. I have been in awe of you since high school, and spending so much time with you this past month has only solidified how incredible I've always known you to be. I'm so dang grateful for Sally's Christmas Cliché list because, in a lot of ways, the list brought us together. I like being together with you. Actually, I-I'm in love with you, Laney. I'm sorry I didn't tell you that until now."

Laney pinched her eyes shut, wanting to tattoo this moment on her soul. Ford loved her. She felt like she could burst with joy. With hope. With love.

"Say something."

Laney popped open her eyes to find Ford looking agonized. She'd been so lost in enjoying his words that she hadn't responded to his declaration.

"Oh! Right." Laney put her hands over his, like frosting on top of a Christmas cookie. She savored the feel of the knobs of his knuckles under her palms, his grip on her cheeks both delicate and secure. "First of all, you should share your feelings with me more often because that was pretty wonderful." She grinned, looking him directly in the eye, but then her smile fell. "It wasn't all your fault, Ford. I was being unreasonable, jumping down your throat when you were just trying to have my back with Dustin. You are not controlling. You're supportive. I also shouldn't have accused you of holding back your feelings. If I would have gotten out of my own head for two seconds, I would have seen that you were *showing* me how you felt about me. I didn't give you enough credit. I'm sorry that I was so self-centered that I ignored what was right in front of me.

Laney gulped for a breath and plowed ahead before she lost her nerve. "I'm in love with you, too. Hopelessly, terribly in love. It scares me. You know how I don't like not being good at something, and this is a big thing that I have very little experience with, and—"

Ford bent his head to hers, cutting her off with an urgent kiss. It was like he needed her lips on his to live. The seconds slowed and may have been years—decades, even. Laney was acutely aware of the hitch in Ford's breathing, the small step forward he took so as to better position them. When she reached up and draped her arms around his neck, pulling him closer, she felt the muscles in his back bunch and then release, as if coming to rest and exhaling a sigh of relief.

She trembled at the feel of his bicep brushing against the indent of her waist as he dropped one hand from her face and drew her nearer. It was euphoric—this connection. There was no question that this was exactly where she wanted to be.

Eventually, Ford pulled back and rested his forehead against hers, his eyes closed. They stood like that, wrapped in each other's arms, breathing heavily, as the snow fell around them. Laney felt entirely safe. Ford was so solid. So steady. She would never doubt his affection or intentions again.

"Laney?" Ford's voice broke the silence.

"Mmhmm." Laney snuggled closer to him as he pressed his hands against her hips, dropping kisses on her forehead, her temple, behind her ear.

"I don't think you have to worry. We're going to be pretty good at this."

Laney chuckled. "You think so?"

"I know so." He kissed her quickly again. "We should go enjoy the ball, and then we'll figure out what to do next. We can plan weekend trips back and forth between here and Madison. I can look into work down there."

Laney pressed her hand against his chest.

"I mean, only if you want me to," he added quickly.

Laney shook her head. "No, it's not that I wouldn't want you to. It's just that I'm going to quit my job."

"What?" Ford's jaw hung down. "With Senator McClaren? Wait, back up. You got the job. Congratulations."

Laney nodded her head in acknowledgement, watching as Ford processed all of this.

"But now you're quitting. After two days? What happened?"

Laney coiled her arm through his and let him lead her around the side of the house toward the barn. "Nothing major happened. I just realized it was never what I really wanted. I liked the idea of it, but the job itself wasn't fulfilling. I'm going to search a little more, but I'm thinking about throwing my name in the hat for the village clerk job."

He pulled her to a stop before she went any farther. The noise from the barn was louder now. "Really? You're interested in the job here? Not just because of me being in Mapleton? Because I don't want you to settle. I want to support you in whatever you want to do."

Laney smiled up at him. "I know. And I know we could make it work if I got a job elsewhere, but I am actually interested. I promise. I want to make a difference with my work. I think I can do that here, in Mapleton. Like you do."

Chapter 46

Ford

Ford stared at Laney. "Thank you for saying that."

"It's the truth. Your work is worthwhile. More than that, *you* are worthwhile. While we're on the subject,"—Laney tilted her chin up and her eyes shone with the determined flicker he loved so much—"I'd like to go on record and state that I don't want you to compare yourself to anyone else. In my eyes, you're it, Ford. You don't have to prove yourself to me. You're everything that's good. If that's hard for you to accept, I'll believe it enough for both of us."

Ford was quiet, letting Laney's words sink in. They were spoken with conviction, and he allowed them to burrow into his heart and take root. He was enough. He made a difference. Laney loved *him*. He wasn't sure he could speak, but he made a silent vow to start believing in himself the way she did.

"I don't deserve you," he whispered into her hair as he wrapped Laney in his arms again.

"Ah, ah, ah. Yes, you do. We deserve each other. We're going to make mistakes, but we're going to show up and we're going to believe in us. Deal?"

Ford nodded. "Deal."

Laney melted into him, resting her head on his shoulder and burying her nose in his neck. "Now that that's settled, do you just want to get out of here?"

Ford eased back and shot her a grin. "You know I'd love to keep you all to myself, but we've got to at least make an appearance.

Isabel will come and hunt us down if we don't. And I told her I would get her this check." Ford patted his pocket.

"God bless Isabel. It's a good thing I called her, or I would have gotten to Mapleton only for you to be halfway to Madison. That would have been awful. She promised she'd get you here and keep you here for me. She also dropped off this dress." Laney stepped back and smoothed the soft red silk of the gown.

"That dress." Ford swallowed. "It's good. It's really good. It deserves to be shown off. It would be my honor to attend the Merry Mapleton Ball with you by my side." He held out his arm for her.

Laney took it, grinned up at him, and Ford felt a giddy smile play at his lips.

Laughter and Christmas music poured from the barn as they made their way across the clearing. Ford pulled the wooden door open, and Laney stepped inside. She gasped, and Ford looked around. They had done well. The lights twinkled overhead. He had to hand it to Isabel. The dangling snowflakes were showstoppers. The usual smell of old wood and pine that he'd grown accustomed to over the past month was enhanced with the fragrance of cinnamon and various perfumes. Laughter rang out along with the music.

Ford bent and spoke directly into Laney's ear. "Looks pretty good in here, doesn't it?"

Laney visibly shivered when he kissed the column of her neck. "It's beautiful."

"It sure is." He didn't try to hide the fact that he was staring directly at her.

Laney grabbed his bicep and squeezed before turning to survey the barn again.

It was packed. Ford spotted Laney's parents talking with Eric and—

"Is that Sally and Ron?" Ford asked at the same time Sally's eyes landed on them. Laney's friend clasped her hands together and hurried across the barn. She grabbed Laney into a ferocious hug and pulled Ford down to join in.

"This makes me so happy!" Sally trilled.

Laney must've caught the slightly stunned look on Ford's face because she hurried to explain. "Sally and Ron insisted on coming with me."

"I predicted this"—Sally stepped back from the hug and waved her hand between the two of them—"was going to happen before Thanksgiving. I was not about to miss the chance to see it through." Sally's face shone as she cuddled into Ron's side. Ron raised a glass of cider to the two of them.

"Pretty sure we had a hand in this, too." Isabel joined them with Daniel.

"I actually had a hunch over a year ago there was something brewing here. I just needed Isabel's knack for meddling to bring you two together," Daniel added, wrapping his arms around Isabel's waist and pulling her close.

"Isabel? Meddle? Never," Ford teased.

"Yeah, yeah. You can say 'thank you' for signing you up to help out at the tree farm anytime, big brother. And for sparing you a trip to Madison tonight." Isabel kicked out a heeled foot and tapped Ford's shin before turning to Laney. "You look amazing."

"It's the dress." Laney winked.

"It's you in the dress." Ford said it under his breath, but he knew Laney heard him when her cheeks flushed. Sally fanned herself, and Isabel grinned, glancing over her shoulder and sharing a happy look with Daniel.

Eric joined them, along with the elder McGregors.

"Well, well, well. Nice of you to finally show," Eric said to Laney.

"Very funny," she replied.

Eric smirked and shot a look to Ford. "Like I said, I'm going to go ahead and take credit for this." He blinked his gaze down to where Ford held Laney's hand.

Laney rolled her eyes. "Get in line. Good grief. Did everyone have us pegged to be together?"

"Yes," the entire circle chorused, and Laney laughed.

After a bit more small talk, the group dispersed. Ford and Laney walked around the barn, sipping hot chocolate and greeting countless other villagers. When the music slowed and couples took to the floor, Ford held out his hand. "Dance with me?"

"Of course."

They set their empty cups down on a table decorated exquisitely with a floating-candle centerpiece and ruby-red tablecloth, and Ford pulled Laney to an open spot on the makeshift dance floor. She draped her hands around his neck, and he flexed his fingers against her hips as they swayed together.

"I've been thinking," Laney said after they danced in comfortable silence for a minute.

"That does not surprise me."

Laney's laugh was soft and sweet. "If I'm going to move back to Mapleton, I'm going to need to find a place to live."

Ford shifted her in his arms so he could look at her.

Her eyes glittered. She took one hand and ran her finger along the stubble on his chin. "Do you happen to know any charming, successful, wildly handsome realtors with a knack for the Mapleton market? I've got to find someone who isn't afraid to spend a lot of time with me so we can find the perfect place."

"Finding someone with all that to his name will be a tall order." Ford kept his voice professional. "But I may have a lead on a guy who is about to open his own agency. I know he'd be happy to help."

Laney grinned. "I knew I could count on you."

"Always." He bent his head and captured her lips with his, right there in the center of the dance floor, underneath the paper snowflakes and twinkly lights, surrounded by the entire town.

Epilogue

LANEY – 11 MONTHS LATER

LANEY POUNDED ON THE back of the minivan belonging to Melly and her family, letting them know their Christmas tree was secured. She waved as they drove down the driveway before she scooted into the barn and out of the chill of the November night air.

It had been another busy opening day to the tree farm season. She was happy to help her parents out, but she was even happier that she didn't have to shoulder all the responsibilities this year.

It was almost unimaginable that it had been a year since she'd been thrown into running the tree farm on her own.

Well, not on her own. She'd had Ford's help.

Laney's lips curved into a full smile at the thought of Ford. This had been the best year of her life, in large part because of Ford's constant support and presence. They'd laughed and teased and worked hard and grew more in love each day.

So much had changed for her. She'd relocated to Mapleton. Ford helped her find a cute little starter home, which was perfect for her for the time being. It was right off of Mapleton Avenue and within walking distance to the municipal center. The location was ideal since she gladly accepted Samson's offer to come on board as the new village clerk. It had taken her some time to learn the ropes of the role, but Laney had hit her stride. She was working to streamline processes and make things run smoother for all involved.

In early November, she'd successfully coordinated and overseen the local election efforts, and she could wholeheartedly say that she was thankful to be in her position in Mapleton and not licking her wounds with a defeated Senator McClaren. She loved being able to put her stamp on the way things were run in Mapleton, and she took great pride in assisting her friends and neighbors with their civic needs.

For his part, Ford's real estate agency was thriving. She'd never doubted that it would, and Laney couldn't wait to see what the future held for him.

She slid the barn door shut and rubbed her frozen hands together. Even the wool gloves she wore didn't ward off all the cold.

Laney's mom sat on the high stool behind the counter, flipping through and facing bills. She glanced up from the register at the sound of Laney entering the barn. "You look cheerful. Was that the last of our customers?"

"Yep. I think we're all set. It was a good day!" Laney shot a gaze around the barn. "Where's Dad?"

"He said something about wanting to trim boughs from the trees along the south lot line. We nearly ran out today." Joan gestured to the table where the homemade garland usually was. There were only two strands left of the thirty they had put together this morning. "I'm sure he could use your help hauling branches back."

Laney checked her watch. She was supposed to watch a movie with Ford and his family tonight, but she had time to spare. "I'll head out that way, and then I've got to run home and get changed."

"Say hi to Val and Dave for me. And please thank Ford for his help again." Laney's mom waved as Laney went back out into the cold.

She set off through the lines of trees, squishing snow under her boots. She ran her hands up and down on her arms and picked up her pace. She expected to hear the slicing of her dad's handsaw as he trimmed the lower branches off of some of their taller trees, but as Laney approached, the night was conspicuously quiet.

When she broke through the tree line, there was no sign of her dad. She glanced down at some of the trees. They were neatly trimmed already. Maybe she missed him. Laney was about to turn back when a light caught her eye across the clearing. Near the trail that led to the ravine, something glowed in the snow.

Laney walked toward it only to find a line of white bags along the path that went through the trees. Inside each, a flameless tea-light candle flickered.

Just then, a duck call shattered the silence with a resounding quack.

Laney burst out laughing and hurried to cut through the woods, following the lit path toward the drop-off.

There, standing with his back to her, surrounded by a ring of glowing tea-light candles, was a figure she could recognize even in the black of night.

Ford turned. "Hey, you."

Laney made her way over to him, letting him pull her into a tight hug and savoring his warmth and the firmness of his body against hers.

"What are you doing here? I thought you had a work thing. And it's not duck season," she joked.

"I know, but I had to get your attention somehow."

Laney felt the rumble of Ford's low voice through his chest. She nuzzled in closer, inhaling his scent. She'd seen him just hours before, but somehow that was too long. "You should know by now that you always have my attention."

"Ditto." Ford pushed her slightly away, and Laney's protest got lodged in her throat when he dropped to his knee.

"Laney McGregor, I have admired you for as long as I can remember, and it has been my greatest privilege to spend this year with a front-row seat to the wonder that is you."

Laney's hands flew to her mouth.

It's *happening*.

She'd hoped for a proposal, sure—pretty much every day for the past year. Now she clung to Ford's every word, letting his voice wrap around her and seep into her skin.

"You are absolute magic. You make me want to be better—and not just because you're freakishly competitive."

Laney snort-laughed, tears streaming down her face and freezing to her cheeks as Ford looked up at her with so much admiration in his eyes she felt like she could fly.

"You are kind and funny. You have a servant's heart, and you're dedicated to the people you love. I have never met someone who is so beautiful—on the outside and on the inside. You have been my wish on every Christmas-tree star I've seen for the last year. I want to spend the rest of our lives challenging each other, and supporting each other, and falling deeper and deeper in love. I will always be here for you, Laney. Will you marry me?"

As if on cue, snow started dropping from the sky, shrouding them in their own little world of white. Laney sunk to her knees, oblivious to the cold, and reached forward to grab Ford's bearded face into her hands. She pulled him into a deep and firm kiss, pledging all of her love along with it.

"Yes! Yes, I'll marry you, Ford."

Ford took off her mitten and slipped a gorgeous round-cut diamond onto her ring finger.

"Wow."

"Do you like it?"

"It's stunning." She smiled up at him. "That was some speech."

"You know me—a big talker."

Laney laughed as Ford pulled her into him, clamping her to his chest. Heat flooded Laney's body—a combination of love, joy, and adrenaline—and she would have been content to stay right there with Ford forever, in their own personal snow globe.

"I meant every word," he whispered.

Laney sighed happily. She knew he did. Better yet, she trusted he'd spend the rest of his life showing her.

Acknowledgments

All glory to God, now and forever.

I keep calling this the Christmas book of my dreams, and it's true, but it wouldn't be anything without you, dear reader, so thank you! Whether you're a friend or family member or someone who randomly stumbled across my work online or in a book store, I'm so grateful to you for spending some of your precious time with my words. I hope *Together With You* made you smile and filled you with the joy of Christmas.

To Jenn Lockwood. Thank you for your care and attention. My books are in the best hands with you.

To Ana Griogoriu-Voicu at Books-Design. I cried when I saw the cover you created for this story. It's beyond perfection. Thanks, again, for bringing Mapleton to life so vividly with your exceptional designs.

To my beta readers. Thanks for your wonderful and constructive feedback. You all are the real MVPs. A special shout-out to Samantha for your excitement and passion for Ford and Laney. You read three drafts of this story, and I hope I did you proud with the finished product.

To my favorite librarians. Thanks for helping me with all my printing needs, even when it means pushing through an eighty thousand word manuscript. Thanks for putting said manuscript on the shelves when it finally made it to book form. Most of all, thanks for all the work you do to raise up readers in our community.

To the members of my book clubs. Book club nights are my favorite nights of the month, and it's such a gift to discuss life and literature with you.

To my family, near and far, you are the very, very best. Thank you for coming to every in-person author event I've ever had (even when you've had the books purchased since they went on sale *and* even though you've already heard me give every spiel I've ever given about writing, publishing, and my stories). I know how blessed I am to have your support, and it makes me weepy every time I think about it. Mom, thanks for reading this one so many times. Dad, Luke, and Ben, thanks for reading all my stuff, even if romance would not be your genre of choice. Bailey, you're my actual hero. Aunt Anne, Rachael, Clare, Sam, and Ashley (and your significant others!), thanks for everything. All my love, always.

To my kids—Miriam, Lyla, Ellen, and Francis. Celebrating Christmas with you is my favorite thing, and I had a blast weaving in some of our traditions throughout this story. I hope you wish on every Christmas tree star you see and then work for your wishes! I am so proud to be your mom. I love you.

Finally, to Nick. Thank you for championing my dreams, for making me laugh, for working so hard for our family, for putting up outdoor Christmas lights just for me...I could go on. Just thank you. I love you madly.

Leah Dobrinska is the author of the Larkspur Library Mysteries and the Mapleton novels. She earned her degree in English Literature from UW-Madison and has since worked as a freelance writer, editor, and content marketer. As a kid, she hoped to grow up to be either Nancy Drew or Elizabeth Bennet. Now, she fulfills that dream by writing mysteries and love stories.

A sucker for a good sentence, a happy ending, and the smell of books—both old and new—Leah lives out her very own happily ever after in a small Wisconsin town with her husband and their gaggle of kids. When she's not writing, Leah enjoys reading and running. Find out more about Leah, join her newsletter community, and connect with her through her website, leahdobrinska.com.

Book Club Discussion Guide

1. What were your initial impressions of Laney and Ford? How did hearing about the history between the pair impact your view of them?

2. Do you have a favorite holiday tradition? Do you have any in common with Ford and Laney and their families and friends?

3. Did you recognize individual character growth in Ford and Laney? How so? How did they mature as a couple as the story progressed? How did their friends and/or families help them to grow?

4. The novel explores the theme of identity and self worth. Both Ford and Laney struggle with how others perceive them—or how they *think* others perceive them. How are their concerns similar? How are they different? Can you relate to their feelings?

5. What are some other themes explored in *Together With You*?

6. Is there anything in the story you wish had gone differently?

7. Share your favorite quote or scene from the book. Why did it stand out to you?

www.ingramcontent.com/pod-product-compliance
Lightning Source LLC
Chambersburg PA
CBHW061614190726
48288CB00007B/2313